CROWD OF WITNESSES

(DEATH AT THE DEMO)

THE 14TH BERNIE FAZAKERLEY MYSTERY

JUDY FORD

Bernie Fazakerley

Publications

COPYRIGHT

CROWD OF WITNESSES

(DEATH AT THE DEMO)

THE 14TH BERNIE FAZAKERLEY MYSTERY

Published by Bernie Fazakerley Publications

ISBN: 978-1-911083-70-2

DEDICATION

This book is dedicated to the staff of the National Health Service, especially those who lost their lives during the COVID-19 pandemic.

'Your new National Health Service begins on 5th July. What is it? How do you get it?

'It will provide you with all medical, dental and nursing care. Everyone – rich or poor, man, woman or child – can use it or any part of it. There are no charges, except for a few special items. There are no insurance qualifications. But it is not a "charity". You are all paying for it, mainly as tax payers, and it will relieve your money worries in time of illness.'

Extract from the leaflet distributed by the government to British households in 1948

CONTENTS

*Therefore, since we are surrounded by so great a cloud of witnesses,
let us also lay aside every weight and the sin that clings so closely,
and let us run with perseverance the race that is set before us.*

Hebrews 12:1

MAPS

This map shows the routes taken by the demonstrators along St Aldate's and The High Street to converge on Carfax.

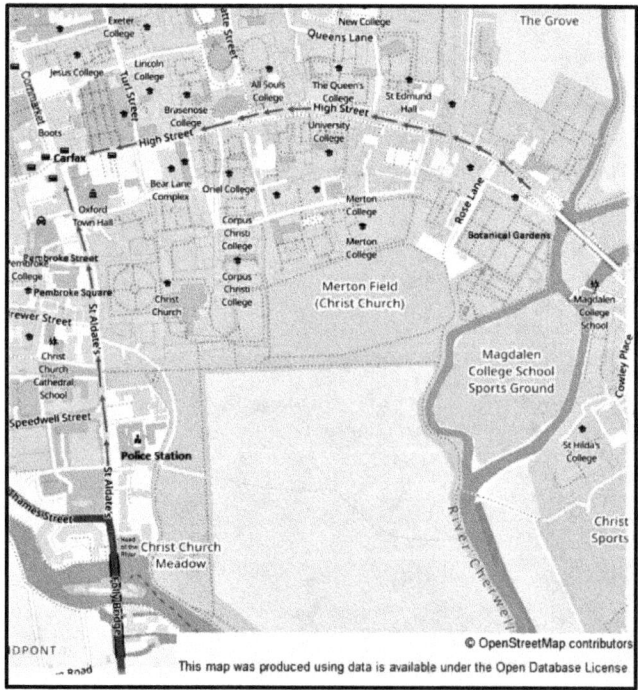

This map shows Oxford and surrounding areas as far as the ring road.

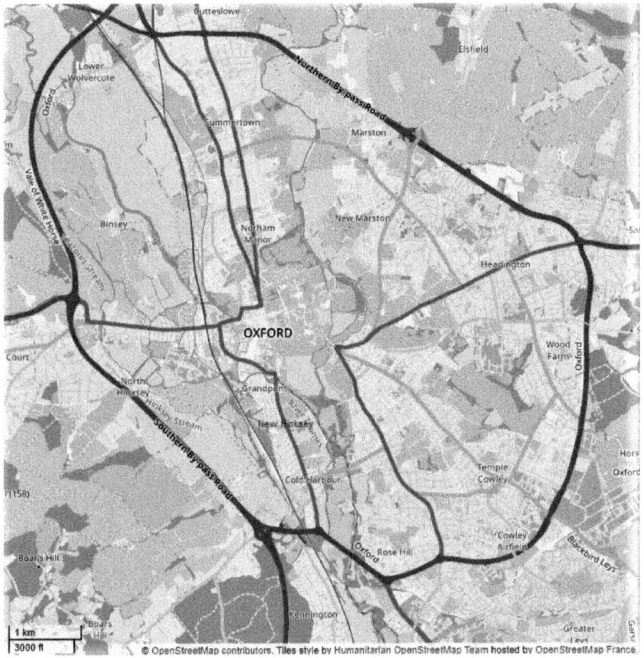

For details of the licence governing distribution of data contained in these maps, see www.openstreetmap.org/copyright.

TIMELINE FOR MAIN CHARACTERS

1940	Richard was born
1948	Richard's mother left home
1950	
1951	Peter was born
1958	Bernie and Jonah were born
1960	
1970	
1976	Bernie's mother died. Bernie began her studies at Oxford.
1978	Peter married Angie.
1979	Bernie graduated.
1980	Peter's daughter, Hannah, was born
1982	Richard's father died and his mother returned. Bernie was appointed Fellow at St Luke's College. Bernie's Father Died.
1984	Jonah's son, Reuben, was born.

1990	Jonah's son, Nathan, was born.
1995	Richard and Bernie met.
1997	Richard and Bernie married.
1999	Richard was killed in accident at work.
2000	Bernie's daughter, Lucy, was born.
2003	Peter's wife, Angie, was killed.
2006	Peter and Bernie married.
2009	Jonah was paralysed in a shooting incident.
2010	
2011	Peter retired
2013	Bernie retired to become Jonah's PA
2014	Jonah's wife, Margaret, died.
2015	Jonah moved in with Peter and Bernie.
2018	Lucy started studying Medicine at Liverpool University

1. LOCKDOWN

'Occupational Health!' DCI Jonah Porter snarled, ending the unwelcome call that had come through on the mobile phone attachment on his wheelchair and looking towards his friend and Personal Assistant, Bernadette Fazakerley ("Our Bernie" to her friends). 'What business have Occupational Health got saying I'm not fit to work? And what does the Chief Super think she's playing at hiding behind Health and Safety like that? If she thinks I'm past it, why doesn't she come straight out and say so to my face?'

It was March 2020. The new coronavirus, first reported in Wuhan – a Chinese city unheard of by most westerners until then – in December, had spread to Japan and various other far-eastern countries by mid-January and made landfall in Europe by the end of that month. During February, cases were reported in Britain, but with all the victims having contracted the disease abroad.

Then things seemed to speed up dramatically. Every day brought new and increasingly worrying news and it began to dawn on the British public that this was not one of those things that only happened to other people.

By mid-March it had become clear that efforts to contain the outbreak had failed. More than a thousand cases had been confirmed in the UK and thirty-five deaths had been reported. There were suggestions in the media that the disease had originated much earlier than first thought and could have been active in Britain as early as the previous autumn. Older people and those with underlying conditions were being advised to stay away from crowded places and employers were considering ways of enabling staff to work at home. And yet, the Cheltenham Festival went ahead and Prime Minister Boris Johnson vowed that he intended to visit his elderly mother on Mothering Sunday. The atmosphere in the country was a strange mixture of impending doom and a determination not to allow "a bit of flu" to affect our way of life.

'Oh Jonah!' Bernie protested with a sigh, raising her eyes from the upturned bicycle that she was engaged in repairing. 'You know perfectly well it's not like that at all. It's all about keeping you safe so that you'll be able to go back once this is all over. It's no good trying to pretend you're not high risk, because you know people with spinal cord injuries are susceptible to respiratory infections and you've even had a fair share of them yourself. You're just going to have to put up with being stuck at home with us for a few weeks.'

'But why couldn't I work from home?' Jonah argued petulantly. 'Other people do. Andy and Monica could do all the leg work.'

'Oh yeah?' Bernie pulled a rag out from the pocket of her overalls and wiped her oily hands. 'They'd do the exciting stuff – interviewing witnesses, viewing crime scenes, interrogating suspects – and you'd be content with the paperwork? You ought to realise by now that you're not even very good at that side of things.'

'I could do interviews by videoconference,' Jonah contended, well aware of the futility of this argument but unable to stop himself from venting his frustration. 'We often do that when suspects are arrested by other forces. And Andy could use his phone to show me round crime scenes.'

'But it'll be a whole lot simpler for everyone if they don't have to organise all that,' Bernie argued, bending down to pick up the bicycle and turn it over on to its wheels. 'Look at it from Alison's point of view. She's already got officers and staff off with coronavirus symptoms or self-isolating because of family members with symptoms. She doesn't need the hassle of sorting out new technology for you, just because you're too stubborn to just take some time off.'

'Jonah stubborn? Surely not?' Peter exclaimed in mock astonishment, coming round the corner of the house with his two grandchildren. 'What's all this about?' he added, sensing that something serious had happened.

'The *great detective* has been sent on gardening leave for his own protection,' Bernie explained, 'and he's afraid they'll try to pension him off again permanently. Try to convince him that the world hasn't ended, will you? I want to take my bike for a spin to test the gears.'

She pushed the bicycle towards the back gate, leaving her husband staring down at Jonah and wondering what to say.

Four-year-old Ricky broke the silence, striding up to Jonah's electric wheel chair and looking him in the eye. 'We've been to the nature reserve. I saw a butterfly!'

'Really?' Jonah adjusted his face and looked benevolently towards the little boy. 'It's early for butterflies. What sort was it?'

'It was orange and white,' Ricky informed him.

'Ah!' Jonah smiled back. 'That'll be an orange-tip butterfly. It must be this warm weather that's made them hatch out.'

'Butterflies start off as eggs,' Ricky told him earnestly. 'And then they hatch out into caterpillars. We've got some of those at Nursery. We've got to feed them the right kind of leaves until they grow big enough to make a cocoon. And then they're going to go to sleep until they turn into butterflies.'

'Like the *very hungry caterpillar*,' his sister, Abigail, added solemnly, holding on to the arm of Jonah's chair and looking up into his face with wide green eyes. Eric Carle's picture book was one of her favourite stories.

'But *that* caterpillar ate lots of silly things,' Ricky declared. '*Our* caterpillars only eat special leaves.'

'Come on, you two!' Peter ushered his grandchildren through the French windows into the house. 'We'd better get you cleaned up. Daddy will be here soon to take you home.'

Once he had seen both children safely inside, he turned back to address Jonah. 'I won't tell you it's for your own good, because you know that already. The way things are shaping up, you won't be the only one confined to barracks for the duration, so just try and get used to the idea, can't you?'

Jonah sat in the sunny garden watching the three figures disappearing into the relative gloom of the house. Then he dropped his eyes to the screen in front of him and pressed keys on the pad beneath his left hand to make a phone call.

'Yes, sir?' Sergeant Andrew Lepage answered after a few seconds.

'How're you getting on with tracing the owner of that car?' Jonah asked briskly. 'And what about the smears on the window latch?'

'No joy with the car, I'm afraid, sir. Either the number plate was false or the witness misremembered something. There's no car fitting the description they gave with a registration that agrees with the partial number.'

'And the smears?'

'Still waiting on forensics,' Andy replied promptly. 'They say it'll be a few days before they can identify the substance. DCI Davenport tried to jolly them along, but they told her they've got a backlog and there's nothing they can do.'

'Anna?' Jonah demanded. 'What's she-?' He broke off, suddenly understanding the import of his sergeant's words. 'Is she the SIO now? Am I off the case?'

'Well … yes, sir,' Andy replied hesitantly. 'I thought it was your idea. I mean … Chief Superintendent Brown told us you were in isolation and Anna was taking over your caseload for the foreseeable.'

'I see,' Jonah murmured, trying unsuccessfully to keep the resentment out of his voice. 'Yes, the Chief Super rang me a few minutes ago to tell me not to come in tomorrow, but I hadn't realised … What time was it she briefed you about all this?'

'The middle of the morning,' Andy answered reluctantly. 'I suppose she wanted to be able to tell you that everything was under control, so you wouldn't feel you were letting anyone down.'

'Yes, I suppose so,' Jonah did not sound convinced. 'OK. I suppose that's it then. I'd better let you get on. I'm sure DCI Davenport has plenty of jobs for you to do.'

'Yes sir. I'm sorry about this, sir. I'm sure the Chief Super's only … Well, as you say, I'd better get on.'

* * *

The weather remained warm and dry for the next ten days, allowing Jonah to spend much of his enforced imprisonment indulging in his second passion (after catching criminals) of gardening. The paralysis caused by a bullet having lodged in his spine (fired from the gun of someone who resented his success in putting away lawbreakers[1]) prevented him from doing any of the spadework, so he had to content himself with directing Bernie and Peter in a programme of clearing overgrown paths, weeding neglected borders and preparing the ground for the planting of vegetables. As panic buying cleared the shops of supplies, growing their own food

---

[1] You can read the full story in *Changing Scene of Life* ©2015 Judy Ford, ISBN: 978-1-911083-09-2

started to feel like a vital necessity and they were fortunate that the house that Bernie had inherited from her first husband had extensive grounds.

Gradually the country took on a siege mentality as more and more calls came from the public for the government to impose restrictions similar to those already in force in Italy. Only days after the Chief Superintendent's phone call, the prime minister announced that schools were to close at the end of the week. Universities hastily put all teaching online. Churches cancelled their services. Restaurants and pubs were deserted. Toilet rolls and flour vanished from supermarket shelves.

On a more personal level, Bernie's daughter Lucy, in the second year of a medical degree at the University of Liverpool, informed them that all her lectures had been put online and that she and her friend Mariam would be continuing their studies from the seclusion of the house that they shared with Lucy's second cousin, Dominic, and Mariam's brother, Ibrahim. Peter's grandparenting duties became increasingly difficult, as it became more and more clear that youngsters, who might be asymptomatic carriers of the virus, should be segregated from adults, such as Jonah, who might be at increased risk from it. In the end, he reluctantly handed Ricky and Abigail back permanently to his son, Eddie, who was by then settled into a routine of working at home.

Finally, after a week that had contained enough news for several months of normal life, Parliament passed the necessary legislation to change government advice into legally-enforceable regulations. Every Englishman's home was no longer his castle but his prison – with excursions restricted to infrequent sorties for provisions or medical supplies, daily exercise and missions of mercy to take necessities to more-vulnerable neighbours.

People over seventy or with certain pre-existing health conditions were forbidden from going out at all and instructed to make arrangements for food and other necessities to be ordered online or brought to their houses by friends and family. Jonah quickly got the legislation up on the screen attached to his wheelchair and scrolled eagerly down the list of underlying medical conditions.

'There's nothing here about spinal cord injuries!' he declared triumphantly.

'You can't expect them to list everything,' Peter argued. 'Your own doctor and the occupational health doctor both say that you may be at increased risk. Why can't you just accept what they say?'

'And in any case, what about "chronic neurological conditions"?' Bernie pointed out. 'I'd say that covers spinal injuries, even if they aren't specifically mentioned.'

'I can't see what you're making all the fuss about,' Peter went on. 'Compared with a lot of people, you're sitting pretty. We've got a big garden as well as plenty of room indoors to get away from one another. Think about Eddie, shut in that tiny flat with two under-fives!'

'And with his wife going into work at the hospital every day and maybe bringing back the virus,' Bernie added. 'For the three of us, it's basically just like being on holiday. Think positive! You'll have time to read all those e-books you downloaded and never got round to starting.'

'Or why don't you settle down and actually write those memoirs of yours that you said you were going to produce when you retired the first time?' suggested Peter, referring to the way in which Jonah had been "persuaded" to leave the police service during a period of cutbacks, and had then managed to secure an invitation to return part-time when increasing police numbers became a political necessity a few years later. 'You claimed to be full of ideas, but nothing ever came of them.'

'It's not as easy as you think,' Jonah complained, shaking his head petulantly. 'If I write about my work, I want to get things right, and I can't be sure of that without having access to the case files. It's all very well trying to remember, but once I started putting thing down in writing I realised that I wasn't always sure what the exact sequence of events was.'

'Do you have to go into it in so much detail?' asked Bernie. 'Isn't the whole point of a memoir that you're telling people what you personally remember – the things that stuck in your mind because they were important to you?'

'That's not how I want to write it,' Jonah insisted. 'I want to show people how a police investigation works: how the little details all gradually add up to make a picture that enables us to solve the crime, and then how we gather the evidence to get a conviction.'

'What about the newspaper archives?' suggested Peter. 'You can get them online. They report all the big cases. You could cross-reference with them to check your facts.'

'And I still don't think you have to treat it like a history thesis,' Bernie insisted. 'People don't want masses of pernickety detail. They just want to get an idea of how your mind works.'

'I wish them luck with that!' Peter snorted. 'Jonah's mind is as convoluted as a French horn.'

'Tell you what,' Bernie said, after a moment's thought. 'Why don't I go up in the attic and get down Richard's diaries? I've been meaning to go through them one day, when I got time. He wrote about what he did every day of his life, including the cases he was working on. He doesn't go into the fine details, but it would help you to be sure about the order in which things happened, at least for those cases where you were working with him.'

Richard Paige, Bernie's first husband and Lucy's father, had been a senior officer in Thames Valley CID, rising to the rank of superintendent before being killed in an unfortunate accident while on duty. Both Peter and Jonah had served under him. It was only several years after his death that Bernie had discovered the hoard of A4 hardback notebooks that comprised his diary, in which he had recorded his daily life from the age of seven until his untimely demise fifty-three years later. On first discovering them, she had read eagerly the entries concerning herself. Then, having satisfied her curiosity as to what Richard had thought of her when they first met and what had motivated him to cultivate her acquaintance, she had laid them aside and thought little more of them. Life was hectic as a single mother of a lively youngster and she had little spare time for browsing through someone else's past.

When Jonah came to live with them, the volumes had been packed away in boxes and transferred to the attic storeroom so that the dining room could be converted into downstairs accommodation for him. There they had lain, untouched for the best part of seven years.

It was not until several days later that Jonah, driven indoors by a bitter north-easterly wind, finally accepted Bernie's offer and consented to look through the diaries in search of a suitable case from his long career in CID to become the basis for his debut in the crowded field of police memoirs. She carried the boxes down to the living room, brushed the dust off them and then settled down on the floor to look through their contents.

'When was it you joined Richard's team?' she asked, looking towards Jonah. 'Nineteen seventy-nine, wasn't it? The same year that I graduated?'

'Well, officially not until nineteen eighty, but of course I was involved in that murder at Margaret's lodgings in seventy-nine. That was really the start of everything, but I was still just a PC then.'

'And everyone already knows all about that case,' Peter put in, 'after that TV interview you did[2]. There's no point writing about that.'

'OK then,' Bernie murmured bending over one of the cardboard boxes and pulling out one volume after another to inspect the dates written in the front of each in Richard's utilitarian handwriting – no flourishes or embellishments, with a slight tendency to leaning towards the right. 'April to September 1979, September 1979 to February 1980, February to August 1980. Would that be the one? When exactly did you join Richard's team?'

'I can't remember the date,' Jonah replied. 'It was after Easter, but not all that long I don't think.'

Bernie opened the book and started thumbing through the pages.

'Here we are! Listen to this. "Porter's first day. He's very keen and eager to please, but still has a lot to learn. I think he was disappointed that the biggest case we've got on at the moment is a break-in at a car show-room on Iffley Road. He probably imagined that we spend all our time chasing murderers and rapists! I had him going through CCTV footage all afternoon, mainly to show him that there's nothing specially exciting or glamourous about being a detective. I could see he wasn't best pleased, but to be fair, he kept his trap shut and didn't complain." Well, there you are!' she smiled up at Jonah. 'That's your first case. You could begin your memoirs by wowing your readers with a description of your valiant efforts to solve the forecourt break-in mystery!'

'Or what about this?' Peter suggested brightly, holding up another of the notebooks. "I had my doubts about Porter when he turned up late looking as if he'd spent a night on the tiles, with his hair sticking up on end

---

[2] See *Changing Scenes of Life* ©2015 Judy Ford, ISBN: 978-1-911083-09-2

and his tie knotted under one ear … He's still a bit wet-behind-the-ears. I could see he didn't have much-'"

'Oh cut it out!' Jonah barked. 'Once! Just once, I sleep through the alarm and you manage to home in on it, as if-'

'Lighten up, can't you?' Peter laughed. 'I remembered it *because* it was so unusual for you to be late or anything less than perfectly groomed.'

'But how did you know where to find that one time out of all this?' Jonah demanded, gazing round at boxes of notebooks strewn across the floor.

'I knew where to look because it was just before Hannah was born,' Peter explained, still smiling. 'Actually, I was glad Richard had decided to expand your horizons by making you his bag-carrier for a while, because I was on tenterhooks all the time in case Angie went into labour and I wasn't there for her. *And* it meant that he was using you to keep my place warm for me while I was off on leave instead of transferring another sergeant, who might have stayed on after I came back.'

'But seriously,' Bernie intervened, 'people will like reading your memoirs better if you include all your faults and failings. Everyone likes to be reassured that their heroes are just as flawed as they are.'

'Not much chance of that!' Peter joked. 'We all know that Super Cop here is practically perfect!'

'Anyway, I don't think we'll find anything worth writing about in *those* diaries,' Jonah declared. 'Put those back and get out something from a bit later on, after I had a chance to get established in the team and be trusted with doing a few things independently. If it's all going to be about old Peter and Richard working together with me tagging along behind, Peter can jolly well write the book himself!'

'Oh! It's a book now, is it?' Peter teased. 'What are you going to call it? The Greatest Detective that Ever Lived? Crimes Wot I Solved? Murders I-'

'Put a sock in it, can't you?' Jonah growled. 'If I'm going to go to the trouble of writing this stuff, I might as well put it out where people will be able to read it. You got your memoirs published, didn't you?'

'Only because Hannah badgered me to do it,' Peter argued. 'And I thought if she was so keen on the idea, perhaps I ought to do it for her and the grandkids.'

'And Jonah's got grandchildren too,' Bernie reminded him. 'That's a good idea of Peter's,' she added, turning to Jonah. 'Whatever you decide to write, do it for Nathan and Reuben and their kids. What would interest them about your work?'

'I don't know,' Jonah mused. 'Maybe they'd like to hear about some of the times their mum got involved. There was one case a couple of years later … in fact, it must've been almost exactly two years, because old Peter was off when it all kicked off celebrating becoming a father for the second time.'

'So that would be September 1982,' Bernie murmured, sorting through notebooks again. 'This'll be the one! July 1982 to January 1983.'

She flicked through the pages, stopping finally and holding up the book where Jonah could read it.

'I could've done with Johns today to help investigate a suspicious death that's cropped up,' he read out with a wry smile. 'It occurred almost on the doorstep of the police station in St Aldates.' He looked up at Bernie. 'Yes, that's the one I was thinking about. Margaret treated the victim in A and E, and she helped with getting to the bottom of what happened too. And it'll be a good story for the younger generation, because it's instructive from a historical point of view too. It all took place at a demonstration against nuclear weapons. I don't suppose they realise what a lot of unrest there was back in the eighties when we were young.'

He continued reading the diary entry to himself. Then he looked up and gestured with his head to Bernie to turn the page. She did so, shaking her head with a thoughtful expression.

'Tell you what,' she said as he nodded to her to indicate that he had read to the bottom again, 'why don't I take this away and scan in the pages so that you can read them on your computer screen? Then you'll be in control and you can refer to whichever entries you want.'

'Thanks,' Jonah smiled back. 'And while you're doing that, I can start making some notes about what I remember about the case.'

'And I'd better start peeling the potatoes,' Peter murmured, also smiling. 'I'm sure world-famous authors need feeding just as much as police heroes do!'

2. DEMONSTRATION

It was September 1982. I had been in Oxford CID for five months, working as part of the team headed up by the legendary DCI Richard Paige. At least, I always think of him as legendary, but he had only been a DCI for just over a year then, so probably he wasn't particularly well-known at that stage beyond the officers at the central Oxford police station on St Aldates. His sergeant (and my line manager) Peter Johns, was on leave following the birth of his second child, and I was fortunate enough to have been picked from among the dozen or so DCs under Richard's command to be his bag carrier until his return.

That warm, sunny morning we headed back to the station shortly before lunchtime, having been in north Oxford interviewing witnesses to an arson attack there. Well, they should have been witnesses, seeing as they admitted to having been out on the streets on the night when it happened, but they all insisted that they'd seen nothing. It's funny how the people who know something about a crime are often reluctant to come forward and tell the police, while there are others who are so keen to be part of a real-life investigation that they imagine that they have information pertinent to the enquiry when in fact they really do know nothing!

But that's all beside the point, and it isn't the setting on fire of a row of lock-up garages in Cutteslowe that I want to tell you about in this memoir. As I was saying, we returned to the police station between eleven and twelve that morning. The sun was shining and it was unusually warm for the time of year. The university term didn't start for another three weeks or so, which should have meant that the street was less busy than normal, but that morning there were plenty of people about, and not the usual groups of Japanese tourists admiring the architecture of Christ Church College, which is almost next door to the police station, or peering in at the "Old Sheep Shop" opposite, holding copies of "Alice in Wonderland" and comparing what they saw in front of them with Tenniel's illustration.

These visitors were mostly younger than the tourists, and they were predominantly female. They were wandering around in small groups, some of them looking a bit lost, as if they didn't know where they were going. Some of the slightly older ones looked rather like hippies, with full skirts, long hair and ethnic-patterned tunic tops. The younger ones were mostly in jeans and tee-shirts topped by patterned jumpers. I noticed one woman wearing a heavy woollen poncho and another with a hat covered in badges.

'Those'll be the anti-nuclear protestors,' Richard remarked as we made our way through the clusters of people.

Then I remembered that we'd been briefed about this planned demonstration earlier in the week. The organisers had been very co-operative. They'd informed the authorities that they were going to meet on Christ Church Meadow and then process to Carfax in two groups: one starting from the botanical gardens and proceeding along the High, while the others approached along St Aldates, setting out from Folly Bridge. They promised that it would be peaceful and that there would be no trouble of any kind.

Of course, that was easier to promise than to deliver. However good your intentions, bringing together a large number of people always carries certain risks, especially if you've publicised in advance that you want as many protesters as possible to march down already busy streets, hemmed in by buildings on either side. For one thing, although your intentions may be peaceful, there is always the danger that your demonstration may be infiltrated by hotheads in search of an excuse for a fight. For another, the sheer quantity of human flesh pressed together in a relatively confined space can be dangerous.

I don't know exactly how the trouble started on this occasion. There was talk afterwards of a bus striking the corner of the makeshift platform that the organisers had set up in front of Carfax Tower for speeches that were to be made once both arms of the procession had assembled there. Attempting to turn right off the High into Cornmarket, the driver had misjudged the corner – or perhaps the platform had been built too close to the road – and knocked one of the boards out of alignment. Someone had fallen off; some equipment had been damaged; harsh words were exchanged and the road was blocked by the bus and several cars, some coming up behind it and others from St Aldates.

Whatever actually caused the blockage, the consequence for the crowd of demonstrators heading up St Aldates from Folly Bridge was that there was nowhere for them to go. The people at the back could not see what was going on at the front, but they could hear what they imagined to be the speeches beginning as one of the organisers tried to calm the chaos at Carfax by speaking to the crowd there on the public address system that they had rigged up.

Richard and I were oblivious to what was going on outside. He set me typing up the results of our morning's interviews while he checked with other members of his team to find out how they were progressing with other investigations. Then, after lunch in the canteen, we sat down together to collate what we knew about the arson attack and to plan our next move. It must have been around mid-afternoon that we were called to help quell what by then amounted almost to a riot in the street outside.

The main crush was near the top of St Aldates, outside the Town Hall, but the road was packed with jostling bodies, right down as far as the police station itself. We joined the army of uniformed officers who were attempting to relieve the pressure by diverting some of the protestors down side streets or into the quadrangle of Christ Church College. It must have been round about half past three when we finally managed to get the crowd to disperse. We were setting up a police cordon to keep pedestrians off the road so that the traffic, which by then was backing up down the Abingdon Road beyond Folly Bridge almost to the by-pass, could start flowing again, when one of the demonstrators called out to us.

I ran over to see what she wanted. She was standing over a young man who was lying motionless on the ground. Another girl was kneeling down beside him slapping him on the cheek and calling out, 'Are you alright? Wake up!'

Both girls looked to be in their teens and my immediate thought was, 'why aren't they in school?' However, I was more concerned about the young man whose face looked strangely grey and whose eyes seemed to be staring into nowhere. As I watched, his limbs suddenly began jerking in rapid spasms and his face took on a series of weird expressions. I'd been told about epileptic seizures during my training, but I'd never seen one in real life. Was this what it looked like? What was it that you were supposed to do?

'It's alright,' I found myself saying, putting as much authority as I could muster into my voice. 'I'm a police officer. Just move back a bit to give him more room.'

I took off my jacket and folded it up to act as a makeshift pillow. Then I turned him over into the recovery position, placing the jacket under his head. The convulsions seemed to be decreasing in strength and becoming less frequent. Perhaps he would recover by himself in a few minutes. I certainly hoped so.

'I'll call an ambulance.' I looked round and saw Sergeant Fuller standing over me. 'Carry on with the first aid, Porter. You're doing a great job there.'

I didn't feel I was doing anything much, but Fuller's words spurred me on and I started talking to the young man, telling him that he was safe and that the ambulance would be here soon. Up above me, I could hear Fuller questioning the two girls.

'Are you friends of his? Can you tell me his name?'

'No. Sorry,' they mumbled back. 'We've never met him before today.'

'I think he was with some other people,' one of them volunteered after a few moments, 'but they aren't here now.'

'We all got mixed up when the pushing started,' the other added.

'Did you happen to see which way the others went?'

'No. Sorry,' they repeated in unison.

'It was all just, such a – a mess!' came the first voice again. 'We were just concentrating on not getting separated.'

'We don't know anyone else here,' the other explained. 'So we wanted to keep together. We weren't expecting it to be like this. We thought it was just a rally, to show we don't want nuclear weapons here.'

'Alright. Never mind,' Fuller said kindly. 'It probably doesn't matter. I expect he'll come round soon and he'll be able to tell us who he is himself and who his friends are. But please stick around. The ambulance crew may want to ask you some questions about what happened to him.'

The two girls retreated to the side of the road and stood leaning against the honey-coloured stone wall that bounded Christ Church College. They appeared very uncomfortable. I'm guessing they weren't looking forward to being cross-examined about what they knew of the unfortunate young man, who was now lying still as if he had fallen asleep with his eyes open.

Fuller kneeled down next to me and started going through the lad's pockets, looking for something that would tell us who he was. He started with the inside pocket of his anorak, presumably assuming that that was the most likely place for valuables such as a wallet or driving licence. No luck there, so he tried the outer pockets.

'Well lookie here!' he exclaimed, holding out a transparent plastic syringe with a hypodermic needle still attached. 'I'd say that puts a different complexion on things, don't you?'

'What's going on here?' Richard had come up behind Fuller and was standing over him staring down at the syringe.

'He passed out in the crush,' Fuller explained. 'I thought it looked like an epileptic fit, but now I'm not so sure. It could well be drugs-related, sir.'

'Hand that over,' Richard ordered, holding out his hand with a clean handkerchief draped over it. 'I'll take care of it for now.'

He wrapped the syringe carefully and stowed it away in his jacket pocket. I rather fancy that even at that stage he suspected that there was more to this than met the eye.

It wasn't long before the ambulance came and took the casualty away. They did their best to revive him at the scene, but none of their efforts had any effect as far as I could see. He remained apparently lifeless with his mouth lolling open and his eyes glazed over, staring at nothing.

As Fuller had predicted, while his colleagues worked on attempting to resuscitate the young man, one of the ambulance men went over and spoke briefly to the girls who had been next to him in the crowd when he collapsed. They gave their names as Tina and Jacqueline. I remember particularly because there had been a Tina in my class at Primary School. Tiny Tina, we called her because she was so much shorter than any of the other girls. This Tina was a "big strapping lass" as my wife would have said, with long brown hair that flopped all over her face as she talked. Her friend Jacqueline was smaller and quieter. I wondered why her parents had chosen such a sophisticated name for such an ordinary-looking girl. She had mousey hair cut in a pageboy style and brown eyes that stared round anxiously reminding me of a frightened deer.

They both insisted that they'd never met the man before and had no idea who he was. They'd only really noticed him at all when the crowd started to thin out and he slid to the floor next to them. Could he have been unconscious for some time before he collapsed, then? Well, yes, they supposed he might. They really hadn't been paying him any attention.

The ambulance left and Richard took over the interrogation. Eventually he teased out from them some sort of picture of the events leading up to the young man's collapse.

He had been in a group with about four or five other people. The rest were all women, the girls thought, but they weren't quite sure about that. There might have been one other man, but probably not, or at least … well he may not have been in the group at all. When the people behind them in the procession started pushing forward, the group had split up. Two – or it may have been three – disappeared to the left. Maybe they went down a side street to get away from the crush. The others all stayed together until the police came and started telling everyone to disperse. Then most of the others slipped out to the right and the girls never saw them again.

The crowd carried on pushing from behind and the girls ended up pressed up against the man. He was just standing there with his hands at his sides. Then someone else moved away from in front of him and he fell down on the floor. Jacqueline got down on the ground to try to revive him – she was in the Girl Guides and had a First Aider badge – and Tina shouted out to the police to come and help.

We thanked the girls for their assistance, took down their names and addresses in case we needed to speak to them again, and then Richard looked round for a WPC[3] to drive them home. His eyes lighted on Alison Brown, a bright young officer who had only been in the force for a couple of years.

Seeing him looking at her, she hurried over.

'Sir!' she began. 'I've got some people here who want to speak to the officer in charge.'

'That'll be Chief Inspector Eddleston,' Richard told her. 'He's responsible for policing the demonstration. What is it they want with him?'

'They've lost one of their friends and they saw someone being taken off in an ambulance and they thought ...'

Richard immediately turned to address the small group of people that was standing at a respectful distance behind Alison.

'Your friend?' he asked briskly. 'Can you describe him to me?'

'He's got dark hair,' one of the two women volunteered, after a moment's hesitation, 'and dark brown eyes. He's a bit taller than John.' She waved her hand in the direction of a young man with straw-coloured hair and pale blue eyes wearing a leather jacket over jeans.

'And he was wearing?' prompted Richard.

---

[3] Woman Police Constable. This term was finally discontinued in 1999.

'Jeans and a CND tee-shirt,' the other woman answered promptly. 'And a blue anorak.'

Richard looked towards Fuller and me. We nodded back. The description fitted.

* * *

'And that's where I thought I'd finish the first chapter,' Jonah concluded, turning his gaze towards the four faces watching him from his computer screen.

It was the daily videoconference between Lucy, and her housemates in Liverpool, and her mother in Oxford. Jonah had been entertaining them with the opening pages of his memoirs.

'You must have a very good memory,' Dominic observed. 'I'm sure I'd never have managed to remember what everyone said word for word like that.'

'Well, I have to admit I couldn't swear to the exact words,' Jonah conceded. 'I remembered the gist and then made the words convey the right message. I thought it gave a better idea of what it was like for us than if I'd just said things like, "Fuller asked the girls if they knew the man and they said they didn't." or "there was a hypodermic syringe in the victim's pocket." Conversation brings it all to life better – or at least that was my idea. Don't you like it?'

'Oh I like it OK,' Dominic said hastily. 'I was just surprised, that's all.'

'So, when you said that Adrian Fuller told you that you were doing a great job, he may not have said anything of the sort?' suggested Peter mischievously.

'You said this was a murder case,' Mariam commented. 'So presumably the young man didn't make it?'

'That's right,' Jonah confirmed. 'As luck would have it, my wife Margaret was on duty at the hospital that day and she pronounced him dead on arrival. The constable that went with them in the ambulance rang Richard to let him know and that's when the investigation really began in earnest.'

'I suppose you'll have started by interviewing his friends,' Ibrahim suggested. 'What did they tell you about him? Was it drugs in the syringe? How did you know he didn't inject himself?'

'Hang on, hang on!' Jonah protested. 'You're getting ahead of yourself! You've got to realise that it takes time to get the contents of a syringe analysed and even longer to get toxicology reports done on a dead person. Not to mention the time it takes for a fingerprint expert to examine an object and tell us who, if anyone, has been handling it! The first thing Richard did was to order the uniformed officers to go round getting names and addresses from everyone who had been on the demonstration, so that we could follow them all up later.'

'I remember that,' Bernie put in, leaning over Jonah's shoulder so that the four viewers in Liverpool could see her. 'I was interviewed by an unpleasant Police Sergeant who seemed very full of himself and very scornful of demonstrators in general and anti-nuclear demonstrators in particular.'

'*You* were interviewed, Mam?' squealed Lucy in surprise. 'You mean you were there?'

'Indeed I was!' her mother declared proudly. 'I made a placard, denouncing Margaret Thatcher and the way she was cosying up to Ronald Reagan.'

'So did you see what happened?' asked Dominic eagerly. 'Were you a key witness?'

'No, I'm afraid not,' Bernie laughed. 'I was in the other part of the procession, the one that started from the Botanical Gardens and went up the High. I didn't see a thing. We just got to within sight of Carfax, hung around for a while waiting for them to sort out the bus that was jammed and then went home for tea. Or at least, we were just about to, when this Sergeant Something-or-other came along telling us all to line up against the wall and wait for one of his constables to take our names. Then he wandered along the line, picking out people he fancied interrogating personally and breathing tobacco fumes all over us.'

'A big fellow, with black hair and a nose that looked as if it'd been broken in a fight?' asked Peter.

'Yes. That sounds about right,' Bernie agreed. 'A friend of yours?'

'Hardly! That must've been Adams. I never understood why anyone thought he merited being made up to sergeant, but I suppose he must've passed the exam and nobody had the courage not to give him his stripes.'

'I remember him,' Jonah nodded. 'He thought the idea of Margaret being a surgeon was highly amusing. His idea of women was that they had no business being anywhere except the kitchen or the bedroom!'

'He was a racist too,' Peter added. 'And when he'd had a skinful he lost all control over his mouth. I nearly punched him in it one time when he started on Angie.'

'He had a down on gypsies and homeless men too,' Jonah continued. 'He was just a mass of prejudices wrapped up in a police uniform.'

'And the worst was that a lot of the younger men looked up to him,' Peter went on. 'They thought he was strong and hard, when he was really just a bully. And if anyone criticised him, there'd be plenty of people – senior officers even – who would say things like, "Lighten up. Can't you take a joke?" and "In a job like this you've got to let the men let off steam now and again."'

'I'm glad things have changed now,' Jonah said fervently, 'You'll still find people who moan about "political correctness gone mad", but mainly we're all singing from the same hymn sheet now and his attitude just wouldn't be tolerated.'

'Or so you hope,' Ibrahim remarked. 'I don't always feel that Muslims are included in this celebration of diversity that we're all supposed to be bought into these days.'

'Too many people believe that our hymn sheet is fundamentally different from yours,' Mariam added dryly.

'But go on,' Dominic urged. 'Tell us what happened next. How did you find out who killed him?'

'Not yet,' Lucy cut in quickly. 'First, *I* want to know exactly what it was Mam was protesting about. Who's Ronald Reagan?'

'He was the President of the United States,' her mother told her. 'Surely you must have heard of him! We were protesting about the Americans being allowed to site cruise missiles at their base at Greenham Common. That's not all that far from Oxford – near Newbury.'

'And what exactly *are* cruise missiles?' asked Lucy.

'Long-range missiles that could send nuclear warheads as far as the Soviet Union,' Bernie explained. 'It was all part of the Cold War. Surely you must have learnt about that at school? The idea was that the Russians wouldn't dare to attack us because if they did we'd destroy them; but the way I saw it, the Russians weren't half as likely to *want* to attack us if we refrained from pointing nuclear weapons at them! Not to mention the danger of a nuclear accident while those weapons were being stored there or moved around from one place to another. So we were protesting against Maggie Thatcher allowing the Americans to base their missiles in Britain.'

'Did it work?' Mariam asked.

'No.' Bernie shook her head. 'Thatcher got her way and the missiles came, but the Greenham Women gave her a good fight. Surely you *must* have heard of them? They set up a peace camp outside the base. Later on that year, thousands of us held hands in a circle all round the perimeter of the base. We were famous all over the world! Don't they teach you any history in schools these days?'

'We did a lot about the two world wars,' Lucy told her, 'and the Tudors and Stuarts.'

'And we did the history of medicine,' Mariam added, 'which was interesting.'

'*I* learned about CND,' Dominic volunteered, 'but that was in RE, not history. Anyway, does it matter what the march was about? I'm more interested in who the guy who died was and why he was killed. Aren't you going to tell us? Or do we have to wait for you to write the next chapter?'

'I haven't got it all planned out yet,' Jonah told him. 'I need to read up more of Richard's diary to check that I'm remembering it right. His account of the first few days of the investigation doesn't say much, but I'm hoping there may be more later, from when we gave evidence at the trial. I just wish I had access to the police files as well. And I wish I'd thought to keep a diary of my own. It would have been really useful for checking my facts.'

'Except that I bet you wouldn't have written down the things you want now,' Bernie commented. 'You'd have written about the things that seemed important at the time – like your wedding plans and whether Richard would support you in doing the Sergeant's exam – not the details of a case that may not even have looked very significant at the start.'

'How did you know it was murder?' asked Dominic. 'I mean, it could have been that the guy injected himself, couldn't it?'

'Yes, it could,' Jonah agreed. 'And that's what we assumed at first. We had to wait for the PM before we even knew whether that syringe had anything to do with his death.'

'So, are you going to tell us?' Dominic persisted. 'You haven't even said who he was yet!'

'Well, I think you ought to wait,' Ibrahim declared. 'It won't be as much fun if Jonah tells us about it in bits and pieces like that. I'd rather have the story set out properly, in the right order so we can see how the police worked out what happened.'

'Well, I'll try to get another chapter done tomorrow,' Jonah promised, pleased to hear that his efforts were appreciated. 'But it's slow work, I'm afraid.'

'Is there anything I could do to help?' asked Ibrahim eagerly. 'Would you like me to transcribe the diaries into Word files, so that you could search them better? Or … how exactly do you write? You don't type it all with two fingers on that little keypad do you?'

'No,' Jonah smiled. 'I dictate using voice-recognition software. Then our Bernie's been going through fixing the places where it heard me wrong – things like words that sound similar but mean different things or where I said one thing and then changed my mind or umm-ed and err-ed a bit; and the punctuation is usually pretty awful at that stage. *Then* I start on the one-finger editing stuff, which is what takes the most time and is the most boring part.'

'*I* wouldn't mind doing the editing,' Ibrahim volunteered. 'To save Bernie the bother. I've got plenty of time, with not being allowed out.'

'I thought Lucy said you were working at home,' commented Peter.

'I am, but that's only for eight hours a day, so there's still evenings and weekends with nothing much to do.'

'You *said* you were going to help us dig a vegetable patch in the garden,' his sister reminded him.

'I can do that too,' Ibrahim insisted. 'There'll be plenty of time for both.'

'OK. You're on!' Jonah smiled at the young man's enthusiasm. 'I'll get the next few pages dictated this evening and send them across to you before we turn in.'

'But mind you don't go giving away the story!' Bernie called over her friend's shoulder. 'Those files are for your eyes only!'

'Can't I help with the editing?' pleaded Dominic. 'My school's closed, so apart from planning online lessons for next term and keeping in touch with people by phone, I've got plenty of time to do it.'

'Tell you what,' Jonah suggested, 'Why don't you split the work? Ibrahim's right: it would be handy to have Richard's diaries typed up so that I can do key-word searches and that sort of thing instead of having to read every line of his long-hand to find out what it's about. How about one of you doing that and the other editing my dictation?'

'Yes!' Dominic agreed eagerly. 'Yes. If you email the files across to us, we can sort out who does what.'

'It sounds as if that's settled then,' said Bernie. 'Now can we set Jonah's literary efforts to one side for a bit and talk about real life? How are your parents doing, Dom? And have you been able to go to see Aunty Dot at all?'

3. FRIENDS

According to his friends, the victim was a Timothy Sudbury. The name agreed with the one on the Bodleian Library reader card that Fuller had found in the back pocket of his jeans before he was carted off in the ambulance. It turned out that he was a postgraduate student at Henderson College, which is one of the twentieth century colleges founded to boost research at the university. It doesn't take any undergraduates – what most people think of as "normal" students.

His friends were all postgraduate students too. Term hadn't started yet for the undergraduates but research students tend to hang around all year, especially if their subject is one of those that needs access to labs.

We interviewed John Goodey (medicine), Diane Winter (Archaeology) and Faith Nelson (also Archaeology). They all shared a house in New Hinksey together with Tim Sudbury. They were able to give us the information that he was from Leicester and that his parents were divorced.

While we were talking to them, a message came through on the police radio to say that Timothy had been pronounced dead on arrival, so now we were dealing with a suspicious death, but we still weren't thinking of murder. It looked more like an accidental drugs overdose (assuming that he'd used the syringe to inject himself) or else that he'd been suffocated by pressure in the crowd. His friends weren't able to tell us the address of either of his parents, so Richard sent me off to contact Leicester Police.

That was about it for that day. After leaving my message with the police in Leicester to find Tim Sudbury's parents and break the bad news to them, I went back and spent a couple of hours helping Uniform with the task of taking down names and addresses of demonstrators and asking them if they'd seen anything. Then I went home to my room in the shared house in Summertown, which is when I discovered that it was Margaret who had seen the victim when he arrived at the hospital and had confirmed his death.

* * *

'So you and Margaret were living together before you got married?' Lucy interrupted Jonah as he paused for breath in reading out the latest chapter of his memoir across the internet link to his eager listeners in Liverpool. 'I didn't think that sort of thing went on in those days.'

'Like I said, it was a shared house,' Jonah explained, 'the same as you're in now. I was on the ground floor and Margaret had her own room upstairs, together with three other women. There were nine of us altogether: three men, four women and a co-habiting couple in a flat in the attic. It was all perfectly proper – well, apart from the couple in the attic!'

'We don't assume you and Ibrahim have got an illicit love-nest,' her mother broke in, 'and even Dom's mam has come round to the idea that it's OK for him to be living in the same house as Mariam, and *they're* engaged!'

'But plenty of couples did live together before they got married, even in those days,' Jonah put in. 'And plenty of them didn't bother with marriage at all. Don't forget, this was after the Swinging Sixties and the Summer of Love and all that.'

'But stop interrupting, Lu!' Ibrahim was impatient to hear Jonah's story.

'Yes, go on Jonah!' Dominic urged. 'You said you were going to tell us about the suspects in this chapter. We don't even know that there's been a crime committed yet!'

* * *

Margaret was very interested when I told her about the syringe that we'd found in the dead man's pocket. She thought that might well have something to do with his death, which didn't have any obvious physical cause. She was sure he hadn't been crushed to death, because there was no sign of bruising on his torso. The ambulance paramedic had described his symptoms as being like some sort of epileptic seizure, but that could easily have been drug-induced. I made a note to myself to check with the victim's friends and family whether he had a history of epilepsy.

I was too excited to sleep much that night. It was the first time that I had actually been there on the scene when a suspicious death was discovered. I have to admit that I was rather hoping that it might be a murder, rather than some sort of sordid drug-induced death. Of course, I now know that there are lots of reasons why people take drugs, but back then I have to admit to a self-righteous feeling of superiority when it came to addiction, especially where students were concerned. After all, they were mostly from privileged backgrounds and they were all well-educated enough to know better than to touch the things!

I wore a clean shirt the next day and gave my work suit a brush down before putting it on; and I took care to be in the briefing room before Richard got there in the morning. I was pleased when he announced that he was now officially in charge of the investigation into the death of Timothy James Sudbury, age 25, studying for a DPhil in biochemistry at Henderson College.

My first task wasn't very exciting. Richard set me looking into Sudbury's university record, which was also not particularly interesting. He'd matriculated in 1976 with a closed scholarship at St Luke's College, which had some sort of historical link with the independent boarding school that he had attended. He'd gone on to get Firsts in Mods and Schools and then a grant to continue his studies under Dr Ivor Williams, a university lecturer and recently-appointed fellow of Holy Cross College. He seemed to have had an exemplary undergraduate career, without so much as a fine for late return of a library book against his name.

Things started looking up later that morning with the arrival in Oxford of Timothy Sudbury's parents and stepmother. Richard took me with him to the station to meet the mother. We watched as the train came in, scanning the platform for likely-looking passengers. It wasn't hard to identify Dr Virginia Sudbury, who was a tall woman with black hair, fastened neatly in a bun on the nape of her neck, and dark brown eyes with which she looked round intently, clearly on the lookout for her promised police escort. She was wearing an immaculate purple skirt suit and carrying a black briefcase. She reminded me of some of the intimidating women who used to come round to the manse when I was a child, intent on discussing the Sunday-School curriculum with my father or to recruit my mother into teams for knitting squares to make blankets for refugees or baking cakes in support of overseas missions.

Richard stepped forward and raised his arm to display his warrant card. He caught Mrs Sudbury's eye and she walked briskly along the platform to meet us.

'Chief Inspector Paige?' she enquired, speaking in a calm, confident tone. 'I'm Dr Sudbury – Timothy's mother. We spoke on the phone earlier.'

Richard confirmed his identity, introduced me and offered his condolences on the death of her son. She paused briefly in her stride to nod acknowledgement towards him, and then continued towards the ticket barrier. Soon we were all out in the weak September sunshine and Richard was holding open the door to allow her to settle into the back seat of the car. Then he went round to the other side and got in beside her.

'We'll take you to the police station first,' Richard told her as I started the car. 'We've got some questions that we'll have to ask you, I'm afraid, and then we'll need someone from the family to do the formal identification. But you might prefer your husband to do that,' he added after a short pause. He was a bit old-fashioned in many ways and probably thought that a man would be less likely to break down at the sight of his son's body. 'He's on his way over here, but he didn't know exactly when he'd arrive.'

'No. I'll do it,' Dr Sudbury said firmly. 'I suppose he's bringing Audrey and the girls with him?'

'He didn't say,' Richard answered. 'They'd be your husband's second wife and their children, I take it?'

'That's right.'

'And Timothy? Does he live with you or with his father – when he isn't in Oxford, I mean?'

'Well, my surgery is in the family home, so I was allowed to keep it when we got divorced, which means that Tim's stuff is all at my house, but neither of us sees much of him these days. He was already up at Oxford when Mark and Audrey got married, so there was no question of custody. It's – I mean, it was – all just up to him.'

It transpired that both of Timothy's parents were doctors. His mother was a GP and his father was a consultant dermatologist. The breakdown of their marriage seemed to have followed the stereotypical pattern of the husband attempting to prove his virility in middle-age by conducting an affair with a younger woman. Audrey White, an English teacher at Timothy's school, had fallen pregnant and Mark Sudbury had been persuaded to leave his first wife in order to provide proper support to her and the child.

'I'm sure she did it deliberately,' Virginia Sudbury told Richard, as I turned the car into the yard at the back of the police station, 'but you can't blame her. Her biological clock was ticking away and Mark must have been her last-ditch attempt to achieve motherhood, which she sees as the pinnacle of every woman's ambition.'

Mark Sudbury and his second family were waiting in Reception for Richard's return. He was a rather portly man with a border of pale grey hair around a shiny bald dome. He was wearing a three-piece suit in a grey pin-stripe material and a black-and-red bow tie. He got up when Richard went over to introduce himself and shook hands, looking directly into his face through rimless spectacles.

Audrey, the second Mrs Sudbury, was shorter than her predecessor and appeared less self-confident. She remained seated, with one arm around a small, golden-haired girl sitting on her lap and the other resting on the shoulder of a slightly older child who was standing alongside her. When Richard suggested that we all went to his office where we could talk in private, she made a great fuss of collecting together their things (plastic drinking cups, a few soft toys and a pile of picture books) and stuffing them into a bulky shopping bag, which she handed to her husband to leave her own hands free for leading the girls.

We made our way down the corridor at the pace of the toddler, who insisted on pausing at each door, patting it with her small fist and announcing, 'door!' proudly to the world. Her mother responded each time with encouraging exclamations telling her how clever she was and confirming to her that this was indeed a door. I could see that her husband was embarrassed by this performance and I was watching him closely to see whether his impatience would finally get the better of him and make him break his silence. However, before he reached that tipping point we were at the door of Richard's office and he ushered us all inside.

Richard found chairs for his guests, arranging them with a diplomatic space between Virginia and her ex-husband's new family, before sitting down behind his desk. There were no more seats, so I perched on a two-drawer filing cabinet in the corner of the room.

It was a good place from which to watch the proceedings, because it gave me a view of everyone's faces. Dr Mark Sudbury looked tired, worried and harassed, and kept looking from his second wife to his first and back again. Audrey seemed to be completely taken up with looking after the children, hugging them and whispering to and taking very little notice of what was going on around her. Virginia remained calm and self-possessed, her expression inscrutable. At the time, I thought that none of them seemed very upset by Timothy's death, but with more experience I now realise that they were probably still in a state of shock and unable to take in the unexpected and almost unthinkable news. I also suspect that Virginia was very determinedly holding in her feelings in order not to give way to any emotion in front of her successor.

Richard summarised the circumstances of Timothy's death and explained that there would have to be a post-mortem examination of his body to ascertain its cause. Of course, none of that can have been a surprise to his parents, seeing as they were both medics. They received the information without comment while Audrey hardly seemed to be listening. Her attention seemed to be single-mindedly on the two children, whom she introduced as Titania and Rosalind. I was glad that my parents had favoured the Bible over the Bard when it came to choosing names for their offspring. *Jonah* was quite bad enough for a young officer to live down – Oberon or Orlando would have been impossible!

Richard was just going on to thank Virginia for agreeing to do the formal identification when there was a knock on the door and one of the secretarial staff came in with a tray of tea and biscuits. That interrupted the conversation while everyone sorted out milk and sugar and the girls were allowed to choose a biscuit each.

Then, at last, we were able to get down to the main business of the interview. I took notes, trying to do so unobtrusively, because we didn't want the parents to feel that they were under interrogation or that we suspected their son of anything illegal – although we did!

The questioning started out on the relatively safe ground of Timothy's medical history and, in particular, whether he had ever suffered from epileptic seizures. Both of his parents shook their heads and declared that he had never experienced any type of neurological disorder.

They both also denied any suggestion that their son was in the habit of taking recreational drugs, and Virginia volunteered the information that her own supplies of medical equipment, including hypodermic syringes, were kept strictly under lock and key in her surgery. Even Audrey looked up from her children for long enough to support the claim that Timothy had been exceptionally clean-living.

'He was a vegan!' she protested. 'He was very into a healthy lifestyle. He'd never have taken drugs.'

I wasn't sure what a vegan was. Veganism hadn't taken off the way it has now. I noted it down, in case it turned out to be important later, and hoped that I'd spelled it right.

Timothy had spent some time staying at his mother's house during August and had not appeared depressed or to have any particular worries. He had told Virginia that his research was going well and he expected to submit his thesis on time. He had a girlfriend whom Virginia had met briefly. She was Irish, but had lived in Oxford most of her life. Her father was a don, Virginia believed. Her name? Virginia couldn't remember. It was very Irish – Maeve, perhaps? And her surname was O'Something. It probably wasn't very serious. It had only started up in the last few months, as far as she knew. Before that he'd been going out with a girl called Faith, who was studying Archaeology.

Faith Nelson?

Yes. That was her name. She seemed a nice girl – very solid and studious with ambitious plans for a career in academia.

And who ended the relationship? Was it Timothy or Faith?

Virginia didn't know. Mark was equally ignorant. I got the impression that he hadn't even known of the existence of either Faith or the Irish girlfriend. I made a note to ask about this when we next interviewed the friends who had been with Timothy on the demonstration. They might be able to tell us the actual identity of his present girlfriend too, and where we might find her.

After that, Mark and Audrey took the girls away to let off steam in the University Parks, while Richard and I drove Virginia to the mortuary to identify Timothy's body, which she did in a business-like fashion without any display of emotion. I was glad not to have to cope with floods of tears, but I did think that a mother would have been more visibly upset at the death of her son. Looking back, I suppose it probably still hadn't properly sunk in with her yet.

She told us that she needed to get back to Leicester for her evening surgery, so we dropped her off at the railway station before heading back to Richard's office to plan our next move.

That next move turned out (for me) to be chivvying up the lab that was testing the contents of that syringe that we found in Timothy Sudbury's jacket pocket, while Richard had another chat with Mark Sudbury. He was waiting for us when we got back. He explained that his wife had found a playground where she could entertain the children so that he could speak to the police without distractions. He wanted to know what we were expecting our investigation to discover and when his son's body would be released for burial.

I imagine that Richard told him the usual stuff about how the PM couldn't happen until after the weekend and we'd be in touch as soon as we knew the cause of death. The coroner's office would be given his name and address so that they could contact him with an interim death certificate and news of when the inquest would take place.

I got back from my phone call just as he was saying that, until the coroner made his decision, there was not much that he could do regarding funeral arrangements, but there would be no harm in discussing with Timothy's mother what sort of ceremony they wanted when the time came. Dr Sudbury looked dissatisfied, but resigned. I wondered how easy it was going to be for him to negotiate funeral arrangements with Virginia.

Needless to say, the lab didn't have any results on the contents of the syringe yet, but they did have some rather interesting news regarding fingerprints on the outside of it: there were none! (Well, only some from Sergeant Fuller when he picked it out of the lad's pocket.) As I said to Richard, if Timothy Sudbury had used it to administer drugs to himself, he'd hardly have bothered to wipe his prints off the syringe afterwards!

I was becoming convinced that this was murder, and not a fatal epileptic seizure or an accidental overdose.

* * *

'But you promised you were going to tell us about suspects!' Dominic complained, as Jonah paused dramatically and looked straight into the camera as if waiting for a reaction from his audience.

'Yes, well I didn't get as far as I was expecting today,' he confessed. 'It's taken longer than I thought to describe what happened with the victim's parents.'

'Aren't most murder victims killed by members of their own household?' asked Ibrahim. 'Presumably in this case, that would be the other students that he was sharing a house with.'

'That's what I thought,' nodded Jonah. 'I wanted to interview them right away, but Richard said that the victim's family had to come first, and that took up most of the first day of the investigation. I'll try and write up what happened when we talked to them tomorrow.'

'Surely whoever killed him *must* have been one of the demonstrators?' suggested Dominic, unwilling to allow the conversation to end without addressing the question of "who done it?" 'And it must've been someone who was near him in the crowd. What about those two girls who were there with him when he collapsed? Did you investigate them?'

'Yes, we did, as a matter of fact.' Jonah sounded slightly annoyed at the question. 'But that was all later. There were hundreds of people there that day, so it took a whole team of officers to take statements and then collate them and follow up on people who might have seen something.'

'OK, so let's see,' Dominic said excitedly. 'We've got those two – what were their names, again?'

'Jacqueline Lancing and Tina Hammond,' Ibrahim answered promptly, looking down at the copy of Jonah's manuscript on his own computer.

'Right,' Dominic murmured, 'and then there's John ...'

'Goodey,' his friend prompted.

'And two more girls: Faith and Diane, was it?'

'That's right,' Ibrahim confirmed, 'Faith Nelson and Diane Winter.'

'That makes five people who were all close to the victim at some point during the demonstration and could've injected him with some sort of poison and then slipped the syringe into his pocket!' Dominic finished triumphantly.

'And I've got another for you,' Bernie said suddenly. 'Did you know about Dawn Farmer? Did you interview her?'

'Not until much later,' Jonah replied tetchily. 'I was going to come to her at the proper time. What do you know about her anyway?'

'And who is she?' asked Lucy.

'She was one of the organisers of the demo,' Bernie explained. 'She made the headlines for a few weeks because she was so young – and some of the tabloids made a big thing of her being neglected by her mother, who was one of the Greenham Common women. She was one of a group of sixth-formers[4] at the march. I saw her before it started, at the rally on Christ Church Meadow. She was one of the speakers – and Timothy Sudbury was another!' she added dramatically.

'Well, we only found out about her a few days later,' Jonah insisted sulkily. 'So you'll hear about her in a later chapter. We didn't get to interview her on the day: she must have slipped away before we started rounding up the demonstrators and taking down their names and addresses.'

'I suppose the two girls that I saw her with must have been the two who were with Timothy Sudbury when he collapsed,' Bernie continued, ignoring his protests. 'I

---

[4] For historical reasons, the last two years of secondary school in England and Wales are known as the sixth form.

hadn't realised that from the newspaper reports. It's funny they told you they didn't know anyone else.'

'Will you just stop interfering?' Jonah demanded testily. 'I'm telling this story, not you. The whole point of finishing this chapter here is that it leaves the readers with a bit of a cliff-hanger wondering who cleaned the fingerprints off the syringe.'

'I bet the syringe doesn't have anything to do with it!' Lucy declared. 'I think you're just trying to lead us up the garden path by making such a mystery of it. I expect the post mortem will show that he died of something completely different.'

'But not an epileptic seizure or a heart attack,' Dominic cut in. 'He's already told us it's a murder investigation, so it can't have been natural causes.'

'Unless this isn't the actual murder victim and the real murder's going to come later,' Mariam suggested. 'I'm with Lucy: I don't think we can trust him not to be stringing us all along, when the real case is about someone quite different.'

'That Dawn Farmer, for instance,' Lucy chimed in. 'He didn't like Mam bringing her up. I bet she's really important and he wanted to use her in some dramatic reveal later on.'

'You can think what you like,' Jonah grinned, his good humour now fully restored. 'I'm telling this story the way I want, and you'll all just have to wait for the next thrilling instalment, won't you?'

4. SUSPECTS

The following day was Saturday, but Richard and I were both on duty. He took me on a visit to the shared house in New Hinksey where Timothy Sudbury had lived with his friends. Faith Nelson and Diane Winter were both at home. They seemed glad to see us. I fancy that any distraction was welcome to take their minds off the tragedy of the day before.

Faith hastily gathered up dirty coffee mugs and empty crisp packets from the low table in the communal living room, while Diane picked up a pile of papers from the settee and brushed crumbs off the chairs. They told us that the third resident of the house, John Goodey, was out. He was a doctor in training and was on a ward round with one of the consultants at the Radcliffe[5]. I made a mental note to ask Margaret if she had come across him. It sounded as if he must have been only two or three years behind her in the medical school.

Soon Richard and I were seated on the sofa, studying the young women across the table. Faith's eyes looked tired and her cheeks were blotchy red and white. She had no makeup on and appeared still to be in her pyjamas, although it was getting on for ten o'clock. Diane seemed more composed, but the thick layer of foundation cream

---

[5] The Radcliffe Infirmary, dating back to 1770, was the main hospital for the city of Oxford until the John Radcliffe Hospital opened in the 1970s. It finally closed in 2007.

on her face did not quite obscure a slight redness around her eyes.

'Is there any news?' she asked eagerly. 'Do you know how it happened?'

'I'm afraid not,' Richard replied gently. 'We need to ask you some more questions I'm afraid, and then we'd like to have a look round Timothy's room.' He turned to Faith. 'His mother says that you and he used to be going steady. Is that right?'

I smiled at Richard's quaint, old-fashioned terminology and wondered idly whether he had ever been "going steady" with a girl. I couldn't imagine it, but then young people always do find it hard to believe that their parents' generation could ever have experienced youthful passion.

'That was a long time ago,' Faith answered. 'It was before we ... We were still undergraduates. I was at Shrewsbury College and he was at St Luke's. We met at a dance at St Luke's. The men's colleges always invite ... I mean, there are so many more men than women in Oxford that they're always glad to have women coming to their events, so they let us in free.'

'And you split up, when?'

'Oh, ages ago! Just after I started my DPhil, I think.'

'And how exactly did that come about?' Richard pressed her gently.

'It's difficult to say. We just sort of ... realised it wasn't working. I mean, we stayed friends, but we just didn't ... Well, I was away for a long time on a field trip. We're – Diane and I are working on a big project excavating an ancient settlement site in Dorset, aren't we Di?' She turned to her friend for support. 'It's very exciting. We think some of the inhabitants may have been Phoenician. If we're right, it could change the whole way we look at life in Britain before the Roman invasion. ... And then after a bit Tim started going out with Niamh.'

'Neave?' I queried. 'How do you spell that?'

'N-I-A-M-H,' Diane spelled out. 'It's Irish.'

'And were Timothy and Niamh still going out together when he died?' Richard asked.

'Yes,' Diane confirmed. 'They were both there yesterday – at the demo. We were all there together: me and Faith, John, Tim and Niamh, and Wendy.'

'Wendy?' This was a new name and I wanted to make sure that I had it right in my notes.

'Wendy Brotherton. She and Niamh share a flat in Temple Street – between Cowley Road and Iffley Road.'

'Yes, I know where you mean,' I nodded. 'Can you give us the address? And Niamh's surname?'

I turned to a blank page in my notebook and handed it over to Diane, who wrote down the information. Meanwhile, Richard was talking to Faith.

'Does Niamh know about what happened to her boyfriend?'

'Oh yes! We went round there as soon as we'd finished talking to you and your sergeant.' She looked towards me and I felt obliged to inform her that I was still a lowly constable. (I know that Old Peter will laugh a lot when he reads that, and say that I was never a lowly anything! But he's quite wrong: I'm very modest and self-effacing; he just doesn't appreciate my particular brand of humility, that's all!)

Anyway, to get back to the interview: Faith insisted that there were no hard feelings between her and Timothy, and Diane backed her up, pointing out that they would hardly have all decided to share a house together if there had been any friction between them. I wondered how Niamh felt about the arrangement. She could be forgiven for feeling a bit anxious about her boyfriend sharing a house with his ex, especially if they were still such good buddies as Faith and Diane were making out.

They repeated their assertions that Timothy would never have experimented with drugs, and confirmed his parents' statement that he had never before experienced seizures. They also told us that he had appeared in good spirits and to be looking forward to completing his studies. He had a job lined up for him at his father's hospital and was planning to visit Leicester the following week to look at flats.

'How did he feel about his parents splitting up?' Richard asked suddenly. Both women looked perplexed.

'I don't know,' Diane answered at last. 'He never talked about it.'

'It all happened ages ago,' Faith added.

'It was while he was an undergraduate,' Richard pointed out drily. 'While you and he were going out together. Did he really not mention it at all?'

'I remember him getting an invitation to the wedding,' Faith said, after a long pause. 'He didn't go. He said it was up to his dad what he did, but he wasn't going to go along and congratulate him on falling for a scheming female with an eye on his index-linked pension.'

'He made a joke about his dad having a shotgun wedding,' Diane added. 'He said with him being a doctor, you'd have thought he'd have known what caused it!'

'So, he blamed his step-mother for stealing his father away from his mother?' I queried.

'Not exactly,' Diane clarified. '*I* think it was more that he thought she was a gold-digger and he was gullible to be taken in. I don't think he would have cared if it had carried on being just an affair. It was marrying her and having kids that he didn't like. If you ask me, *he* was the gold-digger! He was banking on his dad coughing up the deposit to get him on the housing ladder and he didn't like the idea that he might be second in line after a load of new kids.'

'I'm not so sure about that,' Faith protested mildly. 'I think he was upset for his mother – well, maybe "upset" isn't the right word, more "indignant" at the injustice of it all.'

'Personally, I think he was a lot like his father when it comes to relationships,' Diane retorted. 'They both thought they were God's gift to women and resented it if any of them didn't throw themselves at them.'

'No! That's not fair!' Faith's voice rose in indignation and then half-broke as she stifled tears. 'He wasn't like that at all! He just …'

'Well, I'm pretty sure he started chasing Niamh before he'd finished with you,' Diane countered, 'and as soon as he found out John and I were going out together he started sniffing round me. He just can't bear to think that any woman could prefer some other man to him!'

'No!' Faith was almost sobbing now. 'You've got it all wrong! You must have misunderstood what he said to you. He wasn't like that! And anyway, he's dead now, so you shouldn't talk like that about him!'

'I don't believe in all that *never talking ill of the dead* stuff,' Diane declared. Then, turning to Richard, she added, 'and I'm sure you'd rather know what he was really like, wouldn't you, Inspector?'

'Yes,' he agreed impassively. 'We need to build up a picture of what he was like in order to find out how he came to die so suddenly. One thing we need to find out is where that syringe came from that we found in his pocket. Are you sure that neither of you had seen him with such a thing before?'

'Absolutely not!' Faith was adamant. 'He always said drugs were a mug's game and they ruined your health. He was very keen on health – exercise and that sort of thing. His parents were both doctors; they drummed that into him hard.'

'And yet, I've known a lot of doctors who had a drug habit,' Richard murmured as if to himself. 'They have stressful lives and access to prescription medicines. What about your other housemate?' The women stared in surprise as Richard switched his line of questioning abruptly. 'He's training to be a doctor, isn't he? Did he ever bring his work home with him at all?'

'If you mean, "did he take drugs" then the answer is *no*!' Diane answered indignantly. 'And that syringe didn't belong to him either.'

'I see,' Richard was unperturbed by her anger. 'So neither of you have any idea how Timothy Sudbury came to have a syringe containing a small amount of some colourless substance in his pocket?'

'No,' both women declared.

The conversation didn't go on much longer after that. If Faith and Diane knew anything about Timothy's drug-taking, or if they had used drugs themselves, they certainly weren't going to tell us about it!

Diane showed us into Timothy's room, which was the front room on the ground floor. She explained that the house had three bedrooms and a bathroom upstairs and two rooms plus the kitchen downstairs. The other three each had one of the upstairs rooms while Timothy had slept downstairs. There was a lock on each of the study-bedrooms, but they rarely bothered with them.

'We've all known each other for years,' she told me. 'We know we can trust each other.'

It struck me that she hadn't sounded all that trusting of Timothy when she'd been describing his unwanted amorous advances earlier, but I didn't say anything.

His room was large and had a high ceiling. There was a bay window looking out over the tiny front garden – paved with red and black tiles – to the road beyond. The cream-coloured paint on the window-frames was starting to peel off and the floral-print curtains were faded. It felt rather cold and dismal; what little weak sunshine there was on that September day was round the other side of the house.

The furniture was Spartan: a narrow iron-framed bed with a desk next to it and an angle-poise lamp attached to the wall between them (presumably to allow it to double as a bed-side light and a desk lamp), an old-fashioned wardrobe, its varnish chipped and scratched, a chest of drawers with a mirror hanging on the wall above it, one easy chair and one desk chair, and a bookcase.

Richard made a beeline for the desk and started sifting through the contents of its two drawers. I studied the books. Unsurprisingly, there was a large number of serious-looking textbooks on biochemistry and biosciences more generally, but that wasn't all. Timothy's taste in fiction appeared to be mainly of the classic escapist adventure type. Jules Verne, Rider Haggard and Jack London all featured, and a complete set of the original Ian Fleming *James Bond* novels filled the top shelf.

One book caught my eye: Practical Toxicology: a complete guide to harmful substances, including biochemical, pharmacological, pathological and pharmacokinetic aspects. I picked it up and flicked through the pages. Most of it looked very dry, with tables of incomprehensible numbers and graphs that meant nothing to me. There seemed to be a lot about pollution of air and water supplies from industrial processes, which was hardly relevant to our investigation. However, in another chapter, I came across pictures of medical syringes not unlike the one that we had found in the victim's pocket, including a photograph of one being used to take a blood sample from a patient. Could the syringe in Timothy's pocket be related to his work? We ought to visit his supervisor and find out exactly what his research project involved.

Richard, meanwhile, had found an address book and a diary in the desk drawer. He handed them to me. 'Take these back to the station. They may help us to find out who he's been in contact with in the last few weeks and where he's been – or was planning to go.'

Then he set me rifling through the chest of drawers while he tackled the wardrobe. I didn't find anything more interesting than socks and tee-shirts, but Richard came across a shoebox containing bundles of letters tied up with string. He undid one of the packets and unfolded the first letter. It turned out to be a love letter from Faith, dated June 1977. I guessed that this must have been near the start of the first long vac after they met. There was nothing much in it, but it seemed significant that he had kept it after they had split up.

Richard put the letter back in the box, put the lid back on and handed it to me with instructions to take it back to the station and go through all the letters looking for any evidence that might throw light on the nature of Timothy's relationship with his correspondents.

We carried on looking for some time after that, but didn't find anything else of interest. Then we went back downstairs, where I wrote out a receipt for the items that we were taking away with us and handed it to Diane. We didn't mention what was in the box. I watched Faith's expression carefully as we left carrying our booty, and I couldn't see any sign that she recognised it or was concerned about us taking it. So I'm guessing she didn't know that her deepest feelings were about to be pored over by a team of police officers! It's in the nature of the job: we have to ask personal questions and pry into private relationships – often those of quite innocent people – in order to build up a picture of the world in which a murder victim (or the victim of any crime) lived. That's the only way of working out who might have wanted him dead and who might have had the opportunity to kill him.

* * *

'*I* think it was probably the other man who was sharing that house that killed him,' Miss Dorothy Fazakerley said confidently. 'John, did you say his name was? He's got a motive. This Timothy made a pass at his girl; she said so herself! And, working at the hospital, he'd have access to drugs and hypodermics.'

Bernie's Aunty Dot lived in a Care Home in the Wavertree area of Liverpool. Despite her advanced years, she was still very alert and eager to be involved in whatever was going on in the world around her. The isolation that had been imposed on her since the Home had closed its doors to visitors in early March had been extremely trying for her and she had leapt at the suggestion that she might keep in touch with members of her family via video-conferencing. Now, in a three-way conversation involving households in Oxford and Liverpool, she was listening eagerly to Jonah's reading of the second chapter of his memoirs.

'That doesn't seem like a very good motive to me!' Lucy objected. '*I* think Faith's more likely. She used to be going out with him and then they split up. She could've had all sorts of reasons to want to get rid of him. Maybe he knew secrets about her that she didn't want him to tell to anyone else or perhaps she wanted revenge for something he did to her when they were together or-'

'The way Jonah tells it, it's the other woman – Diane – who seems to have it in for him,' Dominic interrupted.

'All the more reason why it can't be her,' argued Lucy. 'Faith is trying to make out that they were still good friends and there were no hard feelings between them. She looks to me like someone who's frightened of being suspected and, as a consequence, is going over the top in saying how well they got on.'

'Ah! But it could all be young Jonah's way of putting you off the scent,' Dot commented. She had a soft spot for Jonah and admired him immensely. '*My* money's still on that John. We haven't been allowed to see what he's like yet. What if that's a ploy to get us to forget about him and concentrate on the others?'

'Hang on!' Jonah protested. 'That's not fair! The reason you haven't met John Goodey is that Richard and

I hadn't met him at that stage either. I'm trying to show you what it was like for us investigating the case. We didn't find things out in a nice orderly way. We never do. We just pick up bits and pieces of information as we go along and then try to put them together to make a picture.'

'Alright then,' Peter intervened. 'So you've told us what you found out so far. Hadn't you better start collating the information and setting it out so that you can see what it tells you?'

'Yes!' Ibrahim agreed eagerly. 'Let's make a table. We'll list all the suspects in the first column and then have columns for motive, means and opportunity – like they do in detective stories.'

'OK,' Mariam agreed, reaching for a pen and paper. 'I'll write down. Who are our suspects?'

'The three people who lived with him,' Ibrahim answered promptly.

'Including John,' Dot said firmly.

'And his girlfriend with the funny name,' Lucy chipped in, 'and I suppose the other girl – Wendy. I don't really see why she'd want to kill him, but she was there at the demo.'

'Then there's those other girls,' Dominic added. 'The ones who found him. They were right by him when he collapsed, which must give them the best opportunity to have killed him.'

'But they said they didn't know him from Adam,' protested Lucy. 'So why would they kill him?'

'Right,' Mariam murmured. 'I've got John Goodey, Faith Nelson, Diane Winter, Niamh – we don't seem to have her second name yet – and Wendy, ditto.'

'Then the girls at the demo were Jacqueline and Tina,' Bernie added, 'but I agree with Lucy, they don't seem likely suspects. If you include them, you'd better have Dawn Farmer as well.'

'No,' Jonah objected, 'because nobody except you even knows she exists at this stage.'

'OK.' Mariam crossed out Dawn's name. 'Now I've got John's motive down as jealousy, because Tim was flirting with his girlfriend, and Niamh might be jealous for the same reason or because she's afraid he hasn't really broken it all off with Faith.'

'And Faith could've found out that he'd been two-timing her before they broke up,' Dominic added. 'What about Diane? Jonah made it sound as if she didn't like him much, but would that be enough to make her want to kill him?'

'They all had opportunity,' Ibrahim murmured, looking down at the table over his sister's shoulder, 'and it's difficult to assess means until we know how he died.'

'If we assume the syringe had something to do with it, the one with the best opportunity was John, the trainee doctor,' Dot pointed out, her breath sounding wheezy as she leaned forward to speak into the microphone on her iPad.

'In my experience, students don't seem to have much trouble getting hold of the necessary gear to inject illicit drugs into themselves,' Peter commented drily.

'It's quite a puzzle, isn't it?' smiled Jonah. 'And I'm not going to give you any clues. You're going to have to wait for me to write the next chapter!'

5. FAMILIES

The next evening, Bernie, Peter and Jonah met Lucy and her friends in the videoconference that had now become a regular daily event. Jonah had a new chapter of his memoir ready to read out, but first Dominic had some worrying news to report.

'Aunty Dot's Care Home's got the corona virus,' he told them. 'One resident has been taken to hospital and two more have symptoms. So far Aunty Dot's OK, but of course some of the people who're looking after her must have been in contact with the people who've gone down with it.'

'The home's been closed to visitors for weeks,' Lucy added, 'so it must've been one of the carers that brought it in.'

'Do they definitely have COVID-19?' Bernie asked anxiously. 'It couldn't just have been seasonal flu or something?'

'Only the one that's gone to hospital has been tested,' Dominic answered, 'and the results aren't back yet.'

'But anyway, even seasonal flu would be dangerous for Aunty Dot,' Lucy pointed out. 'If she hadn't been vaccinated. All the Care Home residents have had their vaccinations, so it's unlikely that it's that – not with three of them all being affected.'

'No. I think it must be coronavirus,' Dominic agreed. 'All the residents are being kept isolated in their rooms to reduce the risk. It's just difficult with not knowing which of the staff could have spread it between the three who've got it now. Mum's going frantic, worrying.'

'Let's invite Aunty Dot to join in with us again tomorrow evening,' Bernie suggested. 'She enjoyed it yesterday. And how about asking your Mum and Dad too, Dom?'

'I've tried, but Mum doesn't trust anything to do with computers and they've only got Dad's phone that he uses for the business, now that James has moved out.'

'OK,' Bernie smiled. 'I'll give your dad a ring tomorrow and see if I can't persuade them to give it a go. Now, unless there's any more urgent news, I suppose we'd better give the floor to the Great Author.'

* * *

Richard was off-duty that afternoon, so he left the interviewing of Niamh O'Halloran and Wendy Brotherton to me – under the supervision of Sergeant Gordon MacBride (we all called him "Big Mac"). I was quite surprised. Often, when there was an important or interesting investigation going on, Richard didn't bother with rest days and just kept working until the case was solved or he'd satisfied himself that no further progress could be made.

I was even more surprised when we stopped off at a petrol station on the way back and he bought a large bunch of flowers. Could it be that he had a date that afternoon? He'd been unusually keen to get off home at the end of the previous day too. I'd assumed at the time that it was probably because he had things to do in relation to his father's death. The funeral had taken place earlier that week and I thought there was probably paperwork that needed sorting out for that or for administering the estate. Now I began to wonder if there was a side to my boss that I'd never known about!

But that's all irrelevant to the case of Timothy Sudbury's untimely demise. Getting back to the investigation, Mac and I found ourselves outside a terraced house in Temple Street. There were two bell pushes next to the door, labelled "Flat 1" and "Flat 2". We pressed the button for Flat 2 and stood back to wait. After a while, we heard the sound of feet coming downstairs. There were voices too, but we couldn't hear what was being said. Then the door opened and a tall, muscular-looking woman with a tanned face and short-cropped dark hair stared out at us belligerently.

'What do you want?' she demanded.

We held up our warrant cards and did our best to sound confident. I don't think we succeeded, but her manner did become less aggressive once she knew that we were police officers. She confirmed that she was Wendy Brotherton and that she lived in the upstairs flat with Niamh O'Halloran.

The soft pad of bare feet on the stairs, and a voice from above signified that Niamh had heard us mention her name and was coming down to see what this visit was all about. We stepped inside and there she was on the way down. She stopped when she saw us and stood transfixed on the first or second step, which brought her face more or less level with Mac's.

She was very different from her friend. While Wendy was almost as tall as me, Niamh was only barely five foot – perhaps not even that – and her slight figure made her appear even smaller. She had ginger hair – not as bright as old-Peter's used to be, more copper than carrot – and greeny-blue eyes. Her skin was almost white with just a hint of colour on her cheeks. She was very much the stereotypical Irish colleen in appearance, even down to the bare feet and her dress, which was below-knee length and of a Victorian-style design that was all the rage back then. However, when she spoke her accent was more reminiscent of Cambridge than Connemara. We learned later that she had lived almost all her life in England, her father having held posts in several British universities, culminating in his current role as Fellow in Irish Literature at Lichfield College.

The women took us upstairs to their flat, which seemed to comprise a tiny hall, with a row of hooks on the wall for coats, two bedrooms and a living room with a kitchen area in one corner. Presumably, there was also a bathroom somewhere, but we didn't see any sign of it. We all sat down at a round wooden dining table. Niamh hesitantly offered us coffee, while Wendy growled at us to get on with the interview.

We declined the offer of refreshment and Mac started by offering condolences to Niamh on the death of her boyfriend. She nodded and smiled weakly back at him.

'Now I'm sorry,' Mac continued in his soft Glaswegian accent, 'but in order to find out how he died we need to ask you a few questions.'

'Surely it's the doctors who'll tell us how he died?' snapped Wendy.

'They'll try to find out the cause of death,' Mac explained patiently, 'but that isn't quite the same thing. We need to know about the events that led up to it – *why* it happened, if you like.'

'I was there,' I put in. 'He seemed to be having some sort of seizure when I got there. Had he had anything of that sort before, do you know?'

Both women shook their heads.

'No,' Niamh confirmed, 'nothing like that.'

'Have you ever seen him injecting himself with drugs?' Mac asked.

'No! Why do you ask that?' Niamh suddenly became agitated and looked round at us both with wild eyes. 'He would never ...! He wasn't like that at all.'

'So he wasn't on any medication from his doctor?' Mac tried to soothe her down. 'There was a hypodermic syringe in his pocket. We thought perhaps he had some condition that needed … painkilling injections, for example?'

'No.' Niamh sounded a little calmer. 'Nothing like that.'

'Of course, we wouldn't necessarily know, would we?' Wendy pointed out, putting her arm around Niamh and staring across the table belligerently at us. 'Why don't you ask the people he lives with – Faith Nelson, for example?'

'We already have,' Mac answered patiently. 'And they said the same as you, which leaves us with the question: how did the syringe get into his pocket?'

'Obviously he must have put it there,' Wendy answered dismissively, 'but I don't know why you're jumping to the conclusion that it's got anything to do with how he died. He probably slipped it into his pocket by mistake when he was working in the lab. You do know that he was a biochemist, I assume?'

'Yes,' Mac confirmed. 'We do know that. Did he often bring lab equipment home with him?'

'How would we know?' Wendy was scornful. 'You keep asking us questions that we can't possibly answer!'

I tried to steer the conversation away from *cause of death*, which we wouldn't know until the PM was completed, and towards the victim's relationships with his friends. I was jumping the gun a bit assuming that this was a murder enquiry, but I couldn't help thinking that the Timothy Sudbury that everyone was telling us about wasn't likely to have taken an overdose or to have suffered a fatal heart attack or stroke. I was convinced that someone had injected him with whatever that colourless liquid was in the syringe and I was keen to establish who it could have been and why.

'How did he get on with his housemates?' I asked casually.

'OK,' Wendy shrugged.

'Very well,' Niamh answered unequivocally. 'We'd all known each other since we were freshers. And we were all lucky enough to get grants to stay on to do research; and then we moved on to Henderson College together – well, all apart from John. He's a medic, so he was still in the middle of his course and he stayed at St Luke's.'

* * *

'Hang on! This is all very confusing.' Dominic interrupted Jonah's narration. 'I know you're trying to tell it as it happened, but why can't you just summarise what all these people were studying and where they were doing it? We've got one medical student and one biochemist; what subjects were the others doing? And why did they move colleges after they got their degrees?'

'Lots of students choose to go to one of the graduate-only colleges if they stay on to do another degree,' Bernie explained. 'Henderson, Nuffield and Wolfson are all twentieth-century colleges with comfortable accommodation and modern facilities. If you've been at Oxford for three or four years getting a BA, you've usually exhausted your desire to live like a mediaeval monk in a draughty cloister and you're ready for some mod cons!'

'But *you* didn't,' Lucy pointed out. 'You did the reverse! You'd been at Shrewsbury, which isn't all that old really, and went to St Luke's for your DPhil, didn't you?'

'I had some inside information from my tutor,' Bernie confided. 'She knew that there was going to be a tutorial fellowship in applied maths coming up in a few years' time and that they'd be keen to have a woman, because they were in the process of going mixed. So she advised me to do my DPhil at St Luke's in order to be waiting there in the wings all ready to step up to the plate when the post became vacant.'

She turned to Jonah. 'I've been trying to remember whether I ever met this John Goodey that you've been telling us about. If he was a peace activist and a member of St Luke's, you'd have thought I might have come across him, but the name doesn't ring any bells.'

'Would you expect to know everyone at your college, then?' Ibrahim asked. 'Even if they were doing quite different subjects?'

'Not exactly *know*,' Bernie admitted, 'but I would expect to have come across the name, on the outside of his door or on a list on a noticeboard or on post left in the pigeonholes or in general conversation. And, even if I didn't come across him while he was there, I'd have expected to have read his news in the *Green Book*.'

'What's that?' chorused Ibrahim and Dominic.

'It's the St Luke's College alumni magazine,' Bernie explained. 'It's sent out annually to all former students of the college, together with a begging letter asking them to donate to support the work of the college. People send in their news. He mustn't have bothered telling people about his latest career move or how his youngest has got a scholarship to the Sorbonne or-'

'Well if you don't want to hear what we found out …,' Jonah grumbled.

'We do!' insisted Dominic, 'but I'd just like to get it clear in my mind who these people all are. Mariam! Can you make another table where we can put down what subjects each of the people was studying and which colleges they were at?'

'I certainly can!' Mariam smiled back. 'And the fact that Jonah is reluctant to tell us suggests that it may be important!'

Jonah sighed, but he waited, while she marked out lines on a piece of paper. Eventually she raised her head and he saw the four expectant faces of the four young people looking out of a small rectangle on his screen.

'OK,' he resumed. 'So far, we have the late Timothy Sudbury, who studied biochemistry at St Luke's College and then went on to Henderson College. John Goodey read medicine at St Luke's College and was now in his pre-registration year at the Radcliffe Infirmary. Faith Nelson did Archeology and Anthropology at Shrewsbury College, where Niamh O'Halloran studied Philosophy and Theology. Diane-'

'Of course!' Bernie exclaimed. 'I knew that name sounded familiar. Why didn't you tell me she was at Shrewsbury? I remember Niamh. She sang in the chapel choir and was a leading light in the Newman Society.'

'What's that?' asked Ibrahim.

'The university Catholic Society,' Bernie explained. 'It's named after Cardinal John Henry Newman, who was a famous convert from the Church of England to Roman Catholicism.'

'So you actually knew her?' Lucy asked. 'I suppose that means she can't have done it.'

'Oh I wouldn't be so sure of that,' her mother smiled back. 'I didn't see any more of her after we both graduated. I didn't even realise that she was still in Oxford after that.'

'As I was saying,' Jonah continued, pretending to be affronted by the digression, 'Diane Winter was another archaeologist and she was working on the same project as Faith, but she did her BA at St Anne's before moving to Henderson. And Wendy Brotherton read Greats at Shrewsbury and then went on to do research into classical philology at Henderson College.'

'What does all that mean?' asked Ibrahim shaking his head in bewilderment.

'Greats is the nickname for Literae Humaniores,' Bernie grinned back at him, 'which is the Oxford name for Classics. Students study Latin, Greek, Philosophy and Ancient History.'

'And philology is the study of the origins of languages,' Dominic added. 'I did a bit about it when I was at uni.'

'Mmm,' murmured Mariam, studying her table. 'So Faith, Niamh and Wendy were all at Shrewsbury College together, and -'

'And so was Mam!' Lucy exclaimed. 'Did you know them?'

'I don't think so,' Bernie replied. 'As I say, I do vaguely remember Niamh, but I can't say the other names ring a bell particularly.'

'What about your college magazine?' asked Dominic. 'Doesn't Shrewsbury have a Green Book?'

'Yes it does,' Bernie laughed, 'but it's not called that. It's called *The Shrew*, but it's the same thing: news about what graduates and dons have been doing – especially scientific breakthroughs and learned publications – births, marriages and deaths and news about building projects and bursaries that need donations from grateful alumni. I've got some of them somewhere. I could look up those people and see what's happened to them. The trouble with women, though, is that most of them change their name when they get married.'

'I think it's a bit of an exaggeration to say that's the *only* trouble with women,' Peter muttered to nobody in particular.

'No!' Ibrahim protested. 'That would be cheating! If you read that they've had five kids or written a seminal work on Phoenician graffiti or whatever, we'll know they can't have been convicted of murder. You might as well get hold of the back issues of the newspapers and find a report of the case!'

'Ibrahim's right,' Lucy backed him up. 'We've got to do this just going from what Jonah writes.'

'Good,' Jonah smiled. 'So, are you ready to hear what happened next?'

* * *

We asked Niamh and Wendy to describe what happened at the demonstration. They told us that the whole group started out together. They met up at their flat for lunch, because that was closer to the city centre than the shared house in New Hinksey. Then they walked across Magdalen Bridge, down Rose Lane and along Deadman's Walk to Christ Church Meadow. When they got there, a woman from the peace camp at Greenham Common was standing on a tree stump giving a rousing speech to the assembled protestors. Wendy's account was that Timothy couldn't resist joining in and giving a speech himself. She clearly had him down as an attention-seeker. Niamh wasn't so sure that it hadn't been pre-arranged.

Either way, they agreed that he got separated from their little group for a while and they saw him talking with some of the women who were in charge of the demo. But he was back with them by the time the processions began. It was a bit chaotic, by all accounts, while they got the demonstrators split up into two groups to walk the two different routes, but they reckoned it all got properly underway by about two thirty. That fits in with the official police account of the demo.

Tim and his friends were in the group that started from Folly Bridge and marched up St Aldates. They weren't at the front, but they thought they must have been nearer the front than the back. That also fits in with police accounts, based on where they were when the trouble started.

They marched along carrying their placards and singing peace songs and everything was very jolly until they got to the Old Sheep Shop. Then the people in front of them started slowing down, but the ones behind still kept coming, so they spread out more across the road to make room for them. But soon the whole road was full and the people in front seemed to have stopped walking altogether.

'We made it as far as the entrance to Christ Church,' Niamh told us, 'but then we just got stuck. Everyone was all crushed together so we could hardly breathe.'

'Were you still with Timothy at that stage?' Mac asked. 'Or had you got separated by then?'

'Oh yes! We were still all together,' Niamh confirmed. 'Or at least … Tim and I were together and Wendy was with us – weren't you Wen? But I'm not sure about the others. I think they may have got squeezed over to the other side of the road. We were on the left-hand side going up – across the road from Christ Church.'

'No. They were still there,' Wendy cut in sharply. 'I remember. John was next to Tim, on the other side from us, and Faith and Diane were with him.'

'I remember a policeman shouting at everyone to stop pushing,' Niamh resumed, 'but nobody took any notice and the crush just carried on getting worse. Then Wendy saw that we were just coming up to Pembroke Square, so we slipped out of the crowd and headed down there. A few other people were doing it too. I thought Tim was with us, but it turned out he wasn't.'

'Could he have already fallen unconscious?' Mac asked. 'When did you last speak to him?'

'Nobody was speaking to anyone at that stage,' Wendy answered, before Niamh could reply. 'We were all getting crushed to death – or that's how it felt! We didn't have any breath left for talking.'

'I can't remember,' Niamh admitted. 'I don't think he was feeling very good, because he handed his placard over to me and said something about not having realised how heavy it was going to be. And then, I don't remember him saying anything much after that.'

'He wasn't the only one,' Wendy put in. 'Quite a few people dropped their placards. That was one of the things that caused the crush. People falling over them and then other people tripping over *them*.'

'About what time was that?' I wanted to get an idea of exactly when Tim Sudbury started to feel unwell. 'Or, whereabouts had you got to at that time?'

'I can't remember.' Niamh shook her head.

'It must've been earlier,' Wendy said firmly, 'before everyone started piling into us from behind. After that, we were all too crushed to be able to hand over a placard.'

'So you took it?' queried Mac. 'He handed it over to you and you carried it after that?'

'Yes,' Niamh nodded. 'I didn't hold it up and wave it about or anything, I just took hold of it and carried it for him.'

'What did you do with it after that?' Mac asked 'Where is it now?'

'I just left it in Pembroke Square,' Niamh admitted. 'We just wanted to get away. It hadn't turned out at all how we'd expected. I propped it up against the railings outside St Aldates and we slipped through to Pembroke Street and across to St Ebbe's.'

'We were going to make our way round to Carfax to listen to the speeches,' Wendy added, 'but in the end, we just slipped away down the back streets and went home.'

'I see.' Mac looked across at me, to check that I was still taking notes of the interview. 'And what time was it when you got back?'

Neither of the women answered. Niamh looked towards Wendy. Wendy looked down at the carpet and seemed to be thinking.

'I couldn't say exactly,' she said at last. 'It took a while, because there was traffic backing up across Magdalen Bridge. And we didn't make up our mind what to do right away, so-o-o …,' she paused. 'I suppose it couldn't have been much before four.'

'Did you notice anyone else close to you and Timothy in the crowd?' I wanted to find out if there was anyone else who could have injected our murder victim with some sort of drug and then dropped the almost-empty syringe into his pocket. 'Particularly anyone who might have had a grudge against him?'

'Are you saying someone killed him?' Wendy demanded, sounding shocked and perhaps a bit angry.

'No, no, not at all.' Mac flashed me a warning look that told me that I'd revealed more than I should have done about the investigation. 'The chances are his death was completely natural. It's just that, with him having been previously healthy and there being no obvious cause, we have to look into every possibility, however unlikely. We'll know more after the post mortem examination. But we would like to know who else was close to him in the crowd, in case they saw anything that might have a bearing on what it was that made him collapse like that. Can you tell us any names at all?'

He looked round hopefully and smiled reassuringly.

'I – I don't think so,' Niamh answered slowly. 'I didn't even notice when we got separated from the others, but they definitely weren't still there when we escaped into Pembroke Square. I think they may have got out the other way – into Christ Church.'

'The college had porters at the gate making sure that nobody went in there,' I told them. 'They only opened up the quad after the police asked them to, to stop people getting hurt in the crush.'

'I saw a couple of teenagers,' Wendy volunteered. 'Girls. A tall one with long straight hair and a shorter one with short hair. They were pressed right up against Tim. And I think John and Faith were still there too. I think they pushed past the girls to get to the Christ Church side of the road at about the same time we escaped the other way.'

'Was Diane with them?' I had my own personal suspicions of Diane, who hadn't seemed particularly well-disposed towards Tim Sudbury.

'I'm not sure,' Wendy shook her head. 'Probably.'

'OK. Thank you. You've been very helpful.' Mac turned to address Niamh. 'Now, Miss O'Halloran, I'm sorry to have to ask you this, but we do have to consider the possibility that Timothy knowingly administered a toxic substance to himself with the intention of taking his own life. So, please: can you tell me how he seemed that day, and in the days leading up to it? Was he anxious or depressed about anything?'

'No.' Niamh looked at us with wide, innocent eyes. 'He seemed just exactly as usual – didn't he, Wen?'

'Yes,' Wendy agreed, 'exactly as usual.' Her tone somehow suggested that she wasn't very impressed with Timothy's normal demeanour. She and Diane appeared to share a low opinion of the young man, but whether this was pertinent to the investigation into his death was another matter!

'So there was nothing in his behaviour in the last few weeks to suggest that he wasn't completely happy with life?' Mac pressed them. 'No problems with his supervisor? No money worries?'

'No.' Both women shook their heads.

'He'd nearly finished writing up his research,' Niamh assured us, 'and he had a job all lined up for him after he'd submitted. He was moving back home – to Leicester. He was going to live with his mum until he got a flat, and then ... and then ...,' she gulped back sobs and only just managed to finish, 'and then I was going to find a job there as well, so that we could get married!'

* * *

'And that's where I thought I'd end the next chapter,' Jonah concluded, closing the window on his computer screen displaying his manuscript. He was now looking at an array of three rectangles: in one he could see himself, with Bernie and Peter on either side looking over his shoulder; another contained the four young faces gathered round Lucy's laptop in her attic room in the Liverpool shared house; and the last showed Aunty Dot's wrinkled features against a backdrop of a wing-backed chair and a crucifix on a white-painted wall. 'Leaving the reader to speculate on what sort of relationships the victim really had with his five friends.'

'At the moment, *I'm* more interested in that bunch of flowers,' Mariam commented. '*Was* Lucy's dad really going on a date?'

'*I* can help you out with that one, 'Bernie smiled. 'It's all in Richard's diary. I suppose it was a date of sorts, but not the kind you're thinking of.'

'What d'you mean?' asked Dominic with a puzzled frown.

'I'll read out what he said,' Bernie offered. They all waited while she flicked through pages. Then, 'Here we are! 17th September 1982: "Rang Mum this evening to arrange to call round. She didn't seem very keen to see me, but she's agreed I can call tomorrow afternoon. I must get some flowers to take and try to think of a nice present for her." So there you have it! He was only going round to see his mother.'

'It's not really *only* though, is it Mam?' Lucy commented. 'It was a big deal for him then, wasn't it?'

'It certainly seemed to be,' Ibrahim added. 'I read that entry – and the one after it where he goes to see her, when I was typing the diary up for Jonah. I didn't understand what was going on. He says he hadn't seen her for years. What happened to her?'

'Oh that's another story altogether!' Bernie replied mysteriously. 'And it took us ages to piece together what actually went on.[6] It'd take too long to tell you everything now. Basically, Richard's mother ran off when he was

---

[6] You can read about Bernie's quest to uncover the great secret of her husband's past in *Despise Not Thy Mother* ©2015 Judy Ford ISBN: 978-1-911083-14-6

eight and then suddenly reappeared at his father's funeral, which must have been only a week or two before this case started.'

'That's right,' Peter confirmed. 'It was the day Eddie was born. That's why I missed the funeral and Jonah went in my place, to represent the team.'

'And I'm jolly glad I did,' Jonah chipped in. 'I wouldn't have wanted to miss seeing old Richard's face when the funeral director escorted her up to the front and sat her down next to him. I could see right away he wasn't expecting her, but it was only later that I realised that she'd been gone for nearly forty years!'

'Well *I've* heard all about that before,' Dot intervened to avoid the conversation being diverted. 'I'm more interested in the puzzle that Jonah's set for us. It sounds to me as if this young man that died wasn't a very likeable person. He sounds like one of those handsome young men that some girls fall for and then regret about it afterwards.'

'So, does that mean you think it's most likely to have been Faith, the ex-girlfriend who did it?' asked Dominic eagerly. 'I was wondering that myself. If she felt passionate about him and then he betrayed her, love might have turned to hate and she could've done it.'

'Show Aunty Dot your table, Mariam,' Lucy urged. 'We wrote down all the suspects and made a grid of motive, means and opportunity,' she explained, looking at her aunt's face on the computer screen. 'All of the people who were near to the victim during the demonstration had opportunity.'

'That's right,' Mariam confirmed. 'We've got Faith, John, Diane, Niamh, Wendy, Jacqueline and Tina all down as having been in a position to inject him with something and then drop the syringe into his pocket. I've put Dawn Farmer down too, because Jonah was so reluctant to let us include her, but we've no evidence yet that she was near enough to him to have done it.'

'Maybe not during the crush in St Aldates,' Bernie put in, 'but how about earlier – when they were rallying the troops on Christ Church Meadow? We don't know how long the drug took to act, so she could've done it then. As far as I remember, there was quite a bit of jostling for the chance to address the assembled masses!'

'We don't actually know yet that a drug was involved,' Peter pointed out drily. 'You're all jumping the gun. Until his nibs sees fit to tell you the outcome of the post mortem, you could still be dealing with a freak medical condition or even compression asphyxia.'

'Like at Hillsborough[7]?' queried Dominic.

'That's right,' Peter nodded. 'For all you know so far, he could simply have been crushed in the crowd so he couldn't breathe.'

'No,' Jonah disagreed. 'I saw him, remember? It didn't look like asphyxiation to me – or a heart attack. He wasn't struggling for breath, he was jerking with muscle spasms and his eyes were flicking back and forth, but he didn't seem to be looking at anything. I'd never seen anything quite like it before.'

'OK. So we're allowed to assume that the victim's death is unnatural,' Ibrahim concluded. 'Can we also assume that he was killed by someone injecting him with that syringe?'

'No,' his sister said firmly. 'The syringe could be a red herring or he could have administered the drug himself. Logically, we can't even be sure it's murder and not suicide or an accidental overdose.'

'And I wouldn't put it past young Jonah to be stringing us all along, pretending that this is a murder case and the twist at the end will be that it turns out not to be after all,' Dot added darkly.

---

[7] The Hillsborough disaster was a fatal crush during the FA cup semi-final between Liverpool and Nottingham Forest. 96 Liverpool supporters died.

'You're dead right there Aunty!' Bernie smiled. 'You've got our Jonah to a T! That's just the sort of underhand trick he would play!'

'I'm just setting out the facts as we found them,' Jonah protested. 'I thought you lot wanted to see how a police investigation actually develops. And it ought to help you to understand why we didn't ask all the right questions at the outset – and why Big Mac was so peeved with me for letting on to Niamh and Wendy that we hadn't ruled out murder.'

'I don't think we can get any further until we know the result of the post mortem,' Mariam murmured, looking down at her table. 'We've got seven suspects – eight if you include Dawn Farmer – all with opportunity, but only John and Faith have a motive-'

'And their motives are pretty weak,' her brother cut in.

'And we don't know what the drug was that killed him – assuming that it was a drug – so we can't tell which of them might have had access to it. So it's all just question marks down the "Means" column,' Mariam added, 'with a tentative tick against John, because he might have been able to get the syringe and whatever drug it was from the hospital.'

'Which makes him the most likely suspect so far,' Dominic commented. 'He has motive, means *and* opportunity. If this was a detective story, that would mean he definitely *didn't* do it!'

'However,' Peter replied drily, 'in real life, it most often *is* the most likely person who committed the crime.'

'But I don't see that this John does have a really convincing motive,' Bernie argued. 'Not unless the witnesses have been playing things down enormously. OK, Timothy was sniffing round his girlfriend, but nobody, including the girlfriend in question, is suggesting that she responded to his advances at all. Why on earth would he take the risk of murdering him? What would be the point? Anyway, I'm more interested in the here and now than what was going on back in 1982. How are you Aunty? Joey told me about one of the residents being taken to hospital.'

'Oh stop fussing Bernadette!' Dot said dismissively, waving her hand in front of the screen and momentarily blocking her face from view. 'It's only Charles making a drama out of a bit of a cough. He always was a hypochondriac.'

'They don't admit people to hospital just for a bit of a cough,' Bernie argued, 'especially not now. It's no good, Aunty. Joey told me what the manager said when she rang him this morning: one resident has been admitted to the Heart and Chest hospital with suspected coronavirus and there are two others with possible symptoms.'

'Are there?' Dot sounded both surprised and interested, but managed to hide any anxiety that she might be feeling at this news. 'They didn't tell us that. Who is it? I bet Fran is one of them. She won't stay in her room, the way we've all be told to. I've had her knocking on my door only a few days ago wanting to come in and have a chat.'

'As you well know, the manager couldn't possibly tell Joey any names.' Bernie tried to keep out of her voice the irritation that she felt at her aunt's refusal to take the situation seriously. 'She was just wanting to make sure that we'd been informed before it got reported in the media and to reassure us that they were upping their infection control measures. You will take care, won't you Aunty?'

'Of course I will!' Dot declared. 'You don't need to tell me about infection control. Don't forget, I was a nurse for more than forty years. I know how to wash my hands properly!'

'I'm sure you do!' Jonah called out. 'Just you make sure all those young care assistants do too, and give them a ticking off if they cut corners!'

'Oh don't you worry, young Jonah!' Dot chortled back. 'I was a ward sister for long enough to know how to put them in their place! I only see two of them now – one for daytime and one for the night. They've sectioned us off so that we only see a few of the staff and they each only see a few residents, to reduce the risk of cross-contamination. I'm with Joan and Betty. *They* must be OK. They told us that anyone with symptoms would be put together in a separate group. I wonder who it is …'

'Well, just as long as you're keeping well.' Bernie decided to change the subject. Her aunt was clearly determined to play down any risk to herself and she supposed that was probably for the best, seeing as there was nothing anyone could do to mitigate it. 'Thames Valley has been calling on recently-retired officers to come back into the police, because they've got so many off sick or self-isolating. Peter's been wondering whether he ought to volunteer.'

'They still won't take me back!' Jonah complained.

'And it's because we're shielding you that I'm not going to put myself forward,' Peter said quickly. 'They're only talking about recent retirees, anyway, not old codgers like me!'

'Mum wanted me to check that you're eating OK,' Dominic put in, suddenly remembering the phone call that his mother had made after hearing the news from the Care Home manager. 'And to ask if there's anything we can send you: books to read, or anything?'

'Tell her to stop worrying,' Dot told him firmly. 'I'm fighting fit and not about to go doolally just because I'm stuck in my room for a while. Now, if everyone's finished cross-examining me, I think I'll sign out and carry on with the e-book I'm in the middle of about the Black Death.'

6. HYPOTHESES

'Mam?' Lucy opened the regular videoconference between Liverpool and Oxford the following evening, 'before I forget, I promised to ask you to set up a Zoom meeting with Ruth and Joey. Ruth's been going frantic about not being able to see the rest of the family – especially Aunty Dot – and we've finally managed to persuade her to download the Zoom app to her phone. We did a call with them this afternoon, but I said I'd ask you to do one before she tries to call Aunty Dot. She thinks Aunty won't be able to manage, although we keep telling her she's fine with it.'

'OK love,' Bernie smiled back. 'I'll add that to my busy social calendar. It seems to me that we're all seeing a lot more of each other, now that we can't go out, than we ever did before! And, speaking of Aunty Dot, here she is just logging in now!'

The rectangle containing Lucy's face moved aside to make room on the screen for another, in which the watchers in Oxford could see Dot's familiar features. Lucy's image moved back away from the camera and Dominic, Ibrahim and Mariam appeared clustered around her.

'Hello Aunty! How're you keeping?' Bernie greeted her aged relative.

'Still in the pink!' Dot replied cheerfully. 'I suppose you'll already have heard that Charles has tested positive?'

'No, we hadn't,' Bernie and Dominic chorused.

'I'd better let Mum and Dad know,' Dominic added. 'What about the other two? Are they still showing symptoms?'

'Yes,' Dot admitted. 'In fact,' she continued reluctantly, in the silence that followed, 'Fran is worse today apparently. But nothing worth troubling the doctor about,' she hurried on, 'just a bad cough and a temperature. And I haven't had contact with her for over a fortnight, so you none of you need worry about me getting it,' she finished defiantly. 'Now, I didn't come here to talk about Charles and Fran. Where's young Jonah? Have you got another chapter for us today?'

'Well, maybe not a whole chapter, but a few pages anyway,' Jonah replied. 'Do you want it now?'

'We certainly do!' Dot cut in before anyone else could respond. 'What are you waiting for?'

* * *

The next day was Sunday. For once, Margaret and I were both off-duty, so after church we went for a pub lunch at the Duke of Monmouth in New Hinksey. As I write that, I can hear old Peter accusing me of never being able to turn off, and suggesting that my choice of venue was contrived with the hope that we might somehow manage to bump into some of the students who shared the house in that suburb of Oxford where Tim Sudbury had lived – and he'd be quite right! Margaret was as keen as I was to discover how her casualty of three days earlier had come to expire in the ambulance on the way to the hospital, and we both thought that his closest friends were the ones most likely to be able to throw light on that question.

We were in luck! It turned out that John Goodey was also entertaining his girlfriend to lunch at the Duke that day. They were already there when we arrived, sitting in the dining area with drinks on the table in front of them.

I pointed them out to Margaret and then she went to order our meal at the bar while I, ostensibly choosing a table for us to eat at, wandered round the room pondering on the best way of opening up a conversation with them.

I was still standing a few feet away from the couple, undecided as to what to do next, when Margaret returned carrying two glasses of orange juice. (She was on call, so alcohol was out of the question.) As she passed John's chair, she clumsily collided with the back of it and juice spilled on to his head. She immediately apologised and, setting the glasses down on his table, began drying his hair with a paper napkin.

'I'm so sorry!' I heard her say. 'I can't think how I managed that!' And then, after much effort with the napkin, 'Don't I know you? I'm sure I've seen you bef-Oh! I know! Do you work at the Radcliffe? You're a medical student, aren't you? I'm Margaret – Margaret Hulme. I'm Mr Gordon's registrar – in emergency surgery.'

'Oh – er – yes,' John mumbled.

'Maybe we could join you?' Margaret suggested, unheeding of the glare that Diane was giving her at the prospect of their tête-à-tête being spoiled by the advent of a talkative doctor and her policeman fiancé. She waved me across and began introducing me to our new friends.

'Jonah, this is – I'm sorry, what did you say your name was?'

'John Goodey.'

'He's a medical student – or ... have you graduated now? Anyway, he's doing his clinical studies at the Radcliffe. And this is ...?' Margaret turned to look at Diane for the first time.

'We've met,' Diane said coldly, looking towards me. 'You're a policeman, aren't you? You came round yesterday morning, asking questions about Tim.'

'Yes, that's right,' I admitted.

'Timothy Sudbury?' Margaret exclaimed. 'What a strange coincidence! I was on duty in Casualty when he came in. I certified him as ... dead ... on arrival.' Her voice faltered as if she had only just realised the insensitivity of what she had just said. 'Oh! I'm sorry! I suppose you must have been a friend of his.'

'John and I live in the same house as him,' Diane confirmed icily, 'as your friend would be able to tell you, seeing as he was writing down everything we said when we were interviewed about it by the police.'

'It must've been a terrible shock for you both.' Margaret sat down at the table and reached out her hand to give Diane's a gentle squeeze. Diane hastily withdrew it and clasped her two hands together under the table. 'Did he have any history of epilepsy? The ambulance crew told me that he looked as if he were having some sort of seizure.'

'No,' John replied, cutting in before Diane could rebuff her. 'I'd known him for over five years. He and I shared a set of rooms in college in our first year. I'd have known if he had anything like that.'

'And I suppose you'd have known if he ever took drugs?' I asked casually, sitting down next to Margaret.

'Yes, I would, and he didn't.' John was unequivocal in his response. 'The girls told me that you found a syringe in his pocket. I just can't make out how it could have got there.' He shook his head slowly, a bewildered look on his face. 'He just didn't do that sort of thing. I'd have known!'

'I agree.' Diane's attitude towards our gate-crashing of their lunch date appeared to be thawing a little. 'He thought far too highly of himself to risk doing anything that might affect his health or make him less attractive to the opposite sex.'

The waitress arrived at this point and placed large plates of roast beef and Yorkshire pudding in front of John and Diane. 'Yours won't be a minute,' she assured

Margaret. 'They just need to make another batch of gravy.'

'We live in a shared house too,' Margaret told them, as if making conversation. 'Until we get married, that is. That's only four weeks away now. We're buying a house in Jericho, but until then there's seven of us all sharing the kitchen and bathroom. If it isn't Susan hogging the washing machine, it's Lyn leaving the oven in a state! I sometimes wonder why I put up with it for so long.'

'I suppose it's easier when there are only four of you,' John murmured through a mouthful of roast potato. 'And we all knew each other before we decided to rent the house together.'

'Ah yes! I suppose that does make a difference,' Margaret agreed. 'Some of us have been there for years, but people are always moving on. Lyn and Susan are PGCE[8] students. They're only here for a year and none of us had met them before they moved in. They seem terribly young compared with the rest of us and they lived in college for the whole of their undergraduate time, so they don't have much idea of how a shared house works. But then, they only moved in a couple of weeks ago, so I expect they'll soon learn.'

The waitress returned with our own Sunday roasts. 'There you are! Sorry for the wait. Is everything alright? Can I get you any more drinks or anything?'

We looked round at each other and then assured her that we were all fine and the food looked delicious.

'How do you organise things?' Margaret asked conversationally, looking towards Diane. 'For meals and laundry and stuff? Do you each do you own thing or do you get together, like a sort of family?'

'A bit of a mix,' John answered. I got the impression that he had rather taken to Margaret. Mind you, she was

---

[8] Post-Graduate Certificate in Education: a one-year course for graduates wishing to teach in English schools.

rather stunning, with her thick plait of black hair reaching down her back to the seat of her chair. It was a Red Day today, by which I mean that her dress – a close-fitting velvet one which showed off her shapely figure – was a deep red colour and her nails and lips were painted to match it. She also had matching red bows at the top and bottom of her plait and the little tailored jacket that she wore over the dress was black with a red collar and buttons. 'We all do our own washing – and sometimes that does lead to arguments about the noise if people put it on at night!' he smiled, 'but sometimes we have meals all together, and sometimes Diane cooks for me, because I have funny hours, with working at the hospital.'

'And sometimes Faith and I eat together, because we work together a lot,' Diane added. She seemed to be warming a little towards us, but maybe it was just that she was resigned to our presence and had decided to make the best of it. 'Tim rather fancied himself as a chef and used to spend hours concocting complicated dinners for us sometimes. It was very irritating if you just wanted to pop into the kitchen to make a coffee.'

'I'm rather hoping that Jonah knows how to cook,' Margaret confided with a little laugh. 'One of us needs to be able to!'

'You'd better start boning up on it then,' I joked. '*Growing* the veg is more my forte than cooking it! If you leave it all to me, we'll be living out of tins.'

'Unfortunately, our house in Jericho doesn't have much of a garden,' Margaret confided to John and Diane, carefully steering the conversation well away from Timothy Sudbury in order to avoid them suspecting that they were being pumped for information. 'It's more just a yard really.'

'But there's still scope for growing herbs and salad crops in containers,' I commented, keeping up the deception. 'It faces south, so at least it gets plenty of sun.'

'Where are you getting married?' Diane seemed to be becoming genuinely interested.

'In my home church back up in Horwich,' Margaret told her.

'Norwich?' echoed John. 'I've got an aunt who lives there.

'No, *Ho*rwich,' Margaret corrected him. 'It's near Bolton - up in the Pennines.'

'Bawlton?' This time it was Diane's turn to be confused by Margaret's strong East Lancashire accent.

'Bolton,' I repeated in my best BBC English. 'You've probably heard of Bolton Wanderers football club.'

'I'd like a church wedding,' Diane murmured, giving John a sideways glance, which he completely missed. 'What's your dress going to be like?'

'It's long, but not quite down to my feet, because I don't want to trip over it coming down the aisle. And there's lace over the bodice which matches my veil and little silk forget-me-nots worked into it and some more round my headdress. And I'll be carrying bunch of blue flowers to match them.'

I couldn't resist adding, 'That was all chosen *after* her dad put his foot down and said he wasn't walking up the aisle with her wearing her motorbike leathers!'

Margaret laughed and the others joined in.

'You weren't seriously thinking of not wearing a proper wedding dress were you?' Diane asked when the hilarity died down.

'No, but I did rather fancy the idea of arriving on my bike. I thought it'd make our wedding a bit different. But Mum said it'd look awful on the photos if I got oil on my dress on the way there, and Dad said he wasn't forking out for any dress if I was going to ruin it before we even got to the church. And that was when I said, in that case, I'd wear my biking gear to the ceremony.'

'At which point they both said that the vicar would have a heart attack if she came into church looking like a Hell's Angel,' I put in.

'Which is complete nonsense!' Margaret declared. 'I'm quite sure he wouldn't have turned a hair. He's known me since I was a baby. In fact, he christened me. He's been in the parish for over thirty years.'

'What about bridesmaids?' Diane was still eager to hear more about the wedding. 'Was it hard to choose who to have?'

'Jonah's sister is going to be the chief bridesmaid, and I've got a couple of young cousins whose mum sort of expected me to choose them. They're all going to wear pale blue dresses with forget-me-nots on them to match mine.'

'It sounds lovely!' Diane gushed, 'Doesn't it, John?'

John nodded dutifully and flashed a look at me, which said, 'Women, eh!'

'And what about a honeymoon?' Diane asked. 'Or is that a secret?'

'We're touring,' Margaret told her.

'On Margaret's bike,' I added. 'I'll be riding pillion.'

'Start as you mean to go on,' Margaret declared, grinning as their mouths dropped open.

'I think I'd like to get married in Oxford,' Diane mused. 'I don't think I'd want to go back home to do it. It's such a tiny village and it's full of old ladies and they're all such gossips! I'd rather it was here with my own friends, not a whole lot of people my parents know.'

'Won't it depend where you go after you finish your DPhil?' Margaret asked. 'You're in your final year aren't you?'

'Yes, but I'm hoping to stay working in Oxford after that. Dr Loftus – our supervisor – has another grant coming up to do more work on the site in Dorset. It includes funding for a research Assistant and he's more or less said that he'll give it to me or Faith.'

'So you and Faith are rivals,' I suggested. 'Doesn't that make things a bit awkward for the two of you?'

'Not really,' Diane shrugged. 'Whoever he goes for, I expect something will turn up for the other one. I'm not even sure Faith wants to stay on after …'

'After what?' Margaret asked, somehow managing to sound interested in a concerned sort of way rather than as if she were interrogating a witness.

'Just everything that's happened here: going out with Tim and then splitting up and now this! She's very upset. And it *is* awful to think of him dying like that – even if he did go off with her best friend when she thought he was still seeing her.'

'It wasn't like that,' John protested mildly. He looked me straight in the eyes. 'Tim told me all about it. Faith couldn't accept that everything was over between them. He tried to break things off with her weeks before he started going out with Niamh, but she just wouldn't listen.'

'No. That's not true. Faith told me she wanted to break it off, but he just carried on following her around and giving her presents. He just couldn't believe that any woman could resist him! Come on, John,' Diane turned on her chair to look her boyfriend in the eye, 'you know what he was like! He even came on to me – just as soon as he realised we were going out together.'

'You mean he made a pass at you when he knew you were seeing John?' Margaret asked, her deep brown eyes wide with amazement. 'And this was when he was going out with your friend Faith?'

'It was after he'd switched to Niamh, but yes. He just couldn't resist trying to split us up, just to prove to himself that he was God's gift to women.'

'And what about Niamh?' Margaret sounded shocked. 'Did she know?'

'I told her,' Diane informed us self-righteously. 'I thought she had a right to know; but she didn't believe me. She said I must have misunderstood what he said, but I know I didn't. It was absolutely crystal clear. But Niamh's very naïve about that sort of thing. It's her family. She was brought up a Catholic, and she doesn't know much about men. She went to a school run by nuns. She was convinced that Tim was going to marry her – in her dreams!'

'Yes,' I agreed, feeling very satisfied at the way the conversation was progressing. 'She told us that she was looking for a job in Leicester so that they could set up home there. Timothy had a job lined up for him there, didn't he?'

'That's right,' John nodded. 'His father's a consultant at a hospital there and he found him a job in their labs. He was due to start in November.'

'So he wasn't going to stay in Oxford for the rest of the academic year?' I asked in surprise.

'He didn't need to. He could finish writing up his thesis while he was working,' John explained.

'His grant had run out,' Diane added, 'and he was already sponging off his parents for his rent. I suppose that's what made his dad pull some strings to get him a job.'

'I suppose you'll need someone else to rent his room now?' Margaret asked. 'Or will the landlord advertise for someone?'

'No. it's up to us,' John answered. 'We rent the whole house jointly, so we'll have to pay Tim's share until we find someone else.'

'I suppose there may be some undergraduates who haven't found anywhere yet,' Margaret suggested

'Faith already has someone in mind,' John told her. 'His lodgings fell through and he's been sleeping on her floor since he came up this term.'

'Faith's been angling for him to have Tim's room ever since they started going out to together,' Diane added. 'She wasn't expecting him to still be here after his grant finished. Personally, I don't think Colin tried very hard to find somewhere to stay, because Faith had as good as promised him he could move in here.'

'So Faith has a new boyfriend now?' Margaret asked. 'How did Tim take that?'

'He was fine with it,' John said at once. 'He'd split up with Faith years ago. Why would he care who she went out with?'

'I was just thinking of what you said, Diane, about him not liking to see women paying attention to anyone except him.'

'He made a few bad jokes about cradle-snatching, because Colin's younger than her, but apart from that … just the usual nonsense. You know: a playful pat on the bum here, an accidental-on-purpose hand on the thigh there.'

'I'm sure you're imagining it all,' John protested, but not very forcefully. I could see that he wanted to defend his friend but wasn't completely confident that there was nothing in Diane's allegations. 'Tim likes larking about, but it's all just a bit of fun. He's not – I mean he wasn't – seriously trying to break up other people's relationships.'

The waitress returned for our empty plates. 'Would you like a dessert?'

John looked at his watch. 'Not for us. We'd better be getting along. Things to do!' He got up and picked up his coat from the back of his chair. 'It's been nice talking to you,' he added, turning to Margaret. 'Maybe I'll see you around.'

'Yes,' she nodded. 'I'll keep a lookout for you.'

* * *

'It looks as if one or other of them was lying,' Lucy observed. 'They can't both be telling the truth about what he was like.'

'I'm not so sure,' Ibrahim was more measured in his assessment of the conversation with Diane and John. 'People come across differently to different people. It's probably more that one or both of them is mistaken about him than that either of them is actually lying. John sounds like one of those people who always wants to see the best in everyone …'

'… and Diane seems to have got it in for Tim,' Dominic finished for him. 'I agree. The question is: is John seeing him through rose coloured spectacles or is Diane just incapable of seeing any good in the guy?'

'What I don't get,' Mariam murmured thoughtfully, 'is how he came to be sharing a house with them, if both women disliked him so much – and especially now we know that Faith wanted her boyfriend to have his room.'

'But did she have a boyfriend when they started renting the house?' Bernie asked. 'How long had they been there?'

'Just over a year,' Jonah informed her. 'They took out the lease at the end of their second postgraduate year, which was when Henderson stopped providing them with a room in college.'

'And how long had Faith been with … Colin, was it?' queried Bernie.

'I dunno exactly, but I found out later that he'd only been in Oxford for just over a year. He did his undergraduate study in Cambridge and then moved to Oxford to do a DPhil at Henderson. You may have come across him, Bernie. He was a mathematician.'

'I don't think …' Bernie's forehead creased in a frown of concentration. 'Oh! You don't mean Colin Anderson, do you?'

'The very one,' Jonah smiled back. 'So you do know him?'

'His supervisor was my old college tutor,' Bernie explained. 'He finished his DPhil in … eighty-four, it must've been, and then he went off to the US on a

Fulbright scholarship[9]. I didn't really get to know him until he came back a few years later and took up a tutorial fellowship at Holy Cross. That must've been in the late eighties or early nineties, I think. I rather fancy he had posts at some other universities before he landed back in Oxford.'

'So he can't be our murderer,' Ibrahim observed, 'which is a pity. I had him down as quite a likely suspect. He had the most to gain, what with Tim being his girlfriend's ex and wanting to take over his room as well!'

'But Tim was all set to leave Oxford,' Mariam pointed out. 'So they were all going to see the back of him quite soon anyway.'

'Apart from Niamh,' Lucy put in. 'She was still engaged to him and expecting to move to Leicester with him. I think she's the most likely. She was there, walking next to him at the demo, and if there's anything in the stalking behaviour that Diane told Jonah and Margaret about, maybe she was finding him too controlling and wanted to get away from him.'

'Except that the others all seemed to think that their engagement was just a figment of Niamh's imagination,' Jonah commented. 'They thought Tim was just stringing her along, because that was the only basis that she'd stay with him.'

'They may have been wrong.' Lucy was unwilling to give up her theory. 'Or, even if he wasn't serious about marrying her, he could still be putting pressure on her to come and live with him in Leicester. People like that will do anything to keep control over their victims.'

'It's Diane who came across as the one who had it in for him the most,' Mariam argued. 'The way Jonah tells it, she doesn't have a single good word for him. What if

---

[9] The Fulbright programme funds academic exchange schemes supporting visits by foreign nationals to American universities and visits abroad by American citizens.

there was a whole lot more than just one-sided flirtation between them?'

'Such as?' demanded her brother.

'Could they have been in a relationship and he dumped her and she switched to John on the rebound?' Mariam suggested. 'And now she's going over the top about how awful he is to cover up the fact that she still feels sore about not having him for herself.'

'Except that none of the others have even hinted that there was anything between them.' Ibrahim was scathing of this suggestion. 'No, I think it's more likely to have been Faith. Everyone agrees that she was going out with him and then they split up. And Jonah hinted that she had some sort of a grudge against him.'

'Well, yes,' Jonah agreed. 'That was what I thought at that stage. I felt sure that they were keeping something back about what happened to make Faith and Tim part company, and yet still decide to share a house together. If she really didn't want him in the house, it would have been simple enough to explain to John and Diane that it was going to be too difficult the two of them being there. So I could only conclude that she *did* want him there at the point when they took out the lease. Which begs two questions: why was that? And when did things change (assuming that they did)?'

'What about you, Peter?' Bernie asked suddenly. 'You must have been back at work by then. What was your theory?'

'I didn't come back off leave until the Monday,' Peter told her. 'And I spent most of that day being brought up to speed with what had happened while I was off. So I'd better not spoil Jonah's story by telling you what I thought after the post-mortem confirmed that it was a murder enquiry.'

'Oh yes!' Dominic shouted eagerly. 'Tell us about the PM. *Was* it a drug overdose?'

86

'No,' Jonah said firmly, shaking his head. 'That's for the next chapter. You'll have to wait.'

'Bernie had an interesting conversation with Angie after church that morning,' Peter contributed mischievously. 'And she passed on some very interesting information to me later.'

'Really mam?' Lucy leaned forward so that her face filled the entire screen. 'Do tell us about it!'

'I don't want to steal Jonah's thunder,' Bernie hedged. 'He's telling the story from the police point of view and this didn't seem to be important, so Angie didn't mention it to Peter at the time.'

'But what was it?' persisted Lucy. 'You can't leave us hanging here like that!'

'Why don't Peter and Bernie both write the story from their point of view?' suggested Dominic. 'Then we can compare their versions with Jonah's.'

'Well, I don't mind telling you about my conversation with Angie,' Bernie replied, 'but I'm not going to tell you what it was that she passed on to Peter that had an impact on the investigation. You'll have to wait until the proper place for that.'

* * *

In reading my account of what happened, you need to bear in mind that I was in the other half of the demonstration: the group that started from the Botanical Gardens and marched along the High with the intention of converging on Carfax at the same time as the others reached there from St Aldates. So I didn't see anything at all of the drama that was going on outside Christ Church.

I was no novice demonstrator, having been brought up during the industrial unrest of the late sixties and seventies. My father was a docker and a staunch trade unionist. At the tender age of nine, I joined him on the picket line during the first national dock strike. In

September 1982 I'd just been appointed to a fellowship at St Luke's – good old Philomena Braithwaite had been right when she advised me to do my DPhil there – conditional on my being awarded my doctorate. I'd submitted my thesis and I was waiting for the viva to confirm that I'd passed. So I didn't have a massive amount of work to do at the time.

I heard about the planned protest against the siting of cruise missiles at Greenham Common through the Christian Union at St Luke's. There were several of us who had greater or lesser degrees of affiliation with CND – that's the Campaign for Nuclear Disarmament, for those of you too young to remember when it was a major movement and often in the news. We cobbled together a wooden placard, packed some sandwiches, and went off down to Christ Church Meadow to join in the fun.

One of the Shrewsbury dons was a leading light in the movement too. I went along to a few meetings that she organised in my first year, but then other things got in the way and I dropped it. Her name was Dr Gwendoline Allett, but she used to insist that we called her Gwen. She was very modern and go-ahead, even though she seemed quite old to us. I suppose she must have been in her fifties then. I looked up her obituary in the *Shrew* and it said that she was born in 1929, and became Fellow in Anthropology in 1958. She had one daughter, called Caroline, who eventually went into politics and became an MEP. Her husband, also a don, died in 1984 and she died two years ago.

But to get back to the day of the demo: we were early – almost the first to arrive. We settled down on the grass to eat our lunch, and watched the other demonstrators arrive. Mostly they came in small groups. They stood around, chatting and comparing placards and banners. There were a lot more women than men, and some of them brought children with them. Our little bunch was quite out of place being all men apart from me. St Luke's was still single-sex as far as undergraduates were concerned and I was one of very few postgraduate women. The first cohort of female freshers wouldn't be arriving for a few weeks yet.

Eventually things started to become a bit more organised. A woman in a long skirt and a woollen poncho got up on a wide tree stump and called for order. Then she gave a speech all about how allowing Ronald Reagan to station cruise missiles at Greenham Common would make us and our children targets for Russian nuclear weapons. Everyone applauded when she finished and there was a lot of shouting and excitement.

She stepped down and immediately a young man got up on the stump and started speaking. It took a while for the commotion to die down, but after a minute or two people started listening to him. I don't remember what he said, but he seemed quite an accomplished public speaker. I put him down as a "Union Type" who had probably cut his polemical teeth in some fancy Public School[10] debating society. (That's what people like me – ordinary students from state schools – used to call a certain breed of student, which we associated with membership of the Oxford Union. Typically they were male, had been to one of the "better Public Schools" – Eton, Harrow, Winchester and the like – and thought extremely highly of themselves.)

He didn't get as much applause as the woman had, but there was still enough clapping and shouting for him to look pretty satisfied with himself when he got off the stump to make way for a very young-looking girl, who must have been skiving off school, I should think. One of my friends from St Luke's knew her. He whispered to

---

[10] In England, the term "Public School" refers to a class of fee-charging schools. The first schools to be officially identified by this title were named in the Public Schools Act 1868, but most of them had been founded several centuries earlier.

me that she was Dawn Farmer, a 6th Former at the High School who was very active in the anti-nuclear movement. He told me that she was one of the people who had organised the Oxford march. There was an amazing reaction to her words, which were all about the need for the younger generation to stand up and be counted, and not let the establishment frighten us into accepting the flawed theory that the threat of mutual annihilation could ever ensure peace. Too many of the people in authority had had their minds warped by memories of past wars. They saw everything in terms of guns and bombs and power. It was time we showed them that killing and threatening to kill never solved anything. She finished with an impassioned plea to everyone present that this march must be a peaceful protest – a demonstration that it was possible to express differences of opinion without resorting to violence.

The Union Type was waiting for her when she stepped off the stump amid rapturous applause, and he slapped her on the back and congratulated her on her speech. At first I assumed that he must know her, but when she shrugged him off irritably and pushed through the crowd to re-join her friends, I started to suspect that he was just trying to attract a bit of her glory by giving the impression that he was one of her intimates.

Then, before anyone else could intervene, he was up on the stump again, calling to everyone to divide into their two groups and assemble at the start points of the two routes. I could see that the older woman was a bit put out at this, although he was quite right in saying that the published start time had already passed. She held up a flag with a CND symbol on it and called out for the High Street contingent to follow her. We'd been allocated to that half of the procession, so we did as we were told and headed off past Merton Field to the Botanical Gardens. That was the last that I saw of Timothy

Sudbury, which turned out to be the name of the Union Type.

I'd brought my Sally Army cornet with me to stir the troops and get us marching in time. I led off playing *We Shall Overcome* and other protest songs. We kept to the left-hand pavement because the traffic was still moving on the road, so we could only walk two-abreast. Everything went fine, as far as I was aware, until we were nearly at Carfax, but of course, being at the front, I wouldn't have seen if there had been any trouble behind me. By the time we got to Catte Street, the traffic had come to a standstill going our way. Then, when we got a bit closer – it must have been round about Turl Street – we saw that there was a bus stopped just where our platform was supposed to be for the big speeches at the end of the rally. We went on a bit further and then, when we could see we weren't going to be able to get through, we all stopped and started looking around and wondering what to do.

These days, we'd all have had mobile phones and we could have contacted the people who were putting up the platform and the people leading the march up St Aldates, but as it was, we just didn't know what was going on. So we stood there, passing messages up and down the long line of demonstrators. People were getting out of their cars to see what the hold-up was and one or two of them shouted at us to get out of the way, which wasn't really fair because we were still all on the pavement – or at least as far as I could see.

I don't remember much after that. We seemed to be just milling around, not knowing what was going on, for ages. After a bit, the traffic started moving again. I suppose they must have got the bus out of whatever fix it was in. Then a group of police officers appeared from the Carfax direction and started taking our names. A few people made a fuss about that and refused to co-operate, until they told us that someone had died and they needed to know who we were so that they could contact us in case they needed to talk to us about it. They split us up into smaller groups and ushered us off the main road into various side streets.

I had the privilege of being interviewed by Sergeant Adams – not that I remember him giving us his name, but Peter's description fits well enough. He was a great lumbering bully of a man – the sort that joins the police because he enjoys pushing people around. I don't know why he picked on me in particular to interrogate. Maybe it was the cornet: he didn't give the impression of having a musical ear. Anyway, he had me up against the wall and, for a moment, I thought he was planning to search me, but he didn't. He just took down my name and address and asked me if I knew Timothy Sudbury. I said "no" because I'd never heard the name at that stage. It was only later that I realised that he was the Union Type: when I saw his photograph in the papers.

After that, the demo disintegrated and we all wandered off home. I didn't think any more about it until Angie commented that she'd recognised me in the TV news footage. I hadn't even noticed that there were any cameras there. I suppose they must have been filming from upstairs in one of the buildings on the High.

Angie broached the subject over coffee in the church hall after the Sunday morning service. That must have been three days later. She wasn't impressed at my having got involved in what she considered to be civil disobedience. I gave her a lot of self-righteous guff about free speech and the right to peaceful protest. She said that it was all very well talking like that, but what about the poor police officers who had to keep order? Apparently, Peter had been put on standby when the trouble broke out on St Aldates and he came close to having his leave cancelled.

You used to often hear on the news when there was trouble of some sort – or in anticipation of disorder – "all police leave has been cancelled" but I'd never thought before about what it actually meant for the officers involved. I suddenly realised the difference between a vocation and a job – or one of the differences. If you're a doctor or a priest or a police officer then you're assumed to be on duty unless you've been given leave of absence (which may be cancelled at any time in an emergency); if you work in a shop or an office or a factory, you only have to work your contracted hours. A vocation defines who you are; other jobs can be left behind at the factory gate.

I wondered where my new job as a tutorial fellow and university lecturer fitted in. There were no specified hours of work and no single place that I was expected to be in order to be considered to be working. I would have a room in college where I would hold tutorials with my students, and another room in the Mathematics Institute for my research, but probably a lot of my work would be done at home, in the house that I was going to look for just as soon as my contract came through and I would be able to convince a building society to give me a mortgage. It was a vocation in the sense that people did it for love of the subject and a desire to pass on knowledge to the next generation, and some tutors at least did work long hours and take great pains to support their students; but there would never be any question of a don being called in unexpectedly to deal with a crisis, and that sacred cow "academic freedom" meant that their employers exerted very little control over how they spent their time outside of timetabled lectures and tutorials. I concluded that being a tutorial fellow was more like the clergy than the police, with probably more opportunity for self-indulgence than either of those professions.

Peter will tell you that no don ever did an honest day's work or even knows the meaning of the word! At least in recent weeks he's had to accept that "working at home" isn't synonymous with not working at all!

I told Angie, with the arrogance of youth, that preventing nuclear war was rather more important than the inconvenience of a few police officers and members of the public. It was a peaceful demonstration and there had been no need for the police to be involved at all. If we weren't careful, we'd be living in a police state, what with Thatcher first trying to destroy the trades unions, and now cosying up to that jumped-up film star over in America. The country had taken a lurch to the right and the next thing we knew it wouldn't be women on the streets marching against nuclear weapons; it would be the National Front campaigning to send people such as Angie back to the West Indies.

Angie wasn't convinced. She thought that writing to my MP would have been a more responsible way of expressing my concern. Her argument was that, if you live in a democracy, there's no need to riot in order to get heard. Moreover, if you resorted to protesting on the streets, you were encouraging the idea that the people who should get listened to are the ones who shout loudest and make the most trouble for everyone else.

I said she wouldn't think that if she'd heard Dawn Farmer talking about how she and her friends at school all felt let down by the older generation, who didn't seem to care that they were putting everyone's lives in danger with nuclear weapons.

Angie remained unconvinced. In her opinion, Dawn would have done better to have gone to school and applied herself to getting the best possible qualifications instead of playing at being a politician. What did she know about how to run the country at her age? I retorted that she seemed to know a lot more about sensible defence policy than John Nott (who was Defence Secretary at the time) with his Trident submarines. They weren't much use in the Falklands war, were they?

After that, I didn't give the demonstration or Timothy Sudbury's death any more thought. I had my viva the next day and then I had to do the corrections to my thesis – mostly just typos and a few extra references that the external examiner wanted included. And then I was kept busy preparing for the influx of new undergraduates as the start of Michaelmas Term approached. Being the only female member of academic staff, I was responsible (together with the Principal's wife) for the welfare of the two dozen women who had been admitted into the first year. My personal opinion is that they were quite capable of holding their own, and it was some of the older tutors who were more in need of having their hands held. The college still had a number of the traditional bachelor dons, who hadn't had any meaningful contact with a member of the opposite sex since they bid a tearful goodbye to nanny as they set off for their prep school at the age of eight!

I do remember reading that the police were treating his death as suspicious and that murder had not been ruled out. And, as I said, I saw his picture, and realised that he was the pompous young ass who had tried to rouse us all from the tree stump in Christ Church Meadow, but I really didn't think any more about it after that.

7. POST MORTEM

After our chance meeting with John and Diane, Margaret and I discussed our own ideas about what might have caused Timothy Sudbury's death. Margaret asked me to describe his symptoms when I first saw him lying in the road. I don't think she considered that I gave a very good account of them. All I could remember was that his limbs were jerking in a strange way and he was staring straight ahead, but not seeming to see us when we called out to him and waved our hands in front of his face. I asked her if it sounded like an epileptic seizure and she said it was hard to tell from my description. The implication was that, if I had described it adequately, she would have been able to give a proper opinion.

Then she admitted that she didn't know a lot about epilepsy and that there were several different kinds of seizure and different people were affected differently. She also said that seizures could be unrelated to epilepsy. He could have had a brain tumour or a stroke. Some people even got the sort of muscle spasm that I'd described as a result of low calcium levels in their blood.

So, just not having a history of epilepsy didn't rule out it having been a natural phenomenon?

No, although finding that syringe was a bit of a coincidence. Margaret didn't give much credence to Timothy's friends' and family's protestations that he never took drugs. She'd come across plenty of people arriving in Accident and Emergency with drug overdoses where their nearest and dearest had been blissfully unaware that they had a heroin habit or regularly snorted cocaine.

Well then, what drug would induce the symptoms that Timothy Sudbury had?

It seemed that seizures feature among the known side-effects for any number of drugs. If we're talking illicit drugs then cocaine would be a likely candidate. Margaret had witnessed a cocaine user exhibiting the sort of muscle spasm that I had described. Opiates, such as heroin, could be to blame too.

Everything seemed to hinge on the post-mortem examination, so I was delighted when Richard asked me to accompany him to the mortuary to watch the proceedings. Peter, who had returned to work that morning, was left among the files bringing himself up to date with the case by studying the paperwork with the help of DS MacBride.

The pathologist, Ernest Stopford-Heyes, was a small, fussy man in his fifties, with a pencil moustache and black hair combed back from a high forehead. His white coat was buttoned up to just below a purple bow tie – an affectation that somehow always annoyed me. I watched impatiently as he pored over the naked corpse, peering down at the skin and occasionally pressing down on it with his fingers. He made small noises to himself as he did so, which made me think that he might have learned something from his examination, but he said nothing aloud to us.

'Mmm-mm,' he murmured as he shone a light into each of Timothy Sudbury's eyes in turn.

'Uh-huh!' he declared as he flexed an arm at the elbow.

'Tch-tch,' he tutted peering down at his patient's right thigh through a magnifying glass. 'Come and have a look at this.'

We both came over and gazed down through the glass. I saw what looked like a small, round bruise. I looked up at Richard, who seemed to understand what Stopford-Heyes was getting at.

'An injection site?' he queried.

'Exactly so,' the pathologist confirmed. 'The only one I've found so far. He certainly wasn't an addict. There are no signs at all on his arms, which is where they usually go first. And this wasn't an injection into a vein, it was intramuscular.'

'Painkillers, perhaps?' Richard suggested.

'Could be,' Stopford-Heyes shrugged. 'Or, based on the analysis of the liquid in that syringe you found on him, ketamine.'

'Ketamine?' we both echoed. I'd never heard of this drug and I guessed from his voice that Richard hadn't either.

'It's an anaesthetic. It's not much used in adult humans, but very common for veterinary procedures and sometimes it's used to sedate children.'

'Does it cause seizures?' I blurted out, remembering what Margaret had said about how lots of drugs did.

'In a minority of cases. Of course it depends on the dose and on the subject's pre-disposition.'

'Is it ever used recreationally?' Richard asked.

'That's quite common in the United States, I believe,' the doctor put down the magnifying glass and began poking around in his tray of instruments. 'It's a hallucinogen. Some people seem to enjoy the feelings of euphoria and "out-of-body" experience that it can create. But it's not used much over here. I can't say I've ever come across it myself. Mind you,' he added picking up a fearsome-looking scalpel, 'I've got a friend in Newmarket who reckons it's rife among the jockeys round there. Easy access, you see. There's a lot of it used for treating horses. That's only anecdotal, mind you. There haven't been any prosecutions. I've taken blood samples for toxicology, so we'll soon know if he had any ketamine in his system when he died. Now, let's open him up and have a look at his insides, shall we?'

I watched with a strange fascination as he expertly cut through skin and soft tissue to reach the internal organs. This was my first post mortem and I wanted to be sure that I took it all in. Glancing round, I noticed that Richard had wandered off and seemed to be studying an anatomy poster on the wall (presumably put there for the benefit of visiting medical students).

Stopford-Heyes examined the heart and lungs, and declared them both to be in good underlying condition. He extracted the liver and weighed it before taking a small sample in a glass bottle, which his assistant fastened, labelled and put on to a tray at the side of the room.

'No sign of liver disease either,' he murmured. 'I suppose we'd better have a look to see what he had for his last meal.'

I have to admit to feeling a bit queasy as he emptied the contents of the young man's stomach into a large kidney bowl and started poking about at them with a spatula. I watched from a distance, noting that they were a reddish orange colour. I declined his kind invitation to take a sniff at what he described as, "a rather interesting bouquet". Even from a distance, the whiff of vomit was unpleasant enough and made me a little more sympathetic with Richard's choice to keep his distance from the proceedings.

'From the smell,' he told us, 'he had consumed a quantity of alcohol. That could explain his reaction to the drug. Ketamine and alcohol *don't* make good friends. It's very much not recommended to take them together. The rest is difficult to identify without analysis. The red colouration could well be tomato soup, and I think I can see some partially-digested bread. So he probably died within a few hours of having had lunch. Would that fit your timescale?'

'Yes,' Richard nodded from the other side of the room. 'According to his friends, they had lunch together and then went off to join the demonstration.'

'Getting back to the alcohol,' I asked, coming a little closer as my interest in the case overcame my nausea. 'Does that mean that it could have been an accident? He didn't realise that his usual safe dose of ketamine would be fatal after he'd been drinking?'

'Perhaps.' Stopford-Heyes pursed his lips, 'but that still begs the question: why did he take the drug at all? However that's your problem, not mine. Now let's have a look inside his head, shall we?'

He took up an electric saw and opened up the skull. The brain, he told us, was in good condition and of average weight. There was no sign of any tumour or other disease that could account for the seizures. He cut out several pieces of tissue from different parts of the brain and sealed them into sample jars.

'Ketamine readily crosses the blood-brain barrier,' he explained. 'We may learn something from the amount of it here compared with elsewhere in the body – always assuming that he did take ketamine that afternoon.'

Eventually, he stepped back from the table and nodded to his assistant to return the body to its refrigerated compartment, peeling off his surgical gloves as he did so. Then he led us into his office and called to his secretary to bring tea.

'The cause of death would appear to be respiratory and heart failure,' he told us. 'Based on the account given by the ambulance crew, it followed a coma, which was probably drug-induced. I'd been half-expecting signs of compressive asphyxiation from his having been caught up in a crush of people, but there are none – which is probably good news for you.'

Richard nodded. 'So his death had nothing to do with any failure to control the crowd?'

'That's right. My guess is that he injected himself with a dose of ketamine from that syringe he was carrying, and either he overdid it or he was particularly susceptible to its effects for some reason.'

'Or could someone else have injected him?' I gabbled. 'There weren't any fingerprints on the syringe, which is odd if he did it himself, isn't it?'

'That's not my area of expertise,' the doctor replied drily. 'Obviously, another person could have administered the drug, but hardly without the victim being aware of it. However, that's your province. I merely examine bodies to ascertain what went wrong with them. It's up to you to decide about who did it and why. I should have the toxicology results back tomorrow. That will confirm – or not – that it was ketamine poisoning that made his heart and lungs stop functioning.'

'How fast-acting is it?' Richard asked. 'If he was already unconscious at three thirty, what time would he have had to have been injected with the stuff?'

'I read up on the pharmacokinetics, after the lab reported that it was ketamine in that syringe. Intramuscular injection of ketamine usually produces sedation or anaesthesia within fifteen minutes and the effect lasts for between thirty minutes and two hours.'

'So he *couldn't* have taken it before the march started!' I cried out excitedly. 'Someone must have stabbed him with the needle when he was already in the crowd. Otherwise, he'd have been unconscious before they got going.'

'Not necessarily.' The pathologist gave me a pitying look, as if he despaired of the ignorance and low IQ of police officers. 'At low doses, ketamine merely produces a dreamy state, similar to mild intoxication. We'll know more when the toxicology tests have been done.'

The PM had taken up most of the morning, so we met up with Peter and Mac in the canteen. They had identified a shortlist of demonstrators whom they thought warranted following up with another interview. So that was our afternoon mapped out. Richard went off in Peter's car to speak to the women who had organised the march, while Mac and I made a tour of various colleges and student lodgings on foot. I don't remember any of this effort turning up any useful information, but it made for a pile of paperwork to be written up and filed when we got back to the station.

The next day (Tuesday) we reviewed the evidence so far. Reports came back from the lab confirming that Timothy Sudbury did indeed have high levels of both ketamine and alcohol in his blood when he died. The pathologist's written report concluded that this combination of drugs was almost certainly the cause of the respiratory and heart failure that led to his demise. It seemed that the only open question was: by whom was the ketamine administered?

* * *

'I thought that would be a nice little cliff-hanger on which to end the next chapter,' Jonah concluded, gazing into the screen, where four young faces were crowded together at Lucy's desk.

'Can't you tell us a bit more about the toxicology report?' Lucy asked. She had ambitions to become a pathologist herself and had read widely on the subject. 'Could they tell anything from the liver biopsy about how long the ketamine had been in his system? And did they test for any other drugs?'

'If you're not going to tell us what you thought when you reviewed the evidence on Tuesday, wouldn't it make more sense to stop at the end of Monday and put what happened on Tuesday in the next chapter?' suggested Dominic.

'But it's more dramatic the way I did it,' Jonah protested. 'I don't want my readers to fall asleep! And it'll be easier to follow if I have all the medical evidence together in the same place.'

'Then why not make this chapter just about the medical evidence?' argued Dominic, 'and cut out the stuff about interviewing other protestors and writing up the paperwork.'

'But I want to take people through the process of the investigation as it happened,' Jonah insisted. 'I want them to see it from the point of view of a raw detective constable working on his first murder case. If I put all the medical evidence together, readers won't realise how much routine work goes on while we're waiting for things like lab reports and stuff. And they won't appreciate how far into the investigation we were before we got confirmation that it really was a murder enquiry. It wasn't until that Tuesday morning – five days after he died – that we could be confident that someone had killed Timothy Sudbury by injecting him with a massive dose of ketamine.'

'And did the report tell you *when* he was injected,' persisted Lucy.

'Well, the pathologist had already told us that it's a fast-acting drug,' Jonah replied, 'which more or less meant it must have been while he was actually in the procession marching up St Aldates. I don't remember anything about the liver biopsy. I think Peter was delegated to read the report and give us edited highlights.'

'Peter?' Lucy asked eagerly.

'What? Oh, yes, I think I did probably read the report, but I don't remember anything about it. It's a long time ago. And I wouldn't have understood the medical details anyway.'

'Anyway,' Bernie broke in, 'now that the Great Author has had a chance to show off his next chapter, perhaps we could turn to more important matters? This meeting isn't supposed to be all about Jonah. It's supposed to be keeping the family together during lockdown. So let's hear everyone's news and how they're doing.'

'I don't think we've really got any news,' Lucy told her. 'Mariam and I have just been carrying on studying online, and Dom's been giving his students lessons online and Ibrahim's been working from home just the same as for the last two weeks. We've been out shopping and taken daily exercise from home, but that's not very interesting to talk about.'

'What about you, Aunty?' Bernie looked at another rectangle on her screen where Aunty Dot's face loomed rather too dark to make out her features clearly and with shadows that made it difficult to assess her state of health based on her complexion. 'Are you still keeping well?'

'Fit as a fiddle!' Dot declared. 'Don't you start worrying about me. We Fazakerleys are tough. It'll take more than a new virus to carry me off!'

'The Home manager told Mum that another resident has been admitted to hospital,' Dominic reminded her, 'and she said there were others with symptoms.'

'Yes,' Dot admitted, 'they took Doris in this morning. But Fran is getting better,' she added brightly, 'and I told you before, they've got us all divided up into small groups so that we only come into contact with two or three staff each to prevent cross-infection. There really is nothing at all to worry about.'

'And you're sure you're still keeping well?' Bernie pressed her.

'Yes. I told you.' Dot sounded affronted at her niece's persistent anxiety. 'Not a hint of a cough and they've been taking my temperature three times a day. So do stop flapping! I'd much rather hear some more of young Jonah's story. Is that as far as you've got?'

'Well, I've made a start on the next chapter, but it's still very rough and ready.' Jonah pretended to be reluctant to continue with his narrative.

'Never mind that. I just want to know what happened next. You can get Dominic to polish it up later, seeing as he's so full of ideas about how it ought to be done.'

* * *

We sat drinking tea in Richard's office, speculating on who could have administered the ketamine to Timothy Sudbury, and trying to decide what we ought to do next. That's Richard, Peter and me: I think Mac was out with some of the other DCs interviewing more of the demonstrators. Stopford-Heyes had told us that it wasn't a street drug of the sort that were readily available to students with the right contacts; so the chances were it had been diverted from some legitimate use.

Which of our potential suspects had access to prescription-only drugs? The obvious candidate was John, the trainee doctor, who was working at the infirmary where such medication was presumably in common usage. But how easy would it be for someone as junior as he was to take any of it away with him? Wouldn't there be more senior colleagues checking up on him all the time? Wouldn't the pharmacy have a system for monitoring the issue of supplies to each ward? Was ketamine used all that much anyway? Hadn't Stopford-Heyes said that it was only really used for sedating children and animals? I made a mental note to ask Margaret about all these things next time I saw her.

Timothy's parents were also doctors. Could Timothy have obtained ketamine from one of them somehow and injected himself with it? But why do it then, in the middle of the demonstration? If he *was* taking drugs for kicks, why pick a moment when he was already on a high after his successful speech? And why risk lapsing into unconsciousness in the middle of the crowd where he might get trampled underfoot?

What about its use in animals? Did any of our suspects have any links to veterinary practices or racing stables? Not as far as we knew.

My personal feeling was that any one of the postgraduate students could probably have got hold of the drug if they wanted it. They were most likely all from privileged families and had more money than they knew what to do with. However, I kept that opinion to myself. It wasn't a good idea in Oxford to give the impression that the police were biased against the students, who made up such a large proportion of the population during term-time. In any case, I had to admit that there were honourable exceptions – Margaret for example – to the posh rich boy stereotype of an Oxbridge graduate.

Peter showed Richard a statement that one of the uniformed officers had taken from a Muriel Rowlinson, who had been at the demonstration but, like Bernie, had marched along the High Street instead of St Aldates. She had seen Timothy arguing with someone shortly before they all set off from Christ Church Meadow. Richard agreed that this certainly ought to be followed up. He sent us off together to interview her again, while he went to the Infirmary to speak to John Goodey and his colleagues there.

Mrs Rowlinson was a housewife – I think that was still an acceptable way of describing a woman who stayed at home to look after her home and children – with a pre-school child who clung to her skirt and peered up fearfully at Peter and me as she led us into the sitting room of her smart detached property in Headington.

'Lynne's very shy,' she apologised, taking the little girl on her lap and holding her around the waist as she waited for us to begin the interview. 'She doesn't like people coming in the house. So unlike her sister! Helen's quite the opposite. I always worry that she makes friends *too* easily. I've told her not to speak to strangers, but …' She sighed. 'Being a teacher, I always thought I'd find it was easy managing my own children, but it doesn't seem to work like that! But I'm sorry: you didn't come here to listen to me going on. What was it you wanted to know?'

'You told WPC Brown that you saw Timothy Sudbury – the man who died – arguing with a woman while you were all waiting in Christ Church Meadow to set off on the march,' Peter began. 'We'd like to know a bit more about that. Do you happen to know who the woman was?'

'No.' Mrs Rowlinson shook her head. 'I'd never seen her before. I hadn't seen the young man before that day either. They weren't part of our group. I think they were students from the university who jumped on the bandwagon when they heard about the demo. I only knew who he was because he insisted on standing up and making a speech before we set off. It was a bit of a nerve actually. It was supposed to be a *women*'s peace march – or that's how Pam and I saw it.'

'Pam?' queried Peter.

'Pamela Lessing. We used to work together. She couldn't come on the march because she had to be in school, but she was planning to be there at the end, for the proper speeches from the platform at Carfax – except that they never happened. She got to Magdalen Bridge and the police turned her back. We've got a little group going, here in Headington, to support the Greenham Women. I'd like to go and camp there myself, but Victor – that's my husband – wouldn't hear of it, and I suppose it wouldn't be good for Helen's schooling. But I do think it's important that women stand up and show the politicians that we aren't going to be pushed around anymore.'

'Getting back to the young woman that you saw arguing,' Peter resumed when she paused for breath. 'Can you describe her to me?'

'I didn't really notice. She was a brunette, I think, and her hair was quite short. Well, I say it was short, but it may just have been hidden inside her coat collar. Yes! I think she had her collar turned up so it covered part of her face. That's why I can't remember it very well. And her hair may not have been as dark as all that. I really can't be sure, I'm afraid.'

'Could it have been red?' I asked eagerly, remembering Niamh's luxuriant locks.'

'No, definitely not. I'm sure I'd remember if it had been.'

'How tall was she compared with Timothy?' Peter prompted. 'Did she have to look up to him? Or were they more on a level?'

'I'm not sure … I *think* … I don't think she was quite as tall as him, but she wasn't a lot shorter either.'

'And do you remember what she was wearing?' Peter asked. 'You said she had a coat with its collar turned up. Do you remember the colour?'

'Dark-ish, but I don't *think* it was black. Maybe a dark green or blue.'

'Thank you. That's very helpful.' Peter glanced across at me to check that I'd written everything down in my notebook. 'Now, can you think back to the argument that you saw. Did you catch what they were saying at all? Do you have any idea what it was about?'

'I didn't exactly hear what they were saying, but I got the impression she was angry with him about something he'd done. She waved her arms around a bit while he just stood there smiling. He looked a bit of a supercilious swine to me, but then I'd just had to listen to him going on about needing to show this Tory government that they couldn't ride roughshod over the will of the people – as if he wasn't quite obviously just the sort of idiot that the Conservative party is full of! Anyway, I think she gave up in the end and then he wandered off and put his arm around this little redhead who was standing around looking a bit lost. Then Gwen called us all to split into our two groups and I went off across the Meadow to the Botanical Garden. That was the last I saw of either of them.'

'Thank you,' Peter repeated. 'You've been very helpful indeed. We'll go now, which I'm sure will be a relief to your daughter.' He looked towards Lynne, who looked back rather fearfully from the safety of her mother's arms. 'I'm sorry we frightened you. We'll try not to have to do it again.'

I was very excited by what we had learned. It looked as if Tim had fallen out with one of the women in their little group only a short time before his death. It was a pity that Mrs Rowlinson's description wasn't good enough for us to tell which of them it was, but it certainly did rule out one of our suspects: little red-haired Niamh O'Halloran. I was inclined to think that Wendy was also an unlikely candidate. Surely, anyone would have noticed her extreme height (for a woman) and striking dark features? So we were left with the assumption that either Faith or Diane had taken him to task over some misdemeanour that he had committed, and he had appeared unmoved by their protestations.

I explained my reasoning to Richard when we re-convened later that afternoon. He agreed that we had obtained some useful new information, but pointed out that the woman that Mrs Rowlinson had seen need not have been one of Tim Sudbury's group of intimates at all. It could easily have been someone that we hadn't come across before – another of the women who objected to him taking the platform the way he had done, for example.

Richard's enquiries at the infirmary had merely confirmed that dangerous drugs such as ketamine were kept under very strict control. The head pharmacist had been affronted at the suggestion that it could be possible for anyone – still less a pre-registration doctor – to obtain a syringeful for his own use. He had insisted on taking Richard through the paperwork to demonstrate how many checks and balances there were to prevent such an occurrence. In the last ten days, ketamine had been supplied to paediatric surgery and to the casualty department. It was all fully accounted for.

The Medical Director had re-iterated this and had also assured him that he took a personal interest in all the trainees and could vouch for the fact that John Goodey was under constant supervision by senior members of the medical staff. He was currently working in rheumatology and had never spent time in paediatric surgery or casualty.

I went home that evening feeling a little deflated. We didn't seem any closer to finding out who had wielded the fatal syringe of ketamine.

Margaret was late in – a not uncommon occurrence – so I whiled away the time by attempting to make a meal for us both. As usual, neither of us had had time to get to the shops, so the available materials were limited. I found a tin of tomatoes and some spaghetti in the cupboard, and a pound of minced beef in the fridge. So I decided to try my hand at spaghetti Bolognese.

It was all coming together brilliantly when I noticed the front page of a newspaper, which one of our housemates had left on the kitchen table. It had a photograph of the demonstration and the promise of a detailed article about the death that had occurred on one of the inside pages. I put the lid on the boiling pan of spaghetti and sat down to read.

'Wow! What on earth are you cooking in here?'

I looked up to see Karen Jones, a medical student who occupied the room next to Margaret's on the first floor of the house, standing in the doorway. She strode across to the cooker and turned off the gas under both of my saucepans. Then she opened the window and made a great show of wafting the foul-smelling fumes outside.

I got up and went over to inspect the damage. The spaghetti had survived, but the mince and tomato Bolognese sauce was a charred mess stuck to the bottom of the pan, which I had omitted to turn down on to a lower heat before becoming absorbed in the newspaper article. I picked it up and immediately dropped it again because the handle had become painfully hot.

'Here! Let me do it.' Karen picked up the kettle holder and, using it to protect her hand, transported the pan across to the sink and submerged it in cold water. 'Better leave it to soak overnight. Then you may, just possibly, be able to get it clean with a Brillo pad.'

At that point, Margaret arrived home. I heard the familiar sound of her motorbike in the road outside, followed by her key in the front door lock and her footsteps in the hall. My heart sank as I realised that she was heading for the kitchen rather than going upstairs to her room. There was no possible way of avoiding her finding out immediately what had happened. In fact, in all probability, it was the odour of my cooking that had prompted her to investigate.

Credit where credit's due, she did manage to stem her hilarity at my culinary failure before the fish and chips that she had brought home for our dinner had gone cold. We sat at the kitchen table eating them out of the newspaper – and it was real newspaper in those days, not a polystyrene box or even the clean food-hygiene approved paper that you get now – with our fingers, while I explained to Margaret what it was that had caught my eye and made me forget to turn down the gas.

The newspaper account was all about "police brutality" and "heavy-handed treatment" of lawful protestors. There was a lot of general stuff about policing policy and injuries incurred by protestors at other demonstrations, followed by a description of Timothy

Sudbury's collapse and subsequent death. It was never said directly, but the implication was that this had been caused by the police attempting to break up the protest in an arbitrary and violent way.

Margaret listened sympathetically and then produced another paper with a very different slant on the incident. According to this correspondent (who, like the writer of the first article, admitted to not having been there at the time), the death had been the result of pushing and shoving by Timothy's fellow protestors, angry at being held up by the bus that was stuck at Carfax. The police had completely lost control of the situation. Had sufficient officers been in attendance from the start, this death could most likely have been prevented.

I sighed. 'And I suppose when it comes out that he actually died from a mixture of ketamine and alcohol, it'll be our fault for not preventing drugs getting on to the streets.'

'Or maybe it'll be *our* fault for not managing to revive him after the ambulance was called,' Margaret commented, trying to raise my spirits. 'Anyway, ketamine isn't classified under the misuse of drugs act. It isn't illegal to possess it – only to administer it except under the direction of a trained medic.'

'And how easy would it be for someone else to get hold of it? Could a pre-registration doctor smuggle some out from the infirmary, for example?'

'I doubt it.' Margaret shook her head. 'The pharmacy have very strict procedures for issuing drugs, and each ward keeps its own record too. About the only way would be to have some issued for a patient and then falsify the records so that it looked as if it had been administered when it hadn't, but that would be incredibly risky. There would be people monitoring the patient constantly and it would be obvious that they hadn't been given the drug. A consultant anaesthetist might get away with it, because the chances were that, if they said the patient needed more anaesthesia everyone would simply accept it as one of the vagaries of medical science and not question their decision. Anyone lower down the food chain would have their work checked up on.'

'They told Richard that ketamine was sometimes used in A and E. Have *you* ever used it?'

'Yes, occasionally. We sometimes use it to sedate someone who needs a quick procedure that's going to be painful – cleaning and dressing wounds, that sort of thing. It's a very good painkiller and it puts them into a trance-like state so they don't fight back through fear and it's less distressing for them, and yet it doesn't put them fully to sleep, so they can still co-operate if we need them to. It's also more fast acting than most analgesic drugs.'

'And if you wanted to steal some to take home with you?'

'No way!' Margaret shook her head emphatically. 'It'd be far too risky. We have to account for every medication that we administer and there are always other people around checking that we've got the dose right.'

'Even when you're frantically busy – on a Saturday night, for example?' I knew that the emergency waiting room filled up when the pubs closed on their busiest night of the week; when the casualties of drunken brawls were picked up by the police and brought in to have their wounds dressed, and opportunistic muggers preyed on those too intoxicated or too careless to defend themselves.

'We-e-ell, maybe,' she conceded grudgingly. 'I suppose you might be left alone with a patient for long enough to fiddle the paperwork and smuggle out a few milligrams.'

* * *

'He's still trying to steer us towards that John Goodey guy,' Ibrahim declared, when Jonah finished his narrative. 'So *he* can't be the murderer.'

'I wouldn't be so sure of that,' Lucy grinned. 'Knowing Jonah, it's at least as likely that he's trying to show off that *he* knew who it was before anyone else.'

'Your mum was very keen to tell us about that girl who made the speech just after Timothy did,' Mariam pointed out. 'Was that because she's very significant or because *she's* trying to lead us up the garden path too?'

'I wouldn't trust anything our Bernadette tells you,' Dot cut in, her voice sounding rather wheezy and strange. 'She always was a troublemaker!'

'That's not fair, Aunty!' Bernie protested. 'I never told lies. Besides, I don't even know how the police investigation went; so I can't mislead anyone about it.'

'You must know who did it,' Lucy insisted. 'It would have been on the news.'

'So if you really don't know whether Dawn Farmer is important, she can't have done it!' Dominic cried triumphantly.

'He's got you there, Mam,' Lucy smiled. 'Get out of that one if you can!'

'I'm not saying anything else,' Bernie retorted. 'You can think what you like. I haven't told you anything that isn't true, and I'm not going to be badgered into spoiling Jonah's story. It's up to you what you believe about whether I've given the game away regarding Dawn Farmer – one way *or* the other!' she added, directing a hard look into the webcam at the top of Jonah's computer screen.

'Where's that table you made, Mariam?' Dominic asked in the lull that followed. 'The one where we wrote down all the suspects and whether they had motive, means and opportunity.'

There was some confusion in the small rectangle where the Liverpool contingent was displayed as Mariam reached across in front of Lucy to pick up a piece of paper from the other side of the desk. For a moment, the watchers in Oxford could see nothing but a lime green blur where her hijab passed in front of the camera, too close for it to focus. Then everything returned to normal and they could see that she and Dominic were holding the paper between them.

'We've got everyone except Dawn Farmer down as having opportunity,' Dominic murmured. 'Do we know whether she was anywhere near the victim in the procession?'

'Mam?' Lucy asked. 'Was she with you or with the St Aldates group?'

'I told you: I'm not saying anything more.'

'We now know he *had* to have been stabbed with the needle while he was marching up St Aldates,' Mariam said firmly, 'because the ketamine would have knocked him out almost immediately. 'So that rules out anyone who wasn't with him then.'

'But all our other suspects were,' Ibrahim sighed, 'so that doesn't get us very far!'

'Let's concentrate on motive and means,' suggested Lucy. 'We said that Faith might have motive because he split up with her and it may not have been as amicable as everyone's leading us to believe, but I can't see how *she*'d have got hold of ketamine.'

'On the face of it, John's the only one of them who would have had any chance,' Ibrahim agreed.

'Could any of them have had it prescribed for them?' suggested Dominic.

'No.' Dot's voice, although still slightly breathless, was firm. 'It's not that sort of drug. If it had been an opiate of some sort, it might have been prescribed as a painkiller, but not ketamine! In all my years as a nurse, I never saw it used except as a sedative in hospital.'

'What about for animals?' Mariam postulated. 'These days, people talk about it as a horse drug. Did any of the suspects have links with stables or vets? Presumably you'd need a much larger dose to sedate a horse, so you might be able to take out enough to kill a human without anyone noticing.'

'That's an idea!' Dominic agreed eagerly. 'I think you may have cracked it, Mariam. The trouble is I don't remember anyone mentioning horses or veterinary practices.'

'I bet a lot of those students had families with "room for a pony" at their houses,' Lucy asserted. 'But we can't know which ones actually had horsey connections until the police team get back out there and ask them some more questions. I think we need to send Jonah back to write up what happened next, before we can have any idea who did it.'

'Well, let's at least have another look at the *motive* column,' pleaded Dominic. 'We've got John down there because Timothy was sniffing round his girlfriend.'

'But we also know that she wasn't interested,' Lucy cut in before he could go on. 'So that motive's looking pretty thin. Why would he risk his whole career – never mind getting a life sentence – when Diane told the police that Timothy's advances just irritated her?'

'They all seem to have found Timothy irritating,' Ibrahim commented. 'The strange thing is that they invited him to share the house with them in the first place.'

'Yes!' Lucy's voice was unusually animated. 'I think you may have got something there, Ibrahim. None of them particularly liked him, and yet they felt obliged to allow him to live there with them. What if that was because he had some sort of hold over them – or maybe just over one or two of them? What if he was a blackmailer? That would be a much more convincing motive than Faith still being angry with him about something that happened when they were going out or John thinking he was out to get Diane.'

'Now that's an idea!' Dominic agreed excitedly, 'but we don't know who he could have been blackmailing.'

'What could one of those youngsters have done that anyone could blackmail them about at their age?' Dot croaked over the airwaves, before breaking off in a fit of coughing.

'Are you alright, Aunty?' Bernie asked anxiously. 'How long have you had that cough?'

For what seemed like an age, they all waited, watching the elderly woman struggling to clear her throat sufficiently to answer.

'It's just a tickle,' she managed to get out eventually. 'It's the dust. I've had the window open because of the heat and it's been blowing in off the trees. Don't – don't ...' she took in a rasping breath, 'don't you worry about me. I told you: they're checking our temperatures three times a day. If I was going down with coronavirus they'd have picked it up.'

'Well mind you take care, Aunty,' Bernie urged. 'Don't go ignoring any symptoms. I think we ought to end this here. We've been on for over an hour. You go and have a cup of tea to get the dust out of your throat and then get some rest. I know you think you're still as strong as a horse, but you can't get away from the fact that once you pass the one hundred mark you're not as young as you once were!'

8. LINES OF ENQUIRY

Palm Sunday. The day that Downing Street announced that Prime Minister Boris Johnson had been admitted to hospital. The day that the Care Home manager rang Bernie's cousin Joey to let him know that his aunt was being treated as a potential COVID-19 patient.

Aunty Dot, still refusing to admit that she was seriously ill, joined the family videoconference from her high-backed armchair as usual and immediately demanded to hear the next instalment of Jonah's story.

'I've done a bit more,' he told her, as she coughed and gasped across the airwaves following the exertion of speaking, 'but it's been slow progress, I'm afraid, and my secretarial team have been letting me down!' he added, grinning into the camera.

Dominic and Ibrahim immediately leapt to defend themselves.

'I've had a lot of work on,' Dominic protested. 'They've got things a bit more organised at school now. We've got to send out work for all the kids to do at home *and* we're going in on a rota basis to teach the children of key workers in school. So it's like doing everything twice!'

'I'm afraid I got a bit diverted,' Ibrahim admitted. 'I've been reading Lucy's Dad's diaries – and typing them up for you,' he added hastily. 'They don't say very much about the case. He seems more interested in talking about his mother.'

'That's because she'd sort of come back from the dead, hadn't she Mam?' Lucy told him.

'Yes,' Bernie agreed. 'As far as I can gather, she just turned up out of the blue after his father died. We can tell you all about it another time, if you're interested, Ibrahim.'

'She sounds a bit of a strange person,' Ibrahim persisted. 'Did you ever meet your gran, Lucy?'

'No. She died when I was a baby.'

'Yes,' Bernie nodded, 'and she never had a good word to say about you, me or even your dad. She wasn't an easy person to like, but Richard did his best. And, to be fair to her, I think she'd been through a lot and hadn't been treated very well by Richard's family. And she left everything she had to us when she died, so she can't have been as set against us as she pretended to be!'

'He seems to think very highly of Peter,' Ibrahim commented. 'He certainly seemed to be pleased when he came back off paternity leave to help with this case.'

'It wasn't paternity leave in those days,' Bernie told him. 'Back then, if fathers wanted to be with their new babies they had to take annual leave, and there was no guarantee their employer would let them. Everyone assumed that it was only the mothers that needed time off.'

'Bernadette,' Dot wheezed, 'I'm sure this is a valuable history lesson for the youngsters, but we're all waiting for Jonah here to read us his next chapter.'

'I'm not sure it's quite a whole chapter,' Jonah smiled back, 'and it's still just a rough draft, but I'll read it to you if you like.'

* * *

After studying the post mortem report, Peter commented that it was important to find out where and when

Timothy Sudbury had consumed the alcohol that had been found in his system.

'He must have drunk quite a lot of it not long before the march started or there wouldn't still have been enough in his stomach for the pathologist to smell,' he said at our morning briefing the next day. 'So how did it get there? Did someone else ply him with drinks or did he do it spontaneously? Did he normally drink at lunch time or was this unusual?'

'You've hit the nail on the head there,' Richard agreed. 'We need to interview his friends again. And we need to contact his family to let them know that this is now a murder enquiry.'

He sat pondering for a few moments.

'I think we'll leave it to Leicester police to tell the parents,' he decided at last. 'I'll take Porter to break the news to the fiancée, and you can go over to New Hinksey and ask to have a look in his room. Ask them about what they had to drink before they went off to the demonstration and what Sudbury's normal drinking habits were.'

We went our separate ways. When Richard and I arrived at the flat in Temple Street, we were once more greeted ungraciously by Wendy, who let us in and led the way upstairs to the living room. Niamh was sitting at the table with a typewriter in front of her and untidy piles of books on either side. There were also two coffee-stained mugs and a plate with an unfinished piece of toast on it.

She had definitely been crying this time. Her eyes were bloodshot and the lids were puffy. She stood up when she saw us and held out a quivering hand to shake ours.

'I'm sorry for the mess,' she apologised, looking down at the table. 'We'd better go and sit over there.'

She pointed towards four easy chairs grouped around a coffee table at the end of the room nearest the bay window. We walked over and sat down. Wendy hurried across the room and sat down next to me, leaving the chair farthest away from us for Niamh. Niamh looked at Richard expectantly, while Wendy stared suspiciously at us, ready to intervene if we over-stepped the mark in interrogating her friend.

'Miss O'Halloran,' Richard began, 'I'm sorry to have to tell you this, but we believe that your fiancé's death was not natural. The post mortem has shown that it was caused by a drug that was injected into him, probably while he was in the crowd at the demonstration last Thursday. It is possible that he administered the substance himself but, on balance, we think it is more likely that it was done by someone else.'

Niamh gave a little gasp and lowered her eyes. Wendy put her arm round her and drew her closer to her. She looked angrily across at Richard over Niamh's head.

'He wasn't her fiancé,' she growled. 'They were just going out, that's all. He wasn't the marrying kind. You know what Diane said about him chatting her up. And you know how badly he treated Faith.'

She turned her attention to Niamh, stroking her hair and murmuring softly in her ear, 'I know you're missing him now, but he wouldn't have been any good for you. He never really cared for you. He never cared for anyone but himself!'

'I know it's a difficult time for you,' Richard said, using the form of words that police officers so often have to employ when they need information from people who have just suffered heart-breaking loss or received devastating bad news, 'but do you think you could answer a few questions – to help us find out who did this to him?'

Niamh lifted her head off Wendy's shoulder and looked towards us. She nodded and wiped her eyes with her hand. Then she pushed Wendy away and reached into her pocket. She drew out a crumpled tissue and dabbed at her eyes. Richard handed her a clean handkerchief from his jacket pocket. She took it uncertainly.

'Go on! Have a good blow. I've got another one here.' He pointed to his other pocket. 'I always carry a spare, in case I meet a damsel in distress!'

Niamh smiled weakly and blew her nose. Scowling, Wendy got up and stalked across the room to the table. She picked up a box of tissues, which she brought back and set down on the coffee table in front of Niamh.

'That's better,' Richard said when Niamh had composed herself. 'Now, can you think back to last Thursday and try to remember what you and Timothy did that day? He and the others came here to lunch – is that right?'

'Yes,' Wendy answered for her. 'We all had lunch together here, because it was more convenient for getting into town than their house. We told you all this before!'

'Can you remember what you had for lunch?' Richard asked gently, continuing to look towards Niamh.

'Soup,' she replied in a hoarse whisper. Then she cleared her throat and repeated, 'tomato soup. And bread. I went out in the morning and got a loaf. Is it important?'

'It helps us to understand what the pathologist found at the post mortem,' Richard explained. 'And did you have anything to drink with the meal?'

'We each had a glass of wine. I don't usually drink at lunch time, but Wendy said she'd won this bottle in a raffle and she wanted us all to help her drink it.'

'It was raising money for the university lacrosse team,' Wendy told us in her sulky voice.

'I see.' Richard still had his attention on Niamh. 'And did Timothy have anything else to drink that afternoon? He didn't drop into the Head of the River, perhaps, while you were down there waiting for the march to start?'

'No.' Niamh shook her head. 'We didn't go near the Head of the River until the march actually started. We passed it on the way to St Aldates, after the speeches, but there wasn't time for a drink there. Tim spoke awfully well, didn't he Wendy?'

'Very well. I could hear every word,' Wendy replied, in a tone of voice that implied that she would have preferred not to have done.

'Why is it important?' Niamh asked. 'Whether Tim had another drink, I mean?'

'He had rather a large amount of alcohol in his system when he died,' Richard told her gently, 'and we were wondering where it came from. Could he have been drinking before he got here, do you think?'

'I think he had some of his own with him,' Wendy put in before Niamh could answer. 'He certainly had something quite heavy in his jacket pocket. I bumped against it while it was hung up in the hall. I couldn't swear he did it on Thursday, but he often used to carry one of those little bottles of vodka around with him and take swigs straight from the bottle. Maybe he took some before he made his speech, to boost his confidence – not that he needed it, the cocky loudmouth!' she added in an undertone. Then, seeing Niamh's pained expression she added, 'I'm sorry, Niamh, I know you liked him, but he really wasn't worth it. Ask Faith! He took her in too – at first!'

'Yes, you said he treated her badly.' Richard turned to address Wendy for the first time. 'How exactly? What did he do?'

'You mean, apart from following her around everywhere and expecting her to ring him three times a day while she was off on a dig – Diane told me about that – and not letting her go to Stratford[11] with us, just because we didn't have tickets for him to come too?' Wendy's sarcasm was bitter. 'And all the time, he had another girlfriend back in Leicester! *And* he started going

---

[11] The Royal Shakespeare Theatre, Stratford-upon-Avon.

out with Niamh before he'd broken it off with either of them.'

'No, that's not true!' Niamh protested. 'He explained all that to me. The friend in Leicester wasn't a girlfriend. She was just someone he'd known since they were at Primary School together. And the first time we went out together was the day Faith dumped him. He needed someone to talk to about it. It upset him a lot.'

'Of course that's what he told you!' Wendy was dismissive of this explanation. 'But don't you see? He was just using you, the same way he used Faith – and that girl in Leicester, too, I expect. Honestly, he wasn't worth it! He didn't love you, whatever he said. He didn't care about anyone but himself!'

'That's not true!' Tears rolled down Niamh's face and she covered her eyes with Richard's handkerchief.

'Oh Niamh! I'm sorry!' Wendy put her arm around her friend again and held her close. 'I didn't mean to upset you. I just can't stand seeing you getting yourself in such a state over him, when he … Look, I know you liked him, but, believe me, you deserve someone much, much better than he ever was.'

Niamh was now sobbing uncontrollably. Wendy glared across at us, as if she blamed Richard for her friend's distress.

'I think you'd better go now.'

Richard nodded and got to his feet, signalling to me to do the same, but before we could leave, there was a ring at the doorbell.

'I'll get that.' Wendy gave Niamh a final hug before heading for the stairs.

We stood in the middle of the room, not liking to make our exit until this new visitor had been dealt with. Niamh wiped her eyes and blew her nose again. Then she looked up at Richard.

'Thank you for ...,' she began, glancing down at the handkerchief. 'I – I'll wash it and ... will I give it in at the police station?'

'Yes. That will be fine,' Richard smiled kindly at her. 'I'm sorry we had to come here disturbing you like this. It's just that we need to ask people questions in order to find out who killed your boyfriend.'

'We *were* going to be married!' Niamh sounded more assured than she had appeared up until now. 'Whatever Wendy thinks, he did mean for us to be together for always. He'd got his job in Leicester and, once I finished writing up my thesis, I was going to get one there too. We had it all planned.'

'Presumably if anyone had threatened Timothy, he'd have told you about it?' Richard suggested gently.

'Yes. I'm sure he would.'

'And I assume he *didn't* tell you about anything like that?'

'No.' Niamh gazed at Richard, wide-eyed. 'Do you really think someone killed him deliberately?'

'Yes. I'm afraid I do. Can you think of anyone one who might have wanted him dead?'

Before Niamh could answer, the door swung open and banged against the wall. Wendy was back accompanied by a woman who bore such a striking resemblance to Niamh that you could easily imagine that she was the Niamh from forty years into the future transported back in time.

'Mum! What are you doing here?'

'Come to see you're alright, of course,' the woman answered in a soft southern Irish accent. 'And I brought some of my chocolate shortbread that you like so much.'

'Thanks, but you needn't. I – I – these gentlemen are from the police.' Niamh waved vaguely in our direction. 'They say someone *killed* Tim.'

'Killed him? How? Why? What's going on? I thought he was crushed in the crowd.'

'Mrs O'Halloran?' Richard stepped forward.

'Yes. I'm Niamh's mother. What-?' She went over to her daughter and put her arm round her shoulders. Then she looked towards Richard again.

'I'm Detective Chief Inspector Paige and this is Detective Constable Porter,' he told her. 'We're here to ask your daughter some questions to try to find out exactly what happened to her fiancé.'

'I don't understand.' Mrs O'Halloran looked round from Richard to me and then back again. 'Why do you think he was killed? Couldn't it have been an accident?'

'It was some drug that killed him, Mum,' Niamh explained. 'Someone injected him with a drug.'

'Who? How? What drug?'

'Ketamine,' Richard told her. 'It's a powerful sedative. We found a nearly empty syringe of it in his pocket.'

'So doesn't that mean he took it himself?' asked Niamh's mother with a bewildered look on her face.

'I can't tell you the details, but there's forensic evidence that suggests that it was administered by another person – probably someone in the crowd at the demonstration – and then the empty syringe was slipped into his pocket.'

'But why? Who would want to kill Tim?'

'That's what we're trying to find out. We were hoping your daughter would be able to help us.' He turned back to Niamh. 'Miss O'Halloran, now you've had a few minutes, can you think of anyone who had a grudge against him at all?'

'No.' Niamh shook he head vigorously. 'Tim never hurt anyone. Nobody could possibly have wanted him dead!'

'Well, if you think of anything else that might help our investigations, give me a ring.' Richard handed her his card. 'This number should get straight through to me or one of my team.'

He led the way to the door. I followed, but Wendy was barring our way.

'You ought to be looking at that old girlfriend he had in Leicester,' she told us, 'and all the others.'

'What others?' Richard asked sharply.

'I dunno,' Wendy shrugged. 'I reckon there must be dozens of them the way he used to carry on.'

'That's not true!' Niamh shouted across the room. 'He wasn't like that at all!'

'Sshhh darling,' her mother murmured, holding her more tightly in both arms. 'Don't get upset. Come home with me – now. You need a few days away from all this.'

'No! *I* can look after her,' Wendy crossed the room at a run and, kneeling down, took Niamh's hands in hers. 'Tell her, Niamh! You're OK here, aren't you?'

We slipped out and went downstairs, but after we got into the car, Richard sat there without turning the engine on. He looked up at the windows of the flat and then fixed his eyes on the door out of which we had just come. After a few minutes, Mrs O'Halloran emerged. We caught a glimpse of Niamh, who embraced her mother and gave a brief wave as she closed the door behind her. Richard got out of the car and went over to intercept her.

'Mrs O'Halloran? Could I have a word, please?'

'Yes?' she looked enquiringly towards him.

'There's a café just round the corner. Can I buy you a cup of coffee?'

'That's very kind of you. I don't mind if I do.'

Richard leaned in at the window and told me to take the car back to the police station. He was going to walk back after his chat with Mrs O'Halloran. I suppose he thought that she was more likely to open up in a one-to-one with someone nearer to her own generation.

When I got back, Peter and Mac were drinking tea together and discussing what they'd learnt from their visit to the shared house in New Hinksey. Faith and Diane had confirmed that the six students had shared a bottle of wine, provided by Wendy, with their lunch. I asked them if they'd mentioned the vodka that Timothy was in the habit of carrying around with him, and they said not.

'There was no bottle in the list of things they found in his pockets,' Peter pointed out. 'Perhaps he finished it and threw it away. We ought to check out the bins at the edge of Christ Church Meadow and in St Aldates.'

I made a mental note to make myself scarce when that job was being allocated. Sifting through other people's rubbish is no fun and rarely yields any significant evidence.

Neither Faith nor Diane had been able to suggest any likely killers. Diane made it quite clear that she believed Timothy to have been a blot on the landscape and unpopular with a lot of people – particularly men – but she stopped short of suggesting that any of them would have borne him sufficient malice to kill him. Faith appeared still to harbour some fond feelings for her ex-boyfriend and was adamant that nobody would have wanted him dead. However, she was unable to suggest any other explanation for the presence of the syringe in his pocket and the ketamine in his bloodstream.

John was once more working in the hospital, so they had not seen him.

At that point, Richard returned from his heart-to-heart with Niamh's mother. It seems that they hit it off right away and she confided much of their family history to him over two cups of coffee and a plate of scones. Niamh was the youngest of their five children, and the only girl. Her brothers all lived in Ireland: three in the South while the other was a lecturer at the new University of Ulster in Coleraine. Two of them were Roman Catholic priests. The others both had wives and families, and, according to Siobhan O'Halloran, were doing very well for themselves.

Niamh's father was Fellow in Irish literature at Lichfield College, a post that he had held for nine years.

They lived in Headington, not far from Richard himself, as it turned out. The house was plenty big enough for Niamh to have based herself there during her studies but of course, young people liked to be independent – even if the result was that her father had had to subsidise her rent for three years. Not that they minded, it just seemed rather wasteful when Niamh might have done better saving up for her wedding.

On the subject of weddings, Siobhan was confident that Tim was intending to marry her daughter, although he hadn't actually bought her a ring or anything like that. But young people these days were so haphazard about that sort of thing, weren't they? He had definitely promised to marry her when … but Richard didn't want to know about that. It wasn't important. It had all turned out to be nothing after all.

After some more skilful probing from Richard, she explained that the previous month there had been an unfortunate incident. Niamh had come to her in tears, sobbing that she was "late" and she was sure that she must have fallen pregnant.

Her father had walked in on them just as she was describing to her mother how it had happened. She told them that it was a single isolated occasion when they had been alone together in the flat and she had had more to drink than she was used to. Tim had been very persuasive, insisting that "just once" couldn't do any harm and that they were going to be married before the end of the year in any case.

Joseph O'Halloran was incensed and it was as much as his wife could do to restrain him from going straight over to the shared house and doing Timothy some damage. Niamh and Siobhan had managed to persuade him to hold fire and wait while they thought things through. He agreed to this on condition that Niamh stayed with them in the interim.

The whole thing blew over two days later when Niamh told her mother that it had been a false alarm. She persuaded her father to allow her to go back to the flat in Temple Street and he agreed that he would not confront Timothy. He did, however, have a private conversation with Wendy, during which he impressed on her the need to keep a protective eye on his daughter, who was very young and naïve in her outlook and might easily be taken in by more experienced men.

'So that explains why Wendy was so protective when we were round there!' I exclaimed. 'I thought she was going rather over the top, but I suppose she felt responsible for her.'

'Mmm,' Richard agreed. 'And maybe now we know why she's got such a down on Timothy. I wonder whether the others in their little group know about all this.'

I put that question to Margaret that evening. She thought that it was unlikely that Niamh would have wanted her scare publicised any further than was absolutely necessary.

'She must have felt an absolute idiot,' she opined, 'getting herself into that fix in the first place and then going running to her mum before she was absolutely certain.'

But to get back to our deliberations: we now possibly had another person with a motive for doing away with Timothy Sudbury, but Niamh's father could not possibly have injected him with the lethal drug because he hadn't been anywhere near the demonstration that morning. We found out later that he wasn't even in Oxford that day, because he was attending a three-day conference in Seattle and did not return until the weekend.

Mac suggested that he could have instigated one of Niamh's friends to do the deed – or even paid someone to do it – but Richard was very sceptical about that idea.

'This is Oxford, not Chicago,' he said scathingly. 'We don't have contract killings or vendettas here!'

In his opinion, based on what Niamh's mother had told him, if Joe O'Halloran had taken a gun to Timothy, it would have been the traditional paternal shotgun employed to encourage reluctant suitors to make an honest woman of their daughter. She had given the impression that they were quite happy about his relationship with Niamh, and expected him to do the decent thing as soon as he was settled in his new job.

Could Niamh herself have done it?' I suggested tentatively. 'I know she says she loved him, but could she be angry with him for backing her into a corner with her parents – I mean, if they were insisting that she had to marry him and, on reflection, she wasn't sure she wanted to?'

'I suppose that's possible,' Richard murmured. 'What do you think, Johns? You have more experience of the fairer sex than the rest of us. Do you think that's how she might have reacted?'

'Difficult to say.' Peter seemed reluctant to commit himself. 'I could see she might be angry with him, but … Well, I suppose it largely depends on how adamant her parents were that, now that she was damaged goods, so to speak, she had to marry the man who'd done it. And, to be honest, I can't imagine many parents taking that line in this day and age – not unless they were some sort of religious fanatics.'

'They *are* Irish Catholics,' Mac pointed out. 'They can have all sorts of queer ideas.'

I remembered that Mac had grown up in a rough area of Glasgow and was a keen (one might almost say, fanatical) Rangers[12] supporter. My own view of

---

[12] Sectarianism in Glasgow is largely defined by the fierce rivalry between the city's two football clubs: Celtic

Catholicism at that stage was more benign, but perhaps more patronising. I looked at their holy water and rosaries and thought their religion was rather childish: largely superstition born out of a lack of education. I imagine that neither Mac nor I had actually known any Catholics or taken the trouble to look beyond the pomp surrounding the Pope and the criticism in the press of their stance on birth control.

'She seemed genuinely upset to me,' I ventured. 'And I don't think she'd have the nerve to do it. Her friend Wendy might have – or Diane! They both seem to have a down on him.'

'Yes,' Richard agreed. 'I must say those two struck me as more like the sort of character who might be able to kill, but their motives aren't very strong.'

'So, are we back to John Goodey?' asked Mac in the long silence that followed this pronouncement. 'He has motive, and whatever the hospital says about how impregnable their systems are, it wouldn't surprise me if he could get hold of the drug from there. *And* we know he was one of the people close to Sudbury in the crowd.'

There was another long silence while we all thought about this assessment of the situation.

'There's someone else I think we ought to consider,' Peter said at last. 'In the accounts of the demonstration, there's mention of three people making speeches on Christ Church Meadow before the march started. One of them was Timothy Sudbury and the others were the organiser of the demo and a younger woman – just a girl, really. Apparently, Timothy Sudbury approached her after her speech and she pushed him away. Could it be that there's some history between them?'

'I suppose it's worth looking into,' Richard nodded. 'What's her name? Did she make a statement?'

(traditionally supported by Catholics) and Rangers (with a predominantly protestant fan base).

'Dawn Farmer,' Peter told him. He had all the details at his fingertips, so I guessed he'd been waiting for the opportunity to put her into the mix. 'She wasn't interviewed on the day, so I reckon she must have slipped away as soon as the trouble started.'

'So we've no idea whether she was anywhere near Timothy in the crush?' Richard looked more doubtful. 'And do we know how to find her? Do you have an address?'

'No, but I know her school,' Peter replied promptly. 'Some of her classmates were there and *did* get interviewed. Shall I go round there and see if I can speak to her?'

'OK,' Richard nodded. 'Take a WPC with you.'

* * *

'And that's as far as I've got,' Jonah concluded.

'So what happened when you got to the school, Peter?' Dominic demanded. 'Did you get to see the girl? I don't think we'd have let you in, just turning up like that. And we'd have wanted to get permission from her parents before you spoke to her.'

'Things were a bit different in those days,' Peter told him with a smile. 'Schools weren't like fortresses where you have to show your ID before you can even get in through the door. We just went to the office and asked to speak to her, and they looked on the timetable and told us which room she was in.'

'And ...?' prompted Dominic.

'It's a long time ago,' Peter hedged. 'I can't remember all the details the way Jonah seems to be able to.'

'I bet he can't remember any better than you can,' Bernie put in. 'He's using his imagination to fill in the gaps. Nobody remembers conversations verbatim the way he'd have us believe he can!'

'So come on, Peter!' Dominic urged 'What did Dawn Farmer have to say for herself?'

'I can't remember exactly what she said,' Peter replied cautiously. 'I do remember that Alison Brown and I were both very impressed by her. She was only seventeen, but she was very articulate. Her form teacher took us into the medical room to talk. It was a small room next to the office, with a low bed in it and four wooden chairs in a line along the wall like in a waiting room. Dawn started off by giving us a lecture on the dangers associated with the proliferation of nuclear arms and telling us that, if we allowed the Americans to base their cruise missiles here we'd be turning our children and grandchildren into targets and risking the obliteration of the whole planet. She talked about the "fallacy of the threat of mutual destruction" and the menace of nuclear fallout. Eventually her form teacher reminded her that we were busy people who had come to ask her questions about a young man who had died, and she stopped talking and asked us what we wanted to know.'

'And …?' Dominic repeated. 'What did she say?'

'She didn't think much of Timothy. She thought he was all talk and only interested in impressing the girls. But then, she didn't seem to think much of any man! I think she rated us slightly above cockroaches, but definitely well below guinea-pigs on the evolutionary ladder. She was very keen on animals and had ambitions to become a vet. She thought that the march should have been women-only and seemed to think that any man who wasn't a warmonger was a hypocrite.'

'But did she want him dead?' Dominic asked impatiently. 'Did she know him before the rally?'

'She said not,' Peter answered, sounding rather tired of this interrogation. 'She claimed that she'd never seen him before.'

'How would a seventeen-year-old have got hold of drugs and a hypodermic syringe, anyway?' asked Mariam.

'Precisely!' agreed Jonah. 'We only left her on the suspect list because of the veterinary connections.'

'Oh?' Ibrahim's interest was aroused by this enigmatic remark – as Jonah had intended it to be.

'Old Peter told you she wanted to be a vet. Well, she was getting work experience helping out at a veterinary practice in New Hinksey.'

'New Hinksey?' repeated Lucy, excitedly. 'Isn't that where you said the victim lived? Could she have met him there?'

'Well she *could* have,' Peter replied, 'but she said she didn't.'

'But, if she killed him, she would say that, wouldn't she?' Dominic pointed out, 'to put you off the scent.'

'And you did say that ketamine was used for treating animals,' added Ibrahim, 'so that's how she might have got hold of some.'

'And she does sound like the single-minded, fanatical sort of person who might go through with killing someone if she thought it was justified,' murmured Mariam thoughtfully.

'Ju-ju-just,' Dot gasped out, her breath rasping in her throat as she tried to speak. 'Just … so long … as – as – young – Jonah here – is-isn't – ha-aving – us – on!'

'Aunty!' Bernie leaned over Jonah's shoulder to get closer to the computer screen where her aunt's face was displayed. 'You don't sound very good. What does the doctor say?'

'Don't – worry – ab – about me!' Dot retorted, before collapsing into uncontrollable coughing.

'Aunty!' Bernie shouted. There were gasps from anxious watchers in Liverpool and Oxford. Then they heard the sound of a door opening and an unfamiliar voice calling to ask if Miss Fazakerley was alright. Then the rectangle that had held Dot's face changed to a green blank as the care assistant's uniform blocked the webcam. There was a one-sided conversation as she helped Dot to a drink of water and offered to help her into bed, while Dot continued to struggle to get her breath. Finally, the care assistant turned round and stepped back far enough from the camera for her masked face to come into focus.

'I'm sorry,' she said. 'It's time for Miss Fazakerley to have her shower and get ready for bed now.'

9. WITNESS STATEMENTS

The next day, all eyes were on Dot when her face appeared on their computer screens in Oxford and Liverpool. She looked pale and her voice was husky, but she insisted that she had nothing worse than a sore throat and a cough.

'My temperature's down,' she told them. 'So I'm through the worst of it. I'll probably be right as rain tomorrow.'

'Well, I hope so,' Bernie tried to make her voice sound more cheerful than she felt. Her aunt was a centenarian, after all. 'Just take care of yourself and don't try to do too much.'

'Did you hear that Boris has been taken into the ICU[13]?' Lucy broke in. 'They said on the news that it was just a precaution, but I don't believe that – unless he's getting special treatment because he's the Prime Minister. The ICUs haven't got the capacity to have people in there who don't absolutely have to be!'

'I agree,' Ibrahim nodded. 'They're just trying to play down how ill he is because they haven't got anyone else in the cabinet who's up to taking over from him.'

'You're talking as if Boris was competent!' Bernie snorted. 'They're a complete and utter shower, the lot of them!'

---

[13] Intensive Care Unit

'Boris deserves it!' Lucy declared. 'Going round hospitals, shaking hands with COVID patients and then boasting about it like that! I'm glad he's in Intensive Care. Maybe now he'll start taking this seriously and do something about giving the doctors and nurses the PPE they need to be safe.'

'I hope so,' Dot wheezed. Everyone else fell silent and listened as she struggled to speak. 'Did you hear about the nurse at Aintree – what used to be Fazakerley Hospital back in my day – who died of coronavirus?'

'Yes, I did,' Bernie replied over the bout of harsh coughing that racked her aunt's body. 'I'm beginning to lose count of how many healthcare staff that makes nationwide.'

'Most of them black or Asian,' Ibrahim added pointedly.

'Bloody immigrants,' Mariam muttered, 'coming over here and running our health service and spoiling our daily death statistics!'

'And now,' Jonah said in the silence that followed this remark, 'perhaps, to take our minds off the dire straits that the country is in today, you'd like another instalment of my cheerful tale of murder from 1982.'

* * *

Good old Peter had been busy collating the witness statements – about a couple of hundred or so – that officers had taken down on the day of the demonstration. You have to remember that back then we didn't have sophisticated software to help us to fit together the evidence that we collected. If the force had a computer at all, it will have been dedicated to running the payroll and keeping track of supplies of stationery. So, to get a picture of what actually went on that day, we had to go through piecing together what each interviewee had said about where they were at the time when Timothy

Sudbury must have been killed. We needed to know which of the demonstrators were close enough to him to inject him with ketamine and then slip the empty syringe into his pocket without being seen by him or the friends that surrounded him.

Most of the statements were quite useless in this regard. Many, like Bernie, had been in the other part of the protest, marching along the High Street with no idea what was going on in St Aldates. Others had been stuck further back, caught in the scrum outside the police station and the law courts, and had seen nothing of what was taking place near the entrance to Christ Church. The organisers of the protest, busily trying to rescue their audio equipment from the onslaught of the double-decker bus, following its collision with the platform that they had set up at the foot of Carfax Tower, were too pre-occupied with that to notice what was going on among the crowds who were approaching from the south.

However, by the time Richard called us all together for our briefing that Thursday, exactly a week after Timothy Sudbury's death, Peter had managed to produce a rough sketch of the relative positions of Sudbury and the people in closest proximity to him during the minutes before his collapse.

The six friends had kept close together from the start of the march, outside the Head of the River pub, until the crush started as those at the front were prevented from moving forward by the presence of the bus across their path. Timothy had been leading the way, holding up a placard bearing the words *Cruise missiles undermine your security*. He had been flanked by Niamh and Wendy. John had been to Wendy's right with Diane next to him. Faith had either been on the other side of Diane or possibly just behind John, nobody seemed very clear on this. Most likely, their precise positions changed during the course of their progress up St Aldates.

The two girls, Jacqueline and Tina, were a little way behind the group of students. They had a banner, which they held up between them, proclaiming *nuclear deterrent = nuclear destruction*. Roughly level with them were two more students, but undergraduates this time and not from Oxford University. Caroline Moreton was studying Politics and Economics at the LSE[14]. Her boyfriend, Howard Grant, was a law student at Bristol University. Both were active members of CND, most likely influenced by Caroline's parents, Geoffrey Moreton and Gwendoline Allett, who were both Oxford dons and both ardent anti-nuclear activists.

Working out who was immediately ahead of Sudbury in the procession was more difficult. TV news footage, shot from an upper room in Pembroke College, showed a large, close-packed group of women marching arm-in-arm, but it seemed that they must have managed to disperse before the police started rounding up the demonstrators and interviewing them, since none of the statements seemed to correspond to any of them.

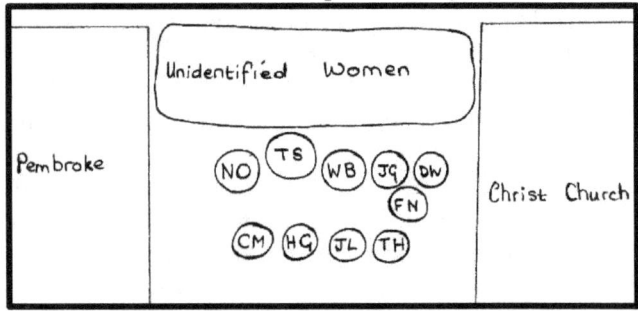

'I can't see how any of *them* could've have done it,' Mac declared as we watched the film, projected on to a screen at the front of the room. 'For a start, they've got their backs to him all the time, and look at the way they've linked arms! If one of them had turned round to stab Sudbury with a hypodermic, the ones on either side would be bound to have noticed.'

'On the face of it,' Richard agreed, 'the people who could most easily have done it are Niamh and Wendy – or possibly those two immediately behind him. What do we know about them?'

'Not a lot,' Peter admitted, looking down at his notes. 'They're both twenty years old and about to start their third year at university. As I said, Caroline Moreton's parents are both dons and both involved in CND.'

'Did they know the victim at all – or any of his friends?' Richard asked.

'Nope.' Peter shook his head. 'Or at least, they didn't say, but I'm not sure if they were told who he was. I mean, we probably wouldn't have revealed his identity until after his family had been informed – even if we knew it by the time they were interviewed. So ...'

'So we could do with talking to them again,' Richard said briskly. 'I doubt if they had a hand in his death, but they may well have seen something significant. They must certainly be the people best placed to notice if someone got unnaturally close to Sudbury or put their hand in his pocket.'

And that's how Richard and I ended up, later that afternoon, standing outside a large detached house in North Oxford waiting for a response to our ring on the doorbell, in the hope of speaking to Caroline Moreton. Peter and Mac, meanwhile, had gone to a similar house a few streets away in search of Howard Grant.

The door was opened by a middle-aged man in a tweed sports jacket and carpet slippers, who identified himself as Dr Geoffrey Moreton, Fellow in Geography at St Luke's College. As he said this, I smiled to myself at the sight of leather patches on the elbows of his jacket, which had been the hallmark – and the source of many jokes – of the geography master at my old school. He invited us into a spacious sitting room, furnished with a large, cumbersome three-piece suite enveloped in floral-pattern loose covers.

'Take a seat. I'll see if I can find Caroline for you. I expect she's upstairs – or she may be in the garden.'

We sat looking round at curtains that matched the loose covers and walls lined with bookcases. The curved bay window looked out on the front garden, which was laid to lawn with a round rose bed in the centre of it. There was a gas fire in the hearth and two small radiators on either side of the window. I got up to inspect a row of photographs on the mantelpiece.

'It looks as if Caroline was an only child,' I observed. 'This must be her with her parents a few years back.' I pointed to a family group comprising a somewhat younger Dr Moreton, a woman of similar age and a girl of about ten. 'And this looks like a school photo from when she was a teenager. And here she is again, receiving some sort of award – school prize-giving do you think?'

Before Richard could answer, the door opened and Dr Moreton came back in.

'Caroline won't be long,' he assured us, shifting his weight restlessly back and forth from one foot to the other and giving us a weak smile. 'She's busy packing. I'm driving her back to university tomorrow. She's at the LSE – in her final year.' He sat down on the arm of one of the easy chairs while he continued to chatter on nervously. 'It's hard to believe that she'll be a graduate next year and setting up with a job and a place of her own. It'll be strange not having her around. We only had one child because we didn't want to contribute to over-population. It's important to be responsible and think of – oh! Here she is now!'

A dark-haired young woman in jeans and a sweatshirt entered the room.

'Dad said you wanted to speak to me about the demo last week?'

'Yes. That's right.' Richard got to his feet and gestured towards one of the armchairs. 'Please – sit down. We won't keep you long.'

'Well, I'll leave you to it.' Her father got up and hurried out of the room, evidently relieved at getting away from the need to make conversation with what were almost certainly unwelcome visitors.

I got out the photographs that we'd acquired of Timothy and his friends and spread them out on the low table that stood in the centre of the room.

'Do you remember seeing any of these people while you were on the demonstration last week?'

Caroline leaned forward to study the pictures. She picked out Timothy's at once.

'This is the chap who died, isn't it? I recognise him from the pictures in the papers. He got up and gave us all a pep talk before we started. Mum was furious. He wasn't on the organising committee or anything, so he had no business trying to take over like that. She'd arranged a programme of speakers for the main event at Carfax – and, needless to say, he wasn't on it! Her talk on Christchurch Meadow was just explaining to everyone what the route was and how important it was not to cause trouble.'

'And did you see him any more after the speeches in Christ Church Meadow?' Richard asked.

'Oh yes! We – that's my boyfriend Howard and I – ended up just behind him and his little gaggle of admirers.

'Can you describe them, please?'

'Well, there was a little redhead who kept very close. This is her, here!' Caroline pointed down at the photograph of Niamh. 'In fact, I think you've got them all. This one,' she indicated Wendy, 'was close too. These two,' she went on, pointing at the pictures of Diane and Faith, 'started out right behind him and then moved up level with him when we started to spread out into the road. They told us to keep to the pavement, so as not to stop the traffic, but there were too many of us.'

'They?' I queried.

'The organisers – Mum and the others. We were trying to make our point without being a nuisance to ordinary people.'

'So, can I be clear about this?' Richard pressed her. 'If someone wanted to drop something into his pocket without him noticing, would you say that any of these people here could have done it?'

'Oh yes! Any of them could have done that. We were all packed together quite close. I shouldn't think he'd have felt a thing.' She gave a nervous giggle. 'Howard or I could've done it! There was some sort of hold-up ahead and we got all squashed against each other when the people behind kept on coming.'

'Including this man?' Richard persisted, picking up John's photograph and holding it out towards Caroline.

'I don't know about him. I don't remember seeing a man with them. I only noticed these four women all clustering round him like bees round a honeypot. As I said to Howard, it's ridiculous the way some women seem to be impressed by that sort of man!'

'What sort of man would that be?' asked Richard with feigned ignorance.

'Show-offs who can't bear it if everyone isn't looking at them. Like I said, Mum was furious with him, trying to take over the way he did.'

'There was a girl who gave a speech on Christ Church Meadow too, wasn't there? Was your mum annoyed about that as well?'

'Oh no! That was all planned. Dawn begged to be allowed to give a speech along with the main speakers – at Carfax – but Mum thought she was too young and it might stop people taking us seriously. She didn't want people to think we were just a load of kids bunking off school. But Dawn still kept asking if she could say something to everyone, so Mum agreed that she could, but she said it would be better if she did it there, rather than on the platform later where there might by television cameras filming. We hoped there would be, because we wanted the publicity, but Mum didn't like the idea of Dawn getting her name in the papers, because she was still at school and it might have affected her chances of getting to the university she wanted and that sort of thing. She wants to be a vet and it's very competitive. So it isn't a good idea to get yourself marked down as a troublemaker. Dawn was a bit disappointed, but she worships Mum, so she did as she was told.'

'It sounds as if you know Dawn quite well,' Richard suggested.

'Yes. Well, Mum does and I've met her because of that. I don't see much of her, obviously, because I'm away at university most of the time.'

'What's she like?'

'She's very enthusiastic about things. I mean things like stopping animal cruelty and banning nuclear weapons and protecting the environment. She's a member of the Ecology Party[15] and says she'd like to stand for Parliament. But, why do you want to know about her? She wasn't anywhere near us. I think she may have been in the other part of the march – the one that went along the High.'

'Someone told us that she had an altercation with the victim shortly before the gathering on Christ Church Meadow broke up,' Richard told her, using deliberately vague language. 'We wondered if they knew each other – before last Thursday, I mean.'

'Not that I'm aware of, but I told you, I hardly knew her. Mum might know.'

'Is your mother at home?'

---

[15] The predecessor of the Green Party

'No. She's in college – Shrewsbury. She's a tutor there.'

'I see. We may want to speak to her later. Was she near you in the procession?'

'No. She was right up the front, leading the way.'

'I see. Now, getting back to the people who were around the victim during the march, did you see anyone getting particularly close to him or looking as if they were putting their hand in his pockets?'

'Well, the little redhead seemed to be clinging on to him. And the tall, dark-haired one was pretty close too most of the time – until the crush got really bad. Then she pulled the redhead away to the side and they disappeared. I think they must have gone off down a side road.'

'That's right,' Richard agreed encouragingly. 'They told me that they escaped into Pembroke Square.'

'That sounds about right. I don't suppose it matters, but I did notice she had something in her hand and she dropped it in the bin on the corner of the street as she passed.'

'What sort of thing?' asked Richard.

'Which of them do you mean?' I demanded at the same time.

'The tall, dark-haired one. I don't know what it was. It looked like a piece of screwed-up paper or maybe a rag or the wrapper off a chocolate bar. Just something small, scrunched up in her hand. Do you think it's important?'

'Probably not, but thank you for telling us about it. It all helps to build up a picture of what happened. Now carry on: you were telling us about how people moved around in the crowd once the crush started.'

'After that, Howard and I were pressed up against him for a while. And then we were forced to the left by those two,' she indicated the pictures of Faith and Diane, 'pushing us from the other side. It was mayhem by then with everyone fighting for space and hardly able to breathe we were so crammed together. And then there was some shouting and the people ahead began to move again.'

'That'll be when the police ordered the college authorities to open up Christ Church to relieve the pressure in St Aldates,' I told her.

'Yes. We saw people getting away that way, so we followed them into the main quad, thinking that we could get out through the college and work our way round to join the march going up the High. But they wouldn't let us out of the quad, once we were in.'

'You said you followed other people,' Richard interrupted. 'Does that include the group of people who were with the victim? These people?' He pointed down at the photographs on the table in front of her.

'Yes, it must have – well, except the two who'd already gone by then.'

'So these three,' Richard indicated John, Faith and Diane, 'all got out of the crush and into Christ Church, leaving their friend behind? Did they say anything to him, did you see? Or do anything to make him go with them?'

'I think they must've been separated from him by then,' Caroline replied after several seconds of thought. 'There were two other girls – quite a bit younger, I think – who got pushed forward when people started shoving from behind. I think they were probably in between those three and the chap who died. So maybe they didn't realise he wasn't following them. Or maybe they wanted to get away from him,' she suggested as an afterthought.

'Good.' Richard got to his feet, and I followed his lead. 'That all fits in with what other people have told us. Thank you for talking to us, you've been very helpful. Now, if you think of anything else – particularly if you remember anyone tampering with the victim's pockets – give me a ring on this number.' He handed her a business card before turning and leading the way out to our waiting car.

We found Peter and Mac waiting for us back at the station. They reported a similar story from Caroline's boyfriend, Howard. It seemed clear that any of Timothy's five friends could have injected him with ketamine and then slipped the syringe into his pocket. And, interestingly, they had all managed to slip away from him before the effects of the drug became obvious, abandoning him in the crowd, just as he began to slide into unconsciousness.

As the most junior member of the team, I was despatched to investigate the litterbin on the corner of Pembroke Square. I established that the bins in the city centre were emptied each Wednesday, which meant that it was impossible to find whatever it was that Wendy had dropped into it. I was secretly rather glad, because it's no fun sorting through the sort of rubbish you sometimes find in those bins!

What might it have been? And how likely was it that it was relevant to the case?

I suggested that it could have been a cloth used to wipe fingerprints off the syringe, and that she had thrown it away in case it had traces of ketamine on it. Peter said that it was more likely to be just a used paper tissue or a sweet wrapper.

Richard decided that the best way to find out was simply to go and ask Wendy herself about it. I was surprised at this suggestion and pointed out that, if Wendy *was* our killer, we would be letting her know that she was under suspicion. However, Richard said that when people thought they were being investigated they often made mistakes and gave themselves away. In any case, he added, if she did come to trial and we sprang the litterbin incident on her unexpectedly, the defence might claim that she hadn't been given an adequate opportunity to explain what happened.

Peter remarked that, if Wendy was innocent then giving her a chance to explain what it was that she had thrown away might save us a lot of wasted effort trying to prove that it was something to do with Timothy's murder. However, I think that Mac and I were both still sceptical of the wisdom of showing our hand too early.

Anyway, off we went to confront Wendy with this new evidence.

This time it was Niamh who came downstairs to admit us to the flat in Temple Street. She explained that Wendy was out getting fish and chips for their dinner, but she would be back soon. Richard and I sat down at the table, which had been cleared of books and papers in readiness for their meal, and Niamh took a seat opposite us.

Richard got straight to the point.

'We have a witness who saw Wendy throw something away in the litterbin on the corner of Pembroke Square, as you escaped that way from the crush in St Aldates. Do you know what it was?'

Niamh looked back at Richard with wide innocent eyes.

'I've no idea. I didn't even notice her do it. I wasn't watching Wendy. I was looking back, trying to get Tim to come with us, but he didn't seem to be listening. I've been thinking about it all. Do you think he was already …? Had he already been drugged? Was that why he didn't hear me calling to him to get out of the crowd?'

'Yes,' Richard nodded. 'That's quite possible. And it's helpful of you to tell us about that. It suggests that we should be looking for someone who was close to him *before* you and Wendy left, rather than later on.'

There was a sound outside and Niamh jumped to her feet.

'That's Wendy!' she declared. 'I'll tell her you want to speak to her.'

She went out, leaving the door open so that we were able to hear the front door closing, a whispered conversation on the stairs and then footsteps hurrying up to the flat. Wendy came in, put the paper packet of fish and chips down on the table and stood staring across it at us.

'Miss Brotherton!' Richard greeted her, getting to his feet.

I made a half-hearted show of following his example and then sat back down in my chair. Richard remained standing.

'We won't keep you long,' he went on. 'We just want to know what it was that you threw away in the litterbin on the corner of Pembroke Square last Thursday afternoon.'

'Why would you want to know that?' Wendy asked. I wasn't sure whether her frown was one of puzzlement or annoyance.

'It's all just routine,' Richard assured her. 'We're trying to get a clear picture of everything that went on that afternoon. Someone mentioned that they saw you throw something away there and we'd like you to tell us what it was.'

'It was just an old crisp packet. It must have been in my coat pocket since the weekend before. Niamh and I had crisps when we went to visit Blenheim that Saturday. I found it there while we were on the demo and I threw it away when we passed a bin. That's all.'

'I see.' Richard looked at me and indicated by a small movement of his head that we were leaving. 'Thank you for clearing that up. We'll go now and let you eat your meal in peace.'

* * *

'I bet she's lying!' Dominic declared the moment that Jonah stopped reading. 'I bet it *was* the hanky she wiped her fingerprints off the syringe with.'

'It doesn't really matter what it was,' Mariam observed drily. 'Once the bin had been emptied, it was too late to prove anything.'

'*I* think it's got nothing to do with the case,' Lucy declared. 'I reckon this is all just Jonah trying to lead us up the garden path. He's making a big thing of this Wendy's suspicious behaviour to put us off the scent. It's not as if she's got any motive at all for killing Timothy Sudbury.'

'Hang on!' Jonah protested. 'I'm not leading anyone up the garden path. I'm just telling it how it happened. Richard was the one who insisted on talking to Wendy about what she threw away. I told you: I thought it was a mistake, remember?'

'That in itself is suspicious,' Lucy replied darkly. 'I don't trust you, Jonah. I won't be at all surprised if the murderer turns out to be someone we haven't even heard of yet!'

'Or if it wasn't murder after all,' Ibrahim added with a grin. 'But, assuming that it was, I reckon it can't have been Niamh who did it. If it was, she wouldn't have drawn attention to Timothy already being woozy before she and Wendy left. She'd have wanted you to believe that he wasn't injected with the drug until after they were safely away.'

'Looking at the diagram, the only people it could have been are Niamh and Wendy,' Dominic mused. 'Or possibly one out of that other couple, who were behind them. But they don't have any obvious motive – unless they knew Timothy better than they're admitting to, which the woman could well do, seeing as her mother was in charge of the whole thing.'

'*None* of them have a decent motive!' Lucy declared. 'According to Jonah – and we only have his word for any of this – practically everyone disliked him, or at least found him intensely irritating, but nobody has any reason to kill him.'

'Especially since he was about to move to Leicester, so they weren't going to have to put up with him for much longer in any case,' agreed Mariam.

'What ... about ... John?' suggested Dot breathlessly.

Everyone else fell silent. They had almost forgotten that she was there, it had been so long since she had spoken.

'What ... if ... Diane was ... lying ... a ... about ...'

The others watched anxiously as she collapsed into a bout of helpless coughing. They saw her taking sips of water from a plastic cup with a lid. How sad that her arthritic hands could no longer be trusted to hold a glass without spilling the contents. After what felt like an age, she put it down and resumed her speech.

'He may ... have ... thought ... she was ... going to ... leave him,' she wheezed laboriously.

'You're right, Aunty,' Bernie agreed, more to deter Dot from further exertion than from any particularly conviction that John was the guilty party. 'We've only got Diane's word for it that she rebuffed him.'

'And John's the only one with access to ketamine,' Dominic nodded. 'But without any fingerprints on the syringe or anyone having seen him put it in Timothy's pocket, I don't see how even Jonah is going to be able to prove he did it!'

'Time to get you ready for bed, Miss Fazakerley!' A cheery voice broke into their conversation and the rectangle displaying Dot's face suddenly turned into a blue blur. There was a confused noise as Dot protested to the care assistant, who had reached out her hand in front of the webcam to switch off her iPad. Then the hand disappeared to reveal a figure dressed in a green uniform with a plastic apron, facemask and blue latex gloves, standing next to Bernie's aunt.

'It's OK, Aunty,' Bernie called out across the airwaves. 'You'd better turn in now. It's getting late. We won't be staying online much longer ourselves. We'll catch up with you again tomorrow, don't worry!'

Dot's rectangle went blank and then disappeared. Everyone else remained silent for a few seconds.

'Dom?' Bernie asked at last. 'Has the Home said anything to your mum and dad about how Aunty Dot's doing? Has she had a corona virus test yet?'

'No.' Dominic shook his head sombrely. 'They're still only testing people who're admitted to hospital.'

'And they're only admitting people from Care Homes if they need intensive care,' Lucy added angrily.

'They did say that her temperature's down to near normal,' Dominic added quickly. 'So maybe she's over the worst of it.'

'Yes,' Bernie nodded. 'Let's hope so.'

'Although, there seem to be lots of stories of people seeming to get better and then relapsing,' Jonah added gloomily. 'I was reading a report just this morning about ...' He trailed off into an uneasy silence suddenly realising that this had not been a useful contribution to the conversation.

'Well, I suppose we'd better sign off now,' Bernie said after a long pause. 'It's time we started getting Jonah ready for bed too. Are you all OK for the same time tomorrow?'

10. NEW EVIDENCE

We seemed to be getting nowhere fast. Timothy Sudbury, while being far from the popular figure that he probably imagined himself to be, did not have any real enemies. It seemed almost certain that he had been injected with the drug during the demonstration, but none of the people who had been close enough to him to do so had any obvious means of obtaining it. And, in the confusion, who could say whether someone quite different could have approached him without being noticed? Or could everyone be wrong in thinking that he could not have administered the drug himself?

Peter and Richard both seemed preoccupied with other things, so Mac and I put our heads together and tried to think of a way of pushing the investigation along. I'd been talking to Margaret again about the effects of ketamine combined with alcohol. She seemed to think that it was possible that Timothy could have been injected up to an hour before he collapsed. That meant that it could have happened while the demonstrators were all still milling about on Christ Church Meadow, before splitting into their two groups. Dawn Farmer and Gwendoline Allett both admitted to having been annoyed at the way he had tried to take the limelight. Could his assailant have been one of them?

'I think we ought to investigate that vet's where Dawn Farmer works,' Mac declared. 'They probably had ketamine stored there and they may not have been as careful with it as the hospital pharmacy.'

'But, by all accounts, she'd never met Timothy until last Thursday,' I objected. 'So why would she have stolen a drug to attack him with?'

'Teenage girls do all sorts of funny things. She could've taken it to experiment with on herself, or to treat a sick animal that she'd come across, or even just for a lark. And then, when this Timothy tried to steal her thunder, she decided to pay him out. She probably didn't intend to kill him-'

'Whoever did it probably didn't intend to kill him,' I agreed, 'but Dawn Farmer seems a particularly unlikely suspect to me. *I* think we ought to look further into Faith Nelson. I reckon *she*'s the woman Muriel Rowlinson saw arguing with Timothy in Christ Church Meadow. From her description, it can't have been Niamh and it's unlikely to have been Wendy. So that only leaves Faith and Diane. Faith had been in a relationship with Timothy, so it's much more likely that she'd have something serious to argue with him about than Diane.'

'Diane claims he made a pass at her and tried to split her up from her boyfriend,' Mac pointed out.

'Maybe.' I was reluctant to let go of my belief that Faith was the person with the greatest reason for hating Timothy Sudbury. 'But the two of them seemed quite well-united when Margaret and I met them in the pub the other day. She was doing her best to encourage him to propose to her,' I added, chuckling as I remembered her performance, 'but he was oblivious to all her chatter about bridesmaids and wedding dresses! Faith, on the other hand, had been two-timed by our friend Timothy when he was going out with her and might well have wanted to make him pay for it. As you said, probably not by killing him, but maybe by giving him a fright or even just hoping he'd make a fool of himself while he was under the influence. Maybe she didn't know that ketamine is dangerous when taken with alcohol. It isn't something everyone would know about, is it?'

'John, the medic would,' Mac pointed out. 'If it *was* his girlfriend having the ding-dong with Tim, there could've been more between them than anyone is letting on.'

In the end, pragmatism took over. Whatever suspicions Mac might have, we didn't have enough evidence to justify questioning the vets about their ketamine supplies; and Dawn Farmer, being a minor, was definitely off-limits for interrogation. However, it was perfectly reasonable for us to approach Faith to ask her about her argument with Timothy only an hour or so prior to his death. So we set off on our bikes to the shared house in New Hinksey. With any luck, John might be there too and we could get an idea of his true feelings regarding the victim.

As it turned out, Faith was alone. John was once more on duty at the infirmary and Diane was working in the Bodleian. Faith still looked red-eyed and miserable, but she was more composed than on the previous occasion when Richard and I had interviewed her. She made coffee and we sat together round the low table in the living room to drink it. Mac opened the conversation in his usual direct manner.

'You had an argument with Timothy Sudbury the day he died. What was it about?'

'I don't remember any argument.' Faith sounded so defensive that we immediately concluded that she not only remembered, but had been hoping to avoid talking about it.

'We have a witness who saw the two of you together,' Mac told her. 'She was quite sure that you were engaged in an altercation. It was while you were on Christ Church Meadow waiting for the march to start.'

'It was nothing.' Faith's assertion was unconvincing in the extreme, but if she kept her nerve and refused to talk, there was no way we could get any evidence that would convince a jury that she was lying.

'If it was so unimportant, there can't be any harm in telling us what it was about, can there?' Mac pressed her.

'It – it was – I – I – oh, I feel so dreadful about it!' Faith suddenly buried her face in her hands and gave way to uncontrollable sobbing. Mac and I exchanged glances over her head, wondering what to do now. We were neither of us good at handling distraught females.

I looked round the room and eventually spotted a box of tissues lying on the battered sideboard. I got up and brought them across for Faith. She looked up briefly and sniffed a hoarse "thanks" as she reached across and pulled one out. She wiped her eyes and blew her nose. Then she looked up at us again, smiling apologetically.

'I'm sorry. I suppose I'd better tell you all about it, but you won't pass it on, will you? I mean, I don't want Colin or Diane to know about it.'

'We won't tell them,' I assured her, 'but, if it turns out to be relevant to Timothy's murder, it might have to come out at the trial. It all depends what it is.'

'I didn't kill him, if that's what you're thinking!'

'And do you know who did?' Mac asked.

'No! I've no idea. I can't think why *anyone* would want to. Don't you think it could've been some sort of dreadful accident?' Faith gave a little gulp and pulled out another tissue. She wiped her eyes again and then crumpled it up in her hand. 'Well, I suppose he could've been … I mean, I may not have been the only person he was … Look, I'd better start at the beginning.'

'Yes please!' Mac urged her. I think he was getting a bit impatient with the way she kept hinting at some big revelation and then stopping short of telling us anything.

'Diane and I are both working on a project run by Dr Loftus.'

'Your supervisor,' I put in for Mac's benefit

'That's right. We're excavating an important iron-age site in Dorset. His grant runs out next July, but he's got another one that will fund a postdoctoral research assistant to carry on working on the dig. He as good as told us that it would be one of us.'

'And do both you and Diane want the job?' I asked when it began to look as if she had changed her mind about continuing. So far, she hadn't told us anything that we didn't already know.

'Yes.' Faith nodded miserably. 'And ever since the summer I wanted it more than ever. My boyfriend, Colin, is going to be in Oxford for another two years, so I want to be here too. I asked Diane if she would stand down, but she said that seeing as John was going to be based in Oxford for the foreseeable, she didn't see why she didn't have just as much reason as me to want the job – which, of course, is true!'

'She told me that she thought you might want to get away from Oxford after splitting up with Timothy,' I commented, perhaps unwisely.

'The lying cow!' Faith's demeanour changed suddenly. She dropped the tissue down on the table in front of her and leaned back with her arms folded across her chest. 'She started sucking up to Arthur – that's Dr Loftus – offering to do extra work on the dig, typing up his notes for him, even inviting him round for dinner when I went home for the weekend once. I thought, two can play at this game, so I – I – I suppose I sort of *flirted* with him. I knew he fancied me because of the way he always used to come up a bit too close when I asked him to have a look at a find, and he once patted me on the bum when I was bending over the bench in the lab. So I – I sort of … worked on it. After a while, he asked me out to dinner and then we went back to his college rooms. His wife and kids live in a house down in Dorset, but he has rooms in college and he only goes there at weekends. I was so desperate to get the job that I – I – I let him do whatever he liked,' she blurted out at last, snatching up the tissue again and covering her face with it.

Mac and I exchanged glances again. This was beginning to get interesting, but it still wasn't clear where Timothy Sudbury came in. For what seemed like ages, she sat there, rocking backwards and forwards with her hands clutching the tissue across her mouth, and her eyes staring blankly ahead, while Mac and I watched helplessly. Then, at last, she gave a jerk and slowly put down the tissue and laid her hands in her lap.

'I don't know how Tim found out,' she resumed, 'but somehow he did. He loved that! It gave him a sense of power being able to threaten that he was going to tell Colin or Diane.'

'He was blackmailing you?' Mac asked sharply.

'We-ell, sort of. I mean – he wasn't demanding money or anything. He just … he just enjoyed knowing he had something over on me.'

'Was that why you let him live here?' It had been puzzling me for some time why she had allowed her ex-boyfriend to live in the same house.

'No. That was before I … Of course, if I'd been going out with Colin then, I probably wouldn't have … The way Tim put it, it seemed sort of … Well, the thing is, we'd got it all sorted before we split up, and then … well Tim might not have been able to find anywhere, so … And Tim could be very nice! I don't suppose he meant anything by it really. I should never have said what I did to him, and now it's too late!'

She dissolved into sobs again. I pushed the box of tissues towards her and leaned back in my chair to wait. We still hadn't quite got to the bottom of what the argument in Christ Church Meadow was all about.

Eventually, Faith composed herself and looked up at us again.

'I'm sorry. It's just … the last thing I said to him was telling him I wished he was dead! He was going on about perhaps he ought to tell Colin about me *playing away from home* as he put it. He was saying it wasn't fair on him that he didn't know. And then he said that Diane ought to be told that I wasn't playing fair with her over the job and sort of hinting that he was going to tell her about it. And that's when I said it. I didn't mean it, I was just so fed up with him going on and on about it, and the way he was really enjoying making me squirm. I told him that I was going to tell Colin and Diane myself and he'd better watch out because then he wouldn't have anything on me anymore and I'd pay him back and ...'

'You threatened him?' queried Mac.

Faith nodded, 'but I didn't mean anything by it. I was just so angry with him for ... You do believe me don't you? I didn't kill him. I wouldn't know how to. I've never even heard of keta – keta – you know, the drug. I just feel so awful about shouting at him like that. I never thought it would be the last thing I ever said to him!'

'Do you think he could've been doing the same sort of thing to anyone else?' Mac asked, after a long pause.

'How d'you mean?'

'Finding out their secrets and then threatening to tell people?'

'I don't know. I don't know who he'd have known anything about. I mean, it must just have been chance that he saw me with Arthur.'

'Or he could've been following you,' Mac suggested. 'Maybe he was hoping to get you back and he was looking for an opportunity to get you on your own or something.'

Faith considered this for a few moments.

'I suppose he could've been,' she conceded at last, 'except that he had Niamh, so why would he care about me?'

'Maybe he didn't trust you not to interfere between him and Niamh, then.'

Mac was full of ideas, but none of them seemed very plausible to me. I thought it was far more likely that Tim simply enjoyed spying on people. However, Mac's suggestion had prompted me to suspect that any one of Tim's immediate circle of friends could have reason to want him out of the way. Who knew what secrets he was taunting them with – and perhaps even actually blackmailing them? Come to that, how could we be sure that Faith wasn't being economical with the truth when she claimed that he wasn't demanding payment of some sort in exchange for his silence?

'Has Dr Loftus decided which of you is going to get the job yet?' I asked.

'No!' Faith looked across at me with wide eyes. I couldn't decide whether she was scared or angry. 'He's still keeping us both on a string, dropping hints one way and then another. I'm almost starting to think he isn't planning to give it to either of us! One of his old DPhil students is due back from America this term on a nine-month contract at Balliol, which would exactly fit in with the start of the new grant. I'm starting to think he may be going to give it to him instead.'

'And what will you and Diane do if that happens?' Mac asked.

'We're both looking out for jobs, but there isn't a lot of money in archaeology so there's not much chance that we'll get something in Oxford. I'm putting in an application to do a teaching certificate, as a backup in case there's nothing else for me. But, if the worst comes to the worst, I'll have to go back and live at home until I find something.'

'And home is – where?'

'East Lancashire, by the sound of it.' I couldn't resist showing off my knowledge of regional accents. Faith's vowels reminded me of Margaret's distinctive way of speaking.

'That's right,' Faith nodded. 'Oldham. My dad works for Ferranti. He'll probably want me to take an office job there. He was never all that keen on me doing a doctorate, but Mum convinced him that I shouldn't turn down the opportunity when it was on offer. I think she wishes she'd been to university. She would've been good enough, but girls just didn't in those days.'

'Well, I think that's about all for now.' Mac got to his feet. I think we were both feeling relieved that Faith seemed to have cheered up a bit and we wanted to get out before there were any more tears. 'Let us know if you think of anyone else that Timothy could have had some sort of hold over. And don't worry; we won't let on what you've told us to any of your friends.'

As we cycled back past the Duke of Monmouth, I got a sudden shock when I saw Margaret emerging from the pub in the company of another young woman. Mac's brakes squealed and he showered me with Glaswegian expletives as I stopped to talk to her and he nearly careered into the back of me.

'What are you doing here?'

'I've been having lunch with an old friend of mine from Bolton.' Margaret smiled enigmatically at me and then turned to her companion. 'This is my fiancé, DC Jonah Porter, and ...?'

'Sergeant Gordon MacBride,' Mac filled in for her. 'You must be Margaret. I've heard a lot about you.'

'Nothing good, I hope!' Margaret quipped. 'And this is Denise Lawson. We were at school together. She went to Liverpool University to study veterinary medicine, and now she's got a job in Oxford. We were catching up.'

'I work just round the corner from here,' Denise added, shaking hands with both of us. 'And I'm afraid afternoon surgery is going to begin in a couple of minutes, so I must dash. It was nice seeing you. We must meet up properly some time.'

I watched her until she turned the corner and disappeared from view. Then I turned an accusatory eye on Margaret.

'She works in the vet practice where Dawn Farmer is getting her work experience?'

'That's right!' Margaret confirmed unapologetically. 'Would you like to hear what she told me about her?'

'You didn't let on that she was under investigation by the police, did you?' I asked anxiously.

'No, of course not! What do you take me for? We just chatted generally and then I brought the conversation round to how difficult it is to get on a vet course and asked what advice she'd give to someone who wanted to do it. And then she said that getting some experience of working with animals was crucial, which gave me the chance to ask whether they ever had teenagers wanting to volunteer with them, and things went on from there.'

We chained up our bikes and accompanied Margaret back inside the pub. Soon we were sitting in a corner drinking virtuous glasses of orange juice, agog with anticipation of what she had to tell us.

'According to Denise, Dawn is a hard worker and very keen. She's been there for six months now and nobody has any complaints about her. She's very earnest and can be quite judgemental of people who don't match up to her high expectations. For example, she was very critical of an owner who brought his dog in to have its tail docked, and she got very upset when a cat was put down after a road traffic accident, instead of a lengthy and difficult operation to try to patch it up.'

'So she might take extreme measures if she thought someone was behaving unethically.' murmured Mac as if to himself.

'I don't know about that,' Margaret replied. 'I got the impression that she definitely wouldn't hesitate to express her views, but as for anything more ...'

'Did your friend say anything about her involvement in the anti-nuclear movement?' asked Mac.

'Yes. She brought some leaflets and posters to the surgery and wanted to have them displayed in the waiting room. She was a bit upset when they told her it wasn't appropriate. Denise got the impression that she couldn't see how anyone who loved animals could possibly be in favour of nuclear weapons. She has a very black-and-white way of looking at everything.'

'There you are!' said Mac. 'I told you we ought to be considering her as a suspect. These black-and-white do-gooders are dangerous. They can't see things from anyone else's point of view. If she thought Timothy Sudbury was a danger to animals or to some cause that she was in favour of, she probably wouldn't hesitate to bump him off!'

'But everyone seems to agree that she didn't know him,' I protested. 'If she'd never clapped eyes on him until last Thursday, she couldn't possibly have come to the demo armed with a syringe full of ketamine intending to do away with him, could she?'

'She could've been planning to use it on someone else,' Mac began. Then he reluctantly shook his head. 'No. You're right. If she did it, she had to have known him before and to have had some sort of grudge against him.'

'Do you want to hear what else I learned?' asked Margaret as he relapsed into a discontented silence. We both looked at her expectantly. 'The vet's had a break-in a few weeks ago. The burglars got away with some expensive equipment and an assortment of pharmaceutical supplies – including several vials of ketamine!'

Margaret looked round at us both triumphantly.

'I'm surprised you didn't know about it. They reported it to the police.'

We sat in silence. Mac and I looked at one-another, shame-faced. She was quite right: we ought to have checked the files for any reports of stolen ketamine. It was surprising that Richard hadn't instructed any of us to do it – this business with his mother must be distracting him more than I'd realised. Of course, Peter, who could have been relied upon to do that job, had been on leave, but that only meant that Mac, his replacement, ought to have thought of it himself.

'Presumably she didn't mention whether any other vet practices have been targeted?' I asked casually.

'She did, as a matter of fact. They were the third in a series of burglaries. The other two were in Abingdon and Witney.'

'And was ketamine taken every time?' Mac asked eagerly.

'She didn't know.'

'We'd better get back and have a look in the files,' Mac announced, turning to me. 'It looks like we may have been mistaken in thinking that ketamine isn't being used as a street drug over here. I wouldn't be surprised if it turns out he took it himself, after all!'

When we got back to the station, we found Niamh O'Halloran talking to the desk sergeant, who was explaining that DCI Paige had been called out on another case. Mac immediately stepped in and offered to deal with her. She looked a bit doubtful, but she must have recognised me, because when I came forward she agreed to speak to us. I took her into an interview room and gave her a cup of tea while Mac hurried off to find the records of the burglaries at the vets.

Niamh sat in silence, clutching her teacup nervously in both hands. I fought back the urge to fire questions at her, remembering Richard's advice that silence was one of our most powerful weapons in extracting information from witnesses. Most people soon become uncomfortable with the lack of conversation and find themselves speaking simply to fill the void. So I contented myself with smiling encouragingly towards her and occasionally sipping my own tea. Eventually, she looked anxiously back into my eyes and gave a small sigh.

'I don't really know why I've come,' she began in a whisper so low that I had to lean closer in order to hear what she was saying. 'It's probably nothing, but ... Well, I just can't get it out of my mind because .... Well, you see, why would she lie about it unless .... But then again, she probably wasn't really lying; it was probably just a mistake!'

'I'm sorry; I don't understand.'

'No. I suppose I'm not making much sense.' She smiled up at me and our eyes met. 'It's Wendy. You remember she told DCI Paige that she threw away an empty crisp packet in the bin on the corner of Pembroke Square?'

'Yes?' I nodded encouragingly.

'Well, she couldn't have. Or at least, it couldn't have been the packet that we ate when we were visiting Blenheim, like she said, because she wasn't wearing the same coat. We cycled to Blenheim, and she wore her yellow cagoule, I'm sure of it! She always wore that when she was on her bike, so that she'd show up in the traffic.'

'That's very interesting. Thank you for coming in to tell us about it.'

'Anyway,' Niamh went on, 'I threw away both packets while we were there. So she couldn't still have had hers last Thursday.'

'Maybe it was from a different occasion,' I suggested. 'When she was wearing her other coat.'

'But it can't have been!' Niamh's eyes widened. I could see that she was both puzzled and disturbed by her friend's claim. 'You see, I collected that coat for her from the dry cleaners only the day before. So it couldn't have had anything in the pockets.'

'Can you think of anything else that Wendy could have been throwing away?' I asked cautiously. 'Something she didn't want to mention to the police, perhaps?'

'No.' Niamh shook her head. '*I* didn't even notice her putting anything in the bin.'

'But we have a reliable witness who says she did. Don't you have any idea what it could've been?'

'No, I don't know. Sorry.'

'I suppose you must have known Wendy for a long time?'

'Oh yes! Well five years. We were at Shrewsbury together. She was in the year above me, but she was reading Greats, so we both finished together.'

'You were doing theology, is that right?'

'Well, philosophy and theology. That's what brought us together. She helped me a lot with the philosophy in my first year.'

'So you had a lot in common?'

'Sort of. Well, not exactly. She knew a lot more than me. Not just because she was in the year above. She'd been to a posh girls' boarding school and knew all sorts of things I didn't – about etiquette and stuff. We've never really bothered with all that at home so I was always afraid of putting my foot in it. Some of the older tutors were rather … well, you know!'

I nodded encouragingly.

'And she's very horsey, which I'm not. You know! She's ridden to hounds and done point-to-point races and stuff.'

'So she helped you to fit in?' I suggested, hoping to draw her out and find out more about Wendy's character. 'She showed you the ropes in your college?'

'Well, not exactly. My dad's a tutor at Lichfield, so he told me all about subfusc and dining on High Table and all that sort of thing. I suppose Wendy showed me that people who'd been to posh public schools weren't all toffee-nosed snobs. She's very kind, and so are her family. They invited me to stay with them a few times in the long vacs. They train racehorses. They've got their own stables. Wendy's been trying to teach me to ride, but I'm not much good!'

She pushed her cup away and got to her feet.

'Anyway, that's it. I don't suppose it was worth bothering you with really. I just thought ... Well, you know! I'm sure it's nothing. Wendy must just have misremembered, only ... Well, I'd better go.'

I escorted her out and then went in search of Richard, feeling rather pleased with myself. A suspect who had lied to the police must be worth further investigation!

* * *

'Another cliff-hanger, eh?' Dot wheezed when Jonah finished reading the next chapter. She looked a little better today and, in answer to Bernie's anxious questioning, had reported that her temperature was back to normal and that some medication from her doctor had helped to suppress her cough.

'I thought that was a good place to stop,' he grinned back, 'to give the reader a chance to digest the evidence and come up with their own theories.'

'It looks straightforward enough to me,' Dominic cut in eagerly. 'This Wendy lied about what she threw away – which must mean that it was something incriminating – and she'll have had access to ketamine through her family's racing stables. It's a no-brainer!'

'Except that she doesn't have a motive,' Mariam pointed out.

'Mariam's right,' Lucy agreed. 'I reckon it's another of Jonah's red-herrings, designed to put us off the scent.'

'I don't know why you all suspect me of trying to lead you up the garden path,' Jonah complained. 'All I'm doing is putting the evidence in front of you in the order in which we gathered it.'

'It seems to me,' Dot said, 'that the question we need to answer is: *why* did Niamh come to the police to tell on her friend?'

Everyone fell silent as she breathed heavily, evidently gathering her strength to say more.

'I think that *either* she suspects Wendy of killing Timothy,' she went on eventually, '*or* ...' Everyone held their breath, waiting for her to continue. '... *or* she knows that she didn't because ... *she* did it herself!'

'I see what you mean,' Ibrahim brought his logical engineer's brain to bear on the problem. 'If *she* killed her boyfriend then she may have seen the police interest in this object, whatever it was, that Wendy threw away as an opportunity to direct their attention towards her. On the other hand, if she knows some reason why Wendy might have wanted to kill him, this discrepancy over the crisp packet could have tipped the balance and made her suspect that she actually did it.'

'If *I'd* killed someone, the last thing I'd want to risk doing was drawing attention to myself with the police,' Lucy objected.

'Rationally, yes,' Ibrahim agreed, 'but I don't suppose murderers always think things through the way you do. She'd probably have been paranoid about the police suspecting her and wouldn't have been able to leave well alone.'

'Absolutely right, young man,' Dot gasped. 'It's a sure sign of guilt – talking about something too mu-uch.'

Her voice cracked and they all waited as she was overtaken by a fit of coughing.

'When I was a sister, I always knew when the junior nurses were lying to me. They just couldn't resist embellishing their ... stories ... with ...'

She began coughing again and the watchers saw her raising a plastic beaker of water to her purple lips with her thin, blue-veined hand. She looked all of her hundred-and-one years and very pale and ill. Had they been mistaken in thinking that she was on the mend?

'I'm – sorry,' she croaked at last, waving her hand across in front of her face. 'Just … carry on. Don't – don't … mind … me.'

'Maybe you ought to have a lie down, Aunty,' Bernie suggested. 'You've been ill, remember. It takes it out of you.'

Dot shook her head vigorously but did not speak, presumably fearful of setting off another coughing spasm.

'OK then,' Dominic said at last, 'what have we got? Let's fill in some more of that table of yours, Mariam. We can add means to both Wendy and Dawn.'

'And Dawn also had opportunity, if we believe Margaret's theory that the injection could have been given before the two parts of the demonstration split up,' Lucy agreed. 'Of course, that also means that Mam could have done it!' she added, grinning towards her mother's face on her computer screen.

'Or a couple of thousand other people!' Bernie retorted. 'But I don't have motive or means, remember, *and*, more importantly, I haven't been convicted of the murder. And you don't really imagine Jonah would choose an *unsolved* case to write about, do you?'

'Hardly!' Peter laughed. 'He'll be wanting to show off how he cracked the case single-handed when everyone else was barking up the wrong tree!'

'I resent that remark,' Jonah protested half-heartedly. He was used to Peter's teasing. 'I am merely describing a typical case for the edification of the public.'

'You said you chose it because Margaret helped to solve it,' Lucy said thoughtfully. 'Does that give us a clue about who did it?'

'No comment!' Jonah smiled back.

'So far, most of the evidence that she's come up with has been pointing towards Dawn Farmer,' Dominic observed.

'Not quite,' Mariam put in quietly. 'What about before? Don't you remember? She was the one who got Diane talking in the pub. What if *that*'s the crucial bit of evidence that she was responsible for?'

'You're all going about this the wrong way,' Jonah complained. 'I'm telling you how we pieced together the evidence and you're ignoring all that and just homing in on *my* motives in telling the story. Put yourselves in my place and work out who you suspect based on the *real* evidence!'

'Alright then.' Dominic took the lead. 'Looking at Mariam's table, pretty well everyone who knew him has a motive for wanting him out of the way, but none of them have a strong enough reason to risk murdering him. All our suspects had the opportunity to stab him with the needle while they were caught up in the crowd or else before that on Christ Church Meadow. So we're left with just the "means" column to play with. John could've got the drug from the hospital; Dawn could have taken it from the vet's surgery; and now we've just discovered that Wendy's family ran a racing stable, where they may well have used ketamine on the horses.'

'And that's the lead that Richard decided to follow up on the next day,' Jonah told them. 'It was Saturday, but we had a case to solve; so he took me off with him down to Lambourn, on the Berkshire Downs, where Wendy's family had their racing stables.'

11. THE END OF THE BEGINNING

It was hard to believe that it was Holy Week. The churches were all closed and none of the usual preparations for Easter could take place. There were plenty of chocolate eggs stacked up in the supermarkets but few people queuing to buy them. Peter selected some for Ricky and Abigail, but his other grandchildren, up in Yorkshire, would have to make do with a card and some money from Granddad this year. Travelling to see relatives and to deliver gifts in person was forbidden (unless, as it turned out later, you happened to be the Prime Minister's favourite aide[16]).

As he drove back past St Cyprian's Church, he saw Father Damien getting out of his battered Ford Fiesta in the car park. He pulled up and wound the window down to call out a greeting. Technically, this was probably illegal, but they were maintaining the statutory two-metre social distancing as they exchanged a few words, so surely that must be OK.

Damien was returning from his second funeral of the day. He had three more booked before the long weekend. No – not all COVID-related. Most of them were elderly

---

[16] On 27th March, Dominic Cummings infamously drove 260 miles from London to Durham with his wife, whom he believed to be suffering from COVID-19, to obtain childcare for their young son from his sister and nieces. They returned to London on Easter Monday.

people whose deaths were not unexpected; but in some ways that only made it more difficult for the families, who had been prevented from visiting their relatives during the last few weeks of their life and now could not even have the funeral that they would have chosen. Not even the priest who knew them. Damien was taking funerals on behalf of several older priests with underlying health conditions who had been advised to self-isolate for their own protection. It was hard comforting families whom he did not know in circumstances that were strange and frightening for all of them, himself included.

Peter nodded and smiled his sympathy. He was about to drive off when a thought struck him. If Niamh's family had lived in Headington in the 1980s then surely the Catholic Church that they had attended must have been St Cyprian's. What if there were still relatives of hers living here? How would they react if Jonah's memoirs were published? He leaned out of the window again.

'Father? Do you have any O'Hallorans in your flock?'

'I don't think so. Why?'

'Oh, nothing much! It's just Jonah's been writing about a case from back in the eighties, and it involved an O'Halloran family who lived near here and I just wondered …'

'That'd be well before my time.'

'I know. I just suddenly thought: what if they were still living here? They might get a bit of a shock if he actually manages to get his book published.'

'I could have a look in the archives if you like,' the priest offered. 'One of my predecessors may have noted down where they went – assuming they moved out of the parish.'

'No, no. Don't go to any trouble. I'm sure it doesn't matter. He'll probably change all the names before publication to save anyone being upset. Besides, it's his job to find people and warn them, not yours. Forget about it. They had connections with the University.

They'll have better records than yours. We can get Bernie to look there.'

He drove home, still pondering on the rights and wrongs of publishing an account of events in the past which some of those involved might have been hoping to keep buried. Where was Niamh O'Halloran now? How would she feel about her relationship with Timothy Sudbury being set out in print for all to read?

When he pushed open the door, struggling with bags of groceries in both hands, he heard a murmur of voices coming from Jonah's sitting room. After a few moments, he recognised the voice of his friend's older son, Reuben. Of course! It was the anniversary of Margaret's death. Reuben and Anne always rang to "check that Dad's OK". No doubt, his younger son Nathan would also be in touch soon. Normally, he and his wife came over from their home in St Albans and took Jonah to visit the grave in South Oxfordshire where Margaret was buried, but that was prohibited this year. Everything was strange and different.

Bernie came out of the kitchen to help Peter with the shopping. As they emptied bags and boxes into the kitchen cupboards and larder, he told her his concerns about the effect that publishing Jonah's memoirs might have on the people who featured in them.

'Most of them were students or staff at the university. Couldn't you use your contacts to find them and give them the heads-up? Niamh, for example: you said you actually knew her. Do you really not know what happened to her?'

'Actually, I do know exactly what happened and she's one person that you don't need to worry about,' Bernie replied enigmatically. 'But I'm not going to spoil Jonah's story by telling *you* – not yet. Let Lucy and her friends have the fun of trying to solve the case themselves first.'

'I'm not asking you to tell the world,' Peter grumbled. 'Just reassure me that we aren't going to have a whole lot of people's lives disrupted if he ever finds a publisher for this book of his. John Goodey, for example. He must still be practising as a doctor. What on earth will his patients think if he suddenly features as a murder suspect?'

'Why would they care, unless he was found guilty? And if he was, he won't be practising. Being a convicted murderer is one of those little things that tends to get you struck off the medical register!'

'You know what I mean. Can't you do a bit of digging so that we're ready to warn them when the time comes?'

'OK. If it'll make you feel better. In fact, I've already made a start. I had a word with Colin Anderson-'

'Faith's new boyfriend – after she broke up with Tim?'

'That's right. And now one of the maths tutors at Holy Cross. He's kept up with most of that little group of friends, and-'

'Including Faith?' Peter interrupted. 'Did they stay together and get married?'

'That would be telling!' Bernie smiled. 'Maybe he beetled off to America to get away from the shame of having gone out with a murderer! I'm sorry, Peter, but I'm really not going to be drawn into giving anything away. Let Jonah have his fun. You'll find out what happened soon enough.'

'Don't forget, I already know what happened,' Peter reminded her. 'You don't have to keep everything secret from me. It's only the youngsters who are still in the dark.'

'Well, just watch what you say. It'd be a pity to spoil it for them. They're enjoying themselves, pretending to be detectives. And so is Aunty Dot. I just hope she survives to hear the end of the story. I'm worried about her, Peter. The number of cases is still rising, and Liverpool seems to be one of the hotspots. I'm scared that if she needs intensive care there won't be the capacity to give it to her. And she *is* over a hundred!'

Progress with Jonah's memoirs slowed down considerably over the next few days, because he found himself surprisingly busy. The warm weather had prompted rapid growth in the garden, and he spent several hours each day directing Bernie and Peter in their efforts to keep it tidy and productive. With the combination of being confined to the house and the anniversary of his wife's death, both of his sons seemed concerned for his mental health. They telephoned several times a day and Reuben arranged a videoconference in which his three children performed an improvised play and showed off the work that they had been doing in their home school. Even Jonah's sister, Sarah, who rarely got in touch, rang to check that he was well and keeping his spirits up.

Maundy Thursday was an especially poignant time, since that had been the day of Margaret's funeral. This year, the usual evening services were cancelled, but Father Damien broadcasted Mass from St Cyprian's. Forbidden to bathe the feet of a symbolic selection of twelve parishioners (as was his normal practice) he made do with washing the bare feet of the statue of Mary, which stood near the front of the church.

© Catherine Young

Good Friday took on a surreal feel as the daily death toll continued to mount. Deprived of their pulpits, clergy talked on social media about the similarities between dying from COVID-19 and Jesus's death on the cross. If we hadn't known before, we were now aware that crucifixion killed its victims by making them unable to breathe. Fluid built up in their lungs and eventually they died of asphyxiation – just like those unfortunates for whom mechanical ventilation had not been the lifesaver that we had been led to expect it would be. Fifty percent of those who went into Intensive Care did not come out alive.

The weather seemed to be determined not to give way to the despondency that everyone else was feeling – or perhaps it was all part of the contrariness of things that the only Bank Holiday weekend that anyone could remember when there was wall-to-wall sunshine for four days should be the only one on which we were all forbidden to leave our homes.

On Holy Saturday, after Jonah was in bed, Peter and Bernie sat in front of her laptop, watching as Father Damien lit the Pascal candle from a fire in the grounds of the church. Then the picture wobbled and became confused as he attempted to continue live-streaming from his phone while carrying the candle into the building. They caught glimpses of the painted ceiling inside the church as he tried to control the selfie-stick with one hand while processing up the aisle towards the altar with the candle in the other. At last he was able to put it down in its place and set the phone on the stand that he had rigged up for broadcasting Mass. He stood, holding his missal in his hand and began to read.

It was a cut-down version of the Easter Vigil, but Damien's voice was noticeably hoarse by the end. Usually there would have been a dozen or so parishioners each taking a turn with the nine Bible readings and the responsorial psalms. This year, it was a one-man show. Bernie looked at Peter when it came to the renewal of baptismal vows.

'This was your big moment,' she whispered.

Peter nodded as he remembered his reception into the Catholic Church at the Easter Vigil two years previously.

This year, any confirmation candidates would have to wait for weeks or perhaps even months before they could take the plunge. Everything was put on hold. The Alleluias of Easter morning rang hollow as we reflected on the fact that the one thousand people in the UK who had died of COVID-19 on Good Friday were not destined to rise on the third day.

This message was hammered home on Easter Sunday morning when the radio news announced the death from COVID-19 of Tim Brooke-Taylor. Bernie looked round at Peter and Jonah as they sat at the breakfast table. It felt like the end of an era. They had all grown up watching the *Goodies* on black-and-white television sets, and then *I'm sorry I haven't a Clue* had been staple listening on Radio 4 over Sunday lunch.

'I suppose he must've been in his eighties,' Bernie commented, 'but he's one of those people who never seems to get any older.'

'He'd have been eighty this year,' Jonah told her. He had been reading an obituary on his computer. 'He was born in 1940.'

'The same year as Richard,' Bernie murmured. 'I suppose, if he hadn't had his accident, COVID-19 might have carried him off now, too.'

Peter left the Easter eggs that he had bought for Ricky and Abigail nestled in the hedge at the end of the drive. As arranged by phone, Eddie took them past, on their permitted daily exercise, so that they could have the fun of finding their presents. It was a very diminished Easter egg hunt compared with the previous year, when they had scoured the large garden for painted wooden eggs concealed in numerous hiding places and then swapped them for the chocolate ones that Peter had kept safe in the larder. No chance of a thank-you hug for Granddad this year! Just a distant wave as he stood watching from the doorstep.

The following day, Aunty Dot was declared "too poorly" to join the family Zoom meeting.

'She's in bed,' the Care Home manager explained to Bernie over the phone, 'and she's too weak and feverish to manage her iPad. Normally, one of the staff would help her with it, but we don't have the time or the PPE[17]. More than a quarter of the care assistants are off sick or self-isolating. We're really struggling just to do the basics. I'm really sorry.'

'Should she be in hospital?' Bernie asked anxiously.

'We're monitoring her every few hours,' the manager promised, 'and we'll call an ambulance if she needs it, but right now, she's better off here. They're even more run off their feet than we are at the Royal[18], as far as I can gather.

Unsurprisingly, the first thing Bernie wanted to know when Lucy's face appeared on Jonah's computer screen that evening was whether Dominic or his father, her cousin Joey, had any more news about their aunt.

'Mum rang them again a couple of hours ago,' Dominic told her, shaking his head, 'but they said there was no change. She's been a bit confused, because of her temperature being so high, but they said she's keeping cheerful and not having any significant trouble breathing.'

'I wonder what "significant" means,' muttered Bernie.

'Mum asked that,' Dominic told her. 'From what Dad said when he phoned me, I think she gave them quite a hard time. *She* thinks Dot ought to be in hospital, but they

---

[17] Personal Protective Equipment. During the COVID-19 pandemic, there was shortage of the clothes needed to protect care workers from infection when treating COVID-19 patients. This was particularly acute in Care Homes, which were not given the same priority as the National Health Service.

[18] The Royal Liverpool Hospital

said the policy is to keep patients in Care Homes unless they need intensive care.'

'Because they're cluttering up the hospitals with people like Boris!' Lucy cut in angrily. 'People who think they're above taking precautions because they're too important to be bothered.'

'And they still can't get enough PPE to the hospitals,' Ibrahim added. 'I was talking to my dad earlier and he says they've been having to wash and re-use stuff that's supposed to be thrown away after a single shift.'

'And what about Care Homes like Aunty Dot's?' Bernie agreed. 'They told me this morning that they couldn't hold her iPad for her to be here with us this evening because they didn't have the right PPE. So what about all the other times they have to be in close contact with residents? What about getting them dressed in the morning, or giving them a shower, or helping them in the toilet? How are they supposed to stop infection spreading, if they don't have the proper equipment?'

'Well, there's nothing we can do about,' Dominic said. 'So how about Jonah reading us some more of his memoirs to give us something else to think about?'

* * *

It was Saturday, but Richard had me out bright and early driving down to Lambourn in the Berkshire Downs, where Wendy's family had their racing stables. We were intercepted at the gate by a lanky stable lad called Gerald who stared at us belligerently and then directed us to park on a gravel area next to a large manure pile.

'Mr Brotherton's in the office,' he mumbled. 'Round the back of the stable block.'

We followed the direction of his pointing finger along a concrete path, which ran beside a very smart looking block of about a dozen loose boxes, to a rather less impressive Portakabin hidden out of view behind it.

Richard stepped up to the open door and knocked on it with his knuckles. A small man with grey hair and striking dark brown eyes looked up from a book of accounts that he was studying and stared at us. Richard held up his warrant card.

'Mr Brotherton? I'm Detective Chief Inspector Richard Paige and this is DC Porter. We'd like to ask you a few questions in relation to the death of Timothy Sudbury in Oxford a week ago last Thursday. May we come in?'

'Be my guest!' Brotherton replied, getting up and moving two chairs into place in front of the desk where he was working. He was dressed in jodhpurs, riding boots and a tweed jacket.

He sat down again and looked expectantly towards us. 'I must say, I don't see how I'm going to be able to help you.'

'He was a friend of your daughter's,' Richard explained, 'and he was engaged to one of her other friends: Niamh O'Halloran. I believe that Niamh comes to stay here sometimes during the university vacation?'

'Yes. That's right. Nice girl. We enjoy having her. A bit timid around the horses, mind you; but of course, she wasn't brought up with them the way our kids were. Wendy was riding before she was walking! The same goes for Keith. I never knew she was engaged! And the boy's died? I'm sorry to hear that. Poor girl! I'm surprised Wendy never told us. How did it happen?'

'It was during that big demonstration in the middle of Oxford, the Thursday before last. Your daughter was one of the protestors. He just collapsed in the middle of it – and we're trying to find out why.'

'Whew!' Brotherton whistled between his teeth. 'Fancy that! That must have been a shock and a half for little Niamh. How is she? I'll bet she's cut up about it!'

'Yes,' Richard agreed, 'which is one reason why we need to find out how he got hold of the drug that seems to have been responsible.'

'Drugs?' Brotherton suddenly became more alert and animated. He was no longer making pleasant conversation; he was on his guard, sensing that he was suspected of something illegal. 'Well he never got them from me or anyone here! And not from Wendy either! She'd dead against that sort of thing. We've brought her up that way. She'd never get involved with anything like that.'

'He had a hypodermic syringe in his pocket when he died,' Richard informed him. 'It still contained a small amount of ketamine. Do you ever have cause to use that on your horses?'

'Only under the direction of our vet,' Brotherton said quickly, his eyes flicking rapidly between the two of us. 'Race horses are very carefully monitored for doping. We'd never risk any of it getting into the wrong hands.'

'But you do have a stock of it on your premises?' Richard suggested.

'Not as a matter of course.' Brotherton was definitely on the defensive now. 'But we have a safe storage facility for medications and sometimes we have horses that need repeated procedures. Our vet might leave a supply there so that it was on hand if a sedative was needed. But there's absolutely no chance of anyone taking any of it. All our medications are kept locked away.'

'Who has a key?'

'Nobody. It's a combination lock.'

'So, who has the combination?'

'I do, of course, and our vet, and my wife does. She and I both train the horses and we would oversee the administration of any medication, if the vet wasn't present.'

'And your daughter, Wendy? Did she have access to the medicine store?'

'No.' Brotherton's easy chatter had died down completely now and he answered Richard's questions as briefly as he dared.

'Did Timothy Sudbury ever come here?'

'No.' Brotherton looked down at his watch and then got to his feet. 'I'm sorry I can't help you, but I really know nothing at all about this young man. Now, if you'll excuse me, I need to see to one of the horses.'

'May we come with you?' asked Richard affably. 'We'd like to see round. And perhaps you could show us where your medicine store is.'

'If you like.' Brotherton clearly did not welcome our presence, but he remained calm and outwardly friendly. 'Although I must say I don't see what you're hoping to find. Like I told you, the lad never came here, and even if he had, he couldn't have got hold of any of our medications.'

'He died from a combination of ketamine and alcohol,' Richard continued, ignoring Brotherton's attempts to close down the conversation. 'We need to find out where it came from so that we can prevent any other young people dying. We've established a link between his girlfriend and your stables, and now you've told me that you do sometimes have ketamine stored on the premises. So now we just have to check things out here in order to eliminate your business as a potential source for the drug. It's all just routine. You and your family aren't under any suspicion.'

'Very well. Be my guest! We have nothing to hide.' Brotherton led the way out of the hut and along the back of the stable block to a large steel-framed building clad in wood.

When we got inside, I was surprised to find that we were in an enormous arena, brightly lit by powerful electric lights attached to the girders above. Looking round, I saw what I assumed was an indoor exercise yard to our right. It was surrounded by a post and rail fence and the floor was covered with sand, which a girl in muddy jodhpurs was raking smooth.

To the left was something even more unexpected: a large pool of water, roughly oval in shape and with an island in the centre. I stood staring as Gerald, the stable lad, walked round the outside leading a swimming horse by a long leash. Another man – slightly older and much shorter – was on the island guiding the horse from the other side with a similar leading rein. Seeing us enter, he called out to his colleague, 'OK. That'll do for now. Take him out and give him a good rub-down.'

I continued to watch as the horse was led from the water, up a ramp at the far side of the pool and out through a door, which seemed to lead into another room in this vast building. The man on the island crossed the water by means of a moveable aluminium bridge and came over to meet us.

When he came closer, I was struck by his resemblance to Mr Brotherton and deduced that this must be his son, Keith. He had the same deep-set brown eyes beneath black brows, and his hair was the raven black that his father's must have been thirty years earlier. I reflected that it was odd that both her father and her brother should be significantly shorter than Wendy, whose Amazonian proportions had been so striking when we first met.

'My son, Keith,' Brotherton introduced us. 'Keith, these are police officers. They're interested in checking that nobody could have taken any ketamine from our medication stocks. Show them whatever they want to see, can you? I've got to check on Hebridean Sunset; his owner's coming round this morning and I don't want any surprises.'

'Sure. No probs.' Keith nodded to his father and then turned to us. 'What was it you wanted to see?'

'Let's start with the place you keep your drugs,' Richard answered, 'and then we'd like to have just a general look around the place. You seem to have quite a set-up here!'

'Yes. We like to think we've got everything our owners could hope for. The hydrotherapy pool has been a big success. Not only does it mean we've got it on hand for our own horses, but we take bookings from other stables. I'll take you through to the veterinary centre. We have a sterile area for undertaking surgical procedures and, as my father will have told you, a secure storage area for medications. The vet centre's another facility that other local stables can book to use. We provide the very best for our own horses and it also means that we have additional income from stables that are less well-equipped.'

He led the way further into the huge chamber: past an enclosure behind the pool, where Gerald was busy rubbing down the horse that we had seen swimming, and then round the back of the exercise yard to a pair of double doors, tall enough to admit a horse and rider. He opened one of them and showed us into a sparklingly clean room with a concrete floor and white painted walls.

'The medicines are stored through here.'

We followed Keith through a door on the right into what seemed very like a doctor's office. There was a desk and chair, several filing cabinets, and a large refrigerator with a padlock hanging from the door. Keith went over to it.

'Drugs that need to be temperature-controlled are kept here,' he explained. 'It has a combination lock on it to prevent unauthorised access. Only my parents and I, and our vets, know the combination.'

'Is that where ketamine would be stored?' asked Richard.

'No. Unopened vials would be kept at room temperature, in this cupboard.' Keith crossed the room and began pressing buttons on a keypad attached to a door set into the wall next to the filing cabinets. He swung it open wide and gestured to us to look inside. 'Again, only the three of us and the vets know the combination.'

'What about your sister, Wendy?'

'I don't think so. She's not here much and she isn't really interested in the business. Polo's her thing. She used to talk about setting up a school, but then she went off to Oxford and forgot about it.'

'How often do you change the combination?'

'I – I don't think we ever have. Do you think we should?' Keith sounded momentarily less sure of himself.

'It *is* good practice,' I informed him.

'I'll tell Dad. We can do it right away.' Keith pulled the door closed and checked the handle to see that it was now locked again. 'Was there anything else you wanted to see?'

'As I said, we'd like to have a general look round and then we could do with speaking to your mother. Is she at home?'

'She's out exercising Parson's Folly, but she'll be back soon. Shall I show you round while you're waiting? Or would you like to come up to the house and I can give you a drink?'

'We'd like the guided tour please.'

Keith escorted us round stable blocks and paddocks, talking amiably all the time. He was clearly proud of his family's establishment and, apart from the brief hiccup over the combination lock, he appeared supremely confident that we would find nothing amiss.

'This is the bunkhouse where the stable lads sleep,' he told us, opening the door to a low, stone-built building and standing back so that we could look inside.

'What about the stable lasses?' I asked, remembering the woman who had been raking the sand in the indoor arena.

'Them too! There are two separate bedrooms with washrooms and showers in between, and a communal kitchen so they can cook for themselves. It's all mod cons here!'

'I'm impressed,' Richard nodded. 'I always pictured stable lads sleeping on straw in a loft over the horses.'

'Is this where Niamh stayed when she came here?' I asked. Our visit to the stables seemed to have done very little to further the investigation so far, and I was keen to push things along.

'No. She stays up at the house with us. We've got plenty of space for guests.'

'How did she fit in? I gather your sister tried to teach her to ride?'

'Yes!' Keith seemed to be amused at the recollection of Niamh's equestrian exploits. 'She does her best, but I don't think poor little Niamh was ever cut out for it. She was too nervous around the horses and they could sense it. You need to be able to assert your authority or they take advantage – just like humans!'

'Do you ever have problems asserting your authority over any of your employees?' Richard asked, picking up on this remark.

'Occasionally, but mostly they toe the line. We did have to let one of the lads go over the summer, though. That was what I was thinking about. He was too cocky by half. Thought he knew it all. It made him careless. I reckon he was responsible for Wendy's collarbone.'

'Wendy's collarbone?' I echoed. This was something new and sounded like a promising line of enquiry.

'She took Niamh out for a hack. She'd put her on an old gelding that she used to play polo on. He was usually steady as a rock, but something spooked him and he took off. Wendy managed to get past them and head them off into a dead-end track, but while she was bending over, reaching for Niamh's reins her saddle slipped and she came off.'

'And broke her collarbone?' I suggested.

'That's right! Collarbones are often the first to go in a fall.'

'And what about Niamh?' Richard took over again. 'Was she hurt at all?'

'No. She was fine. The horse calmed down and she was able to dismount. Then they walked the horses to the road and telephoned from the kiosk on the corner. Mum and I went out to get them, and then I took the horses back while she drove them both to hospital.'

'And the stable lad?' I queried, 'the one you had to let go? Where did he come into it?'

'He was the one who saddled up the horses. Like I said, he'd got careless. He should've checked the girth before letting them ride out. We'd had to speak to him about that sort of thing before. We can't afford to have sloppy work when we're dealing with horses worth hundreds of thousands of pounds!'

'Not to mention your sister's life,' Richard commented drily.

'Exactly! He had to go.'

We rounded the corner of the bunkhouse and found ourselves back in front of the line of loose boxes where we had started. A tall woman was in the act of dismounting from a chestnut thoroughbred while a ginger-haired stable lad stood holding its head. A second lad was standing by with a horse blanket. Once she had both feet on the ground, she nodded to them and they draped the blanket over the animal's back and then led it away. She patted it on the rump as it passed.

'Mum!' Keith called out to her. 'These men are police officers. They'd like to speak to you.'

Mrs Brotherton turned to look at us. She was tall – perhaps even taller than her daughter – with blue eyes and fair hair constrained by a net. Her complexion was pale with just a faint blush to the cheeks – what we used to call "Peaches and cream" – which struck me as strange in someone who evidently led very much an outdoor life.

She came across the yard, pulling off her riding gloves to shake hands.

'I'm Norma Brotherton,' she told us. 'How can I help you?'

There was something about the set of her jaw and the way that she spoke which reminded me of Wendy, despite the stark difference in colouring. Perhaps it was only the unusual experience of feeling that a woman was towering over me.

'We're investigating the death of Timothy Sudbury,' Richard told her. 'He was engaged to be married to Niamh O'Halloran, who I believe came to stay here several times, including quite recently.'

'That's right,' Mrs Brotherton nodded. 'She was here for three weeks at the end of July. She's a friend of my daughter's. I saw about Timothy's death in the papers. Poor Niamh! But I don't see where we come into it.'

'He was killed by a combination of ketamine and alcohol. It's purely routine, but we have to investigate any possible source of the drug. Your establishment came up during our enquiries and so we have to satisfy ourselves that Niamh couldn't have got it from here to give to him.'

'I see.' Mrs Brotherton looked down at her riding boots and seemed to be thinking. Then she raised her head again and called to her son, 'OK Keith! I'll look after these gentlemen now. Can you go and check that the pool's ready? Clarissa Willoughby's bringing her mare over for a session this morning.'

'Right you are!' Keith nodded towards his mother and glanced briefly at us. 'Goodbye officers. I hope you find out what happened to Niamh's boyfriend. She's a nice girl.'

'Come up to the house and have some coffee,' Mrs Brotherton invited us. Then, without waiting for a response, she set off at a brisk walk across the yard, through a gate and up a steep path towards an impressive stone-built house with a climbing rose over the front door, the last red blooms of summer showing bright against the pale walls.

She led us round the back and in through the kitchen door. She left her boots in the large porch and went inside in stockinged feet. As we followed her example and removed our shoes, I hoped fervently that my socks were not one of the many pairs that I owned with holes in the toes!

'Please, sit down.' She indicated a large wooden table with long benches at either side. 'I'll put the coffee on. You do both drink coffee? Or would you prefer tea?'

We assured her that coffee would be very nice.

I gazed round the room while Mrs Brotherton poured beans into a coffee grinder and set it whirring. It was very much what you think of as a traditional farmhouse kitchen: uneven low beams that you could bang your head on – especially if you were as tall as Norma Brotherton and her daughter – a massive Welsh dresser arrayed with plates, a solid-fuel Aga in a huge fireplace, with horse brasses hung on the walls on either side and washing draped over one of those clothes airers that you wind up and down with a pulley system. There were even strings of onions hanging from one of the beams!

Mrs Brotherton poured the coffee grounds into a percolator and plugged it in. Then she heated milk in a pan on the Aga hotplate. An aged dog – a beagle I think – uncurled from a basket in the corner of the room and came over to see what she was doing. It limped as if it had arthritis in its joints. Mrs Brotherton looked down and patted the animal and then poured some milk into a bowl on the floor. The dog lapped enthusiastically and then returned to its basket.

'Poor Bertie! He used to enjoy coming out with us when we exercised the horses, but now he spends almost all day curled up in his basket. Old age! It comes to us all in the end!'

She poured the milk into a jug and set it down on the table together with three mugs, each embellished with a picture of a racehorse surrounded by the words "Brotherton Racing Stables", and a bowl of demerara sugar. Then she poured coffee from the percolator into each of the cups and invited us to help ourselves to milk and sugar.

'How's Niamh coping?' she asked solicitously. 'I should think this will have knocked her for six. She always seemed so sensitive and kind.'

'I think it probably hasn't really come home to her yet,' Richard told her. 'It's often like that with a sudden death. It takes a while for the news to sink in. Your daughter, Wendy, seems to be looking after her very well.'

'Oh yes! She's very fond of Niamh. We were so pleased when they became friends. Wendy's always been a bit of a loner. She doesn't mix well. We used to worry about her when she was at school. I always tried to encourage her to have one of the other girls to stay in the holidays, but she never had anyone she wanted to invite.'

'She went to boarding school, I gather.'

'That's right. Bexington College. It's my old school. It's in a lovely setting down on the coast, not far from Weymouth.'

'In Dorset?' I asked.

'That's right. Do you know it?'

'No.' I shook my head. 'It's just funny the way Dorset has kept cropping up recently. That's where two of Niamh's other friends have got an archaeological dig going on – *and* where their supervisor has a house.'

'It's a small world, as they say,' Mrs Brotherton laughed. 'As I was saying, we were really pleased that Wendy had a friend at last, and Niamh seems such a nice girl. It's a pity this had to happen to her.'

'She came to stay here a few weeks ago, I gather?' Richard carefully steered the conversation back on track.'

'That's right. She's been coming every year since the end of Wendy's second year at Oxford. The last couple of years, ever since she started her DPhil, Wendy's hardly spent any time here, but she always brought Niamh for two or three weeks over the summer.'

As she spoke, I was becoming more and more curious about Wendy. Why had she gone to Oxford University when she could clearly have joined the family business, which appeared to be lucrative and thriving? And what had drawn her to little Niamh, who seemed so different in character and background?

'What's Wendy planning to do after she finishes her degree?' I asked. 'Is she hoping for a university post?'

'You'd better ask her about that,' her mother smiled. 'You don't think she'd tell me, do you? After all, I'm only her mother! No, actually she did say something about it while they were here last. She asked us whether our offer was still open that we'd lease Bradley Hollow to her to start her own business.'

'She was thinking of coming back here permanently?'

'Well, not exactly. She was planning to live there, in the cottage and set up some sort of riding school. She'd had that kind of idea before, when she was still at school. We encouraged her then because we really didn't know what else she'd be able to do. She was so withdrawn at that stage; we thought she'd never cope with working for anyone else and she was determined she wasn't going to work for us! It was a polo school she was hankering after in those days, but I think now she's thinking more of just general riding lessons. I think she got a buzz out of teaching Niamh and thought she'd turn it into a business.'

'And this *Bradley Hollow*?' Richard enquired. 'What exactly …?'

'It's a small house – a cottage really – with a few farm buildings and twelve acres of grazing. It was my grandfather's holding: a mixed sheep and arable farm. My

Dad grew up there and it gave him a base for expanding into horses. He developed this business and I inherited it from him.'

'So, you're the owner, not your husband?'

'We both own it now. George was one of Dad's jockeys. When we got married, he gave us each a one third share in the business as a wedding present. I inherited his third when he died, so technically I'm the majority shareholder, but we do everything jointly. It's probably about time we made Keith a partner too: he puts a tremendous amount of effort into the business; but we've been waiting to see what Wendy decided to do. We always try to treat them fairly, but it's not always easy. It would quite suit us if she wanted to take over Bradley Hollow, because we could give her that and give Keith a share in the business at the same time.'

This was all very interesting background information, but it didn't get us any further in respect of the source of the ketamine that had killed Timothy Sudbury. I tried to steer the conversation back in that direction.

'Getting back to when Niamh was here in the summer: did any of your horses need ketamine injections during that time? Would you have been storing any on the premises?'

'Not one of our horses, but we did have one in from one of our neighbours. I expect Keith told you that other people sometimes pay to use our facilities. This was a horse that needed surgery and their vet recommended hydrotherapy for rehabilitation afterwards. The vet brought everything he needed in advance and stored it here ready for the op. I remember particularly because Niamh was very interested in it all and asked the vet a lot of questions. I think she liked the idea that the horses got just as good medical treatment as people do.'

'So Niamh was interested in the horses?' Richard asked. 'I got the impression from your son that she didn't know much about them.'

'She didn't. She was a complete novice, but she made a real effort to fit in here. The lads were all falling over themselves to look after her. She looks so tiny and vulnerable, but she was a real trier and surprisingly tough when she needed to be. She was very good when Wendy broke her collarbone. She somehow got them both – and two horses – to the telephone box on Wantage Road to phone for help. And afterwards, she took charge of giving her the painkiller injections that she needed. She was marvellous!'

'Your daughter seems to have made a full recovery now,' Richard remarked.

'Yes. Well, she's young. People do at that age. And Wendy isn't one to let on that there's anything wrong. She doesn't like people to see any sign of weakness. She's like her father in that respect. He's always a nightmare to deal with if he's ill or has an accident. He'll never rest up and give things time to heal.'

She drained her coffee mug and looked towards Richard.

'Now, what exactly was it you were wanting to know? How is this all connected to Timothy's death?'

'We need to establish if there was any way that the ketamine that was found in his bloodstream after death could have come from your supply,' I explained. 'Young people have been known to take it for fun. It can produce a sort of out-of-body experience that some people enjoy.'

I had been reading up on ketamine abuse and the effects of taking it, and I was pleased to have the opportunity to display my new knowledge.

'We think that he may have taken it because he wanted the high, without realising how dangerous it can be in conjunction with alcohol.'

'I'm sure Keith or George will have shown you how careful we are about keeping all our drugs locked away securely.'

'But accidents do happen,' I suggested, trying not to sound accusatory, 'when someone gets distracted, for example.'

'Your husband said that only the three of you – you, your husband and Keith – and your vet know the combination to the drug store,' Richard intervened. 'Is there any possibility that anyone else could have found it out? One of the stable lads, for instance? If they'd been watching while one of you opened it, perhaps?'

'We do try to be careful,' Mrs Brotherton hedged, 'but … well I suppose it's impossible to be absolutely sure.'

She thought for a moment and then went on, 'but I am sure that the vet would have told us if any had gone missing. He keeps a very close watch on all the prescription meds.'

'Yes, I'm sure he does.' Richard got to his feet as if he was satisfied with her answers. 'Thank you for the coffee. We'll go now and leave you all in peace. I'm sorry to have disturbed you, but we do have to look into every possibility.'

✳ ✳ ✳

'Hang on a minute!' Peter called out. 'I think that's the phone.'

Jonah stumbled momentarily in his reading and then resumed the story while Bernie hurried out into the hall to answer the landline. It was Joey.

'The Home just rang,' he told her. 'They say that Aunty Dot's condition has worsened. They've been trying to persuade her to let them ring for an ambulance, but she's still well enough to refuse to go.'

'I suppose that's a good sign,' Bernie said, trying to sound more confident than she felt. 'If she can still argue, she can't be at death's door, but …'

'I know,' Joey agreed. 'I can't help thinking this may be the end of the road for Aunty Dot. She's had a good innings but … Well, I'd better let you get on. I'll let you know if there's any more news.'

Bernie replaced the receiver and stood silently digesting the information that she had just received. Then she took a deep breath and went back into the living room to convey Joey's message to the others.

'Well *I* think the ketamine probably came from somewhere quite different and this is just Jonah trying to put us off the scent!'

Jonah had evidently finished reading his current chapter and the youngsters were dissecting it in search of clues to the identity of the murderer.

'No Lu, I think this *is* where the drug came from,' Ibrahim disagreed, 'but I reckon he's giving us lots of stuff about all the family to cover up whatever it is that tells us *who* took it and why. The way I see it, it could have been either Niamh or Wendy, and they could've taken it to give to Timothy to use himself *or* so that they could inject him with it themselves.'

'So you're saying-,' Lucy began, but her mother interrupted.

'That was Joey on the phone.' The room fell silent. 'Aunty Dot's taken a turn for the worse.'

'Is she in hospital?' asked Lucy.

'She won't go. I told Joey it's a good sign that she's still being as stubborn as ever, but …'

'Can't they make her?' asked Dominic. 'If it's for her own good?'

'Not unless she loses mental capacity to decide for herself,' Bernie told him. 'And even then … well, she's made it pretty clear that she thinks they ought to prioritise younger people. She told me very definitely that she didn't want to take up a ventilator that could have been used for someone with their whole life in front of them.'

'Do you think she's going to die?' Lucy asked in her usual direct way.

'I hope not, but …,' Bernie sighed. 'Well, she *is* over a hundred. It's been on the cards for the last twenty years.'

'This seems like a particularly nasty way to go, though,' Ibrahim commented.

There was a long silence.

'I'd better ring Dad,' Dominic said at last.

Lucy broke the connection and the four young faces disappeared from Jonah's screen. He twisted his neck to look up at Bernie.

'Are you OK?'

'Yes. Well, no. I don't know.' She sighed again. 'I always knew she can't go on for ever, but somehow it's difficult to imagine her not being there. It's silly really. It's not as if I bothered to see her much since … well ever since I came up to Oxford, I suppose; but I always knew she was there. And now …'

12. THE BEGINNING OF THE END

Jonah worked flat out the next day, determined to finish writing his story of the "death at the demo", as he described it. Everyone felt a new sense of urgency and the need to *do something* for Aunty Dot before it was too late. While her friend sat in his room dictating his memoirs, Bernie sorted through old photographs from her parents' album, hunting for pictures from her childhood in Liverpool.

'This is their wedding,' she said to Peter, holding the album up so that he could see it while he chopped carrots for a stew. 'Aunty Dot was chief bridesmaid. Mum didn't have any sisters or cousins, so she chose Dad's sister instead.'

Peter looked down at the faded black-and-white picture, curling a little and going brown at the edges. He saw a group of people standing on the steps of a redbrick building, which he recognised as the Catholic church in Toxteth that Bernie had taken them to when they visited Liverpool a few years earlier. The groom smiled self-consciously as he held the hand of his bride. He was wearing the baggy trousers of the era with a prominent crease down the centre of each leg and large turn-ups. His bride, clutching a posy of flowers in her other hand, looked equally nervous.

Peering closer, Peter examined the faces of the two other young people in the picture. The Best Man looked very similar to the groom: one of Bernie's many uncles on her father's side, no doubt. And yes! The other woman was undoubtedly Dot. Her hair was thicker and darker and she stood upright with no need for the support of a stick, but there was that familiar look of determination on her face and those same penetrating eyes.

'I've been on to the Home,' Bernie told him, 'and the manager has promised that someone will help her with her iPad this evening. I thought she might like to see some of these. There's one of my christening too. She was my godmother as well as my aunty.'

'I should think Lucy would be interested in those too,' Peter remarked. 'Has she seen them before?'

'No. I'd forgotten I'd got this album. It was hidden away in a trunk of Dad's things that I brought down to Oxford when he died and never looked at again. I only thought of it when Jonah started talking about how he *must* finish his book so that Dot would know the end of the story, and it brought home to me that there soon won't be anyone left who remembers my childhood. Well, I suppose there's still Joey. God willing, he'll be around for a good few years yet. But it's not the same. I mean, he's my generation, only fifteen months older than me. That must be him here!' Bernie pointed at another of the photographs. 'And that's Aunty Rose holding him. He can only have been a few weeks old.'

'Any chance of a cup of tea?' They both swung round at the sound of Jonah's voice. He had glided silently into the kitchen in his electric wheelchair. 'All this dictating makes my throat dry.'

'I'll put the kettle on,' Bernie said at once.

'I've nearly finished the rough draft. I've sent a chunk off to Ibrahim and Dom to edit. Lucy and Mariam have said they'll all pitch in to get it done by lunchtime. By then, I hope I'll have the last section to send to them, and then this afternoon I can tidy up the stuff I've just emailed to them. I'd be grateful if one of you could give it a read-through too, before Dot hears it. I don't want her to get the impression I'm illiterate!'

'Yes, of course.' Bernie smiled. She understood that this was Jonah's final gift to a woman whom he liked and admired, and he wanted it to be as close to perfect as he could make it. Was this really the end of the road for Aunty Dot? If not quite the end, she certainly seemed to be getting to the part where the tarmacked road gives way to a muddy track. Soon the track would narrow to a path and then the path would gradually become more indistinct before petering out altogether. Please God let it not be alone and in pain, fighting for breath.

No rest for the wicked, as they say, and there is certainly very little rest for police officers during a murder enquiry. The next day was Sunday, but Richard and I were both on duty. I'm sure that Richard had already made his plans, but he waited to reveal them until I had been given the opportunity to voice my opinion on what we should do next.

'I reckon it has to be between Wendy and Niamh,' I told him confidently over an early morning cup of tea in his office. 'The stables are the most likely source of the ketamine, and either of them could've got hold of some from there.'

'The Brothertons were all very clear that neither of them knew the combination,' Richard pointed out.

'But they admitted that it had been the same for years. Wendy could easily have watched when one of the others opened the door and memorised the numbers. So could Niamh. Or she could have taken some without going into the store room at all. Don't you remember? They said she was very interested in that operation they did while she was staying. She could've taken some from the stuff they got out to anaesthetise the horse with. You must need an awful lot more to sedate a horse than a human!'

'OK. Let's suppose one out of Wendy and Niamh took some ketamine from the stables and brought it to Oxford. What then? Did they give it to Sudbury because he'd asked for it? Or did they keep it ready to inject him with it at an opportune moment?'

I thought hard. I wanted to make a good impression and show that I was capable of weighing up the evidence and coming to conclusions.

'Everyone who knew him was absolutely definite that he didn't take drugs and wouldn't have done if they were offered to him,' I said at last. 'Some of them could've been just saying that because they didn't like to criticise someone who can't defend himself; or they could be seeing him through rose-coloured spectacles; but even the people who didn't like him very much were in agreement on that point.'

'So you think it's more likely that someone else injected him than that he did it himself.'

'Yes, sir. And there's the lack of fingerprints on the syringe too. It makes sense that the murderer wiped it before dropping it into his pocket. If he took the drug himself, why would he bother?'

'So your theory is that either Niamh or Wendy took some ketamine from the stables and injected Sudbury with it?'

'Yes, sir.'

Richard appeared to be waiting for me to say some more, so I marshalled my thoughts and continued.

'But we don't have any evidence to tell us which of them it was. Niamh *seems* devoted to him and genuinely upset at his death; whereas Wendy clearly didn't like him and, if anything, is glad he's dead. On the other hand, Wendy doesn't really have a motive for killing him, and Niamh could have – if she's not being frank with us about their relationship. And,' I added with sudden inspiration, 'she could be so upset *because* it was her fault. If the enormity of what she's done didn't strike her until after he was dead. Or – or maybe she didn't intend to kill him, just to send him on some sort of hallucinogenic trip.'

'Very well argued. You're right: we need more evidence. So what do you suggest we do to find it?'

I thought for a few moments. I was still desperately trying to impress a man whose work I admired and who could have influence over my future career.

'I'd like to get some more background on Niamh O'Halloran,' I said at last. 'I don't think we know enough about her and her relationship with Timothy Sudbury. I think we ought to speak to her parents. They only live in Headington, so it would be easy enough to go out there and see what they can tell us. Mrs O'Halloran knew all about Niamh's pregnancy scare. Maybe there's more that she could tell us about their relationship.'

I suspect that Richard already intended to visit the O'Hallorans, but he allowed me to think that it was entirely my proposal that led to us pulling up outside a large house in Headington shortly before noon. I'd been keen to rush off straight away, but Richard pointed out that lots of people have a lie-in on a Sunday and we might not be welcome.

The door was opened by a rather rotund, balding man in his late fifties or early sixties with a round, cheerful face and twinkling blue eyes. When Richard explained why we were there, he welcomed us in, speaking in a soft southern-Irish brogue. It was so strong as to be almost comical, and I wondered briefly if it could be a deliberate affectation.

There was a delightful smell of roasting lamb pervading the hall and I began to feel very hungry as he led us into the lounge and invited us to sit down.

'Siobhan's in the kitchen,' he told us. 'I'll just get her. Do make yourselves at home. I'll not be long.'

We settled ourselves on a comfortable settee upholstered in green velvet and I got out my notebook and pencil ready for the interview. Looking round the room, I noted that one wall was entirely lined with book cases crammed full of what looked like weighty academic tomes. Against the centre of the opposite wall, there was a small rectangular table covered with a white, lace-edged cloth. A black Bible lay on it, open at the Psalms. There was a small statue of the Virgin Mary with a candle in a glass dish next to it on one side and a necklace of beads on the other. On the wall above, a crucifix was flanked by icons of two saints that I didn't recognise. I concluded that at least one member of this household must be a devout Catholic.

'Good morning officers!' Siobhan O'Halloran greeted us, wiping her hands on her apron as she came in. 'You're lucky to find us in: we've only just got back from Mass. We attend St Cyprian's. You may have passed it on the way. It's just along the street.'

'Yes,' Richard replied. 'I know the church. I live not far from here myself. I'm sorry to disturb you at the weekend, but we need to ask you a few questions I'm afraid. We're hoping you may be able to tell us a bit more about Timothy Sudbury's relationship with your daughter. We're trying to get a picture of his state of mind on the day that he died, and of course how he was getting on with Niamh must be a big part of that.'

'Are you suggesting he killed himself?' asked Niamh's father.

'Well,' Richard answered, 'we know that he died from a combination of ketamine and alcohol in his blood. What we don't know for certain is whether he administered the drug to himself and, if so, why? If he was feeling depressed – perhaps because he'd fallen out with his girl – then an overdose of a powerful sedative might seem like an easy way to go.'

'As far as we knew, they were doing fine,' Siobhan said at once. 'They came to lunch the Sunday before and everything seemed absolutely fine between them, didn't it Joe?'

'Yes,' her husband agreed.

'So, there was no hint that either of them was getting cold feet about marrying?' Richard probed.

'Well, I did notice that Timothy didn't seem that keen on discussing dates for the wedding,' Siobhan admitted after a short pause, 'but I assumed he was just being cautious. He said he wanted to get settled into his job in Leicester before fixing up anything definite, which seemed reasonable enough to me.'

'And how did you both feel about having him as a son-in-law?'

'We-ell,' Siobhan hesitated.

'I'll not lie to you,' Joseph intervened. 'He wasn't exactly the man we'd have chosen, but he seemed a nice enough boy and Niamh liked him. So we'd have made him welcome.'

'There's no point being heavy-handed with young people over who they choose,' his wife backed him up. 'We learned that early on with our eldest. Parental disapproval only makes them all the more determined to go their own way. And it turned out we were wrong about Jean. She's been a good wife to Patrick.'

'Our eldest, Patrick, married a protestant from County Down,' Joseph explained. 'We made the mistake of telling him what we thought of mixed marriages and he said in that case they'd be married in her church and he'd go over to Church of Ireland himself.'

'And did he?' I asked. My own father, a Baptist pastor, was scathing in his opinion of "popery" and I could imagine that his reaction had I stated my intention of marrying a Catholic might have been similarly hostile.

'In the end, Jean worked it all out,' Siobhan smiled. 'They both work at the new University of Ulster in

Coleraine. That's how they met. It's supposed to be a place where everyone is treated equally, protestant and catholic alike. The Troubles were just starting at that time – which was another reason we'd been hoping he'd move back to the South – and the university was trying to be a … well there were lots of people there who wanted to build bridges if you like. It was full of young go-ahead people who wanted to change things for the better. Anyway, Jean managed to persuade two of the chaplains there to marry them in a joint service – Catholic *and* Church of Ireland.'

'Why wouldn't Timothy have been your choice for Niamh?' Richard asked. I think perhaps he wasn't impressed by my question having prompted this digression.

'Naturally, we'd have preferred a Catholic.' Siobhan's reply seemed straightforward enough, but somehow I felt that she was holding something back.

'And he was an arrogant young man,' Joseph added. 'He thought very highly of himself and he seemed to me to be taking Niamh for granted. But I daresay he'd have grown out of it.'

'One of his housemates told us that he had a habit if flirting with other women,' Richard informed him. 'Did you see any evidence of that?'

'We only really met him when Niamh brought him round here,' Siobhan replied. 'So we wouldn't. She never mentioned anything like that.'

'It could just be the way he has with him,' Joseph added. I got the impression that he was trying hard to be charitable towards the lad, whom he hadn't greatly liked. 'He was always throwing compliments around: telling Siobhan what a pretty dress she had on and how much he liked her cooking and that sort of thing. Some people might take it as flirting.'

'I can't say I was ever convinced he cared quite as much about Niamh as she did about him,' Siobhan confided, 'but then, we're biased. I don't suppose any man would appear good enough for our only little girl!'

'Your daughter and her flatmate seem to be very close,' Richard observed in an abrupt change of subject.

'Yes,' Siobhan nodded. 'Wendy's been a tower of strength for Niamh these last few weeks – ever since … well … you know!' She inclined her head towards me and I gathered that she was unsure whether I knew about Niamh's "false alarm".

'I'm afraid I had to record what you told me in the case files,' Richard admitted. 'It's unlikely, but it could be pertinent to the case. However, I can assure you that it won't go any further. All our records are strictly confidential and all of our officers are aware that they mustn't discuss any case with anyone outside the police force.'

He glanced towards me and I had a momentary pang of conscience over having got Margaret involved. Had I revealed anything to her that I should have kept to myself? But then, she was in a confidential profession herself *and* she was already involved because she'd examined the victim and pronounced him dead. And often our investigations depended on other people saying things to us that were perhaps a little indiscreet, so didn't that sort of thing cut both ways …?

'How did Wendy get on with Timothy, do you know?' My thoughts were interrupted by Richard's next question. I pulled myself together and sat, pencil poised, waiting for the O'Hallorans to respond.

'Well, you saw for yourself, didn't you?' Siobhan exclaimed. 'I don't know how it was between them when he was alive, but after he was dead, she certainly didn't hold back in telling everyone how much she despised him.'

'She struck me as a very opinionated young woman,' Joseph commented. 'Very black-and-white. With everything, she's either passionately in favour or passionately against. Take the nuclear question, for example. She's absolutely obsessed with the idea that having cruise missiles in Berkshire will lead to Armageddon.'

'She's very intense,' Siobhan agreed. 'I did worry at one point that she was having an undue influence over Niamh. Niamh never likes to upset anyone, so she tends to go along with whatever other people want. I did worry a bit about her getting so involved in this CND and Greenham Common stuff, but give Wendy her due, she never let it interfere with their work and she has been *very* attentive to Niamh since ... well ever since her little scare and now with Timothy's death. Do you really think someone killed him deliberately?'

'We don't know. That's why we have to ask so many questions,' Richard told her. 'We know that he was killed with a drug that is often used on horses. What we don't know is whether he took it himself or someone else injected him with it. And either way, we don't know if the intention was to kill or just to send him on some sort of hallucinogenic trip.'

'A horse medicine?' asked Joseph sharply. 'Is that why you're so interested in Wendy? Do you think that *she* did it?'

'Is there any reason why she might have wanted to?' Richard came back at once.

'Not that I know of,' Joseph replied equally quickly. 'It's just that I know her family keep horses and I wondered if that was what you thought.'

'I'm sure she would never have done anything to harm Timothy,' Siobhan said earnestly. 'She knew how fond of him Niamh was, and she was ... she *does* care so much for Niamh. She'd never have done anything to upset her.'

'You said that your daughter doesn't like to say "no" to people.' Richard looked solemnly at Siobhan and their eyes met. 'Is there any possibility that she would have agreed to get some ketamine for Timothy if he asked her to?'

'No! She would never get involved in that sort of thing! And anyway, how could she? She wouldn't know where to start!'

'There were supplies of it at the stables where she went to stay with Wendy last summer. If Timothy had asked her to bring some back for him, do you think she might have obliged?'

'No! It would have been stealing. Niamh would never ever do that. And that's quite apart from the fact that she'd never have got involved in drug-taking or anything of that sort.'

'No, of course not.' Richard's voice was apologetic. 'I'm sorry I had to ask. It's just that we do have to explore every possibility, however unlikely.'

'And *somebody* must have got hold of the drug,' I put in. I was trying to be helpful, but in retrospect I'm not sure that I wouldn't have been better keeping quiet.

'Not our daughter,' Joseph said firmly.

Richard brought the conversation to an end shortly after that. He apologised again for any upset that his questioning had caused and assured them that Niamh was not under suspicion. I rather doubted the wisdom of that assurance, since I was becoming increasingly convinced that Niamh was the most likely out of our list of suspects to have been responsible for Timothy Sudbury's death – either intentionally or through having supplied the drug to him at his own request.

* * *

'You're not stopping there, are you?' demanded Dominic, as Jonah paused and looked up at the webcam.

'No, of course not. I've got one more chapter to go, and that's all ready, thanks to you all pulling together to get it finished. I just thought maybe we could do with a break before the final dénouement. Especially Dot – and Carys. How're you doing there? Do you need to give your arm a rest? It must get tiring holding the iPad like that.'

The rectangle in which Dot's pale face was displayed became a blur and then another face came into focus. This one had a protective eye shield and a mask covering nose and mouth giving it a strange, science-fiction appearance. It was Carys, the care worker who was assigned to look after Dot during the day. She smiled and nodded.

'It's fine,' she assured him. 'I've been resting my arm from time to time while you've been talking. We can listen without watching the screen all the time.'

'And what about you, Aunty?' Bernie called from behind Jonah. 'Do you need a rest before Jonah goes on?'

There was a long pause. Everyone waited, listening to Dot's laboured breathing as she struggled to draw enough air into her inflamed lungs to speak. When her answer came it was husky and there was a sort of whistling sound beneath the words, which made them difficult to understand.

'I … *am* …resting.' She leaned her head back on her pillow and opened her mouth to draw in more air. They could hear it rasping in her throat as she prepared to speak again. 'I'm … in … bed … aren't I?'

'Here! Have some water.' The watchers in Oxford and Liverpool were treated to a view of the ceiling of Dot's room as Carys laid the iPad down on the bed so that she had her hands free to hold a plastic beaker of water up to Dot's dry, feverish lips. They heard various sucking and wheezing sounds as she took in a little water through a spout in the lid of the cup, in between more gasps for air.

'I reckon Niamh took the ketamine from the stables,' Dominic said, making conversation to cover the sounds coming from his aunt's room. She would be embarrassed to think that everyone was waiting for her and listening to her noisy attempts at both drinking and breathing. 'But she could've been getting it for anyone. She sounds like the sort of person that never likes to say "no" to anybody who asks her for something.'

'You mean, if Faith, for example, asked her to get her some, she'd just do it, without asking any questions?' asked Lucy sceptically. 'It doesn't sound very likely to me!'

'I agree,' Ibrahim backed her up. 'If Niamh took the drug, it was for Timothy: either because he asked her for it or because she intended to use it on him.'

'And if she injected him with it, I bet she didn't mean to kill him,' Lucy added. 'I don't suppose she knew that alcohol made it more dangerous. I certainly didn't.'

'But, suppose the killer *did* know,' Mariam put in quietly. 'Suppose whoever it was did their homework first. If you wanted to kill someone, you'd need to read up on it, wouldn't you? So that you used the right dose and that sort of thing. Who was it who was responsible for Timothy having so much to drink before the march started?'

Nobody could remember. Ibrahim started flicking back through the pages of Jonah's book, which he had stored on his laptop, searching for the students' accounts of their lunch party.

'Didn't someone say something about winning a bottle of wine in a raffle or something?' hazarded Dominic.

'And there was that bottle of vodka that Timothy was supposed to carry about with him,' contributed Lucy.

Carys interrupted their debate. 'I think you'd better go on with reading your book. Miss Fazakerley will need to sleep soon.'

* * *

Our next port of call was the shared house in New Hinksey. Diane and John were there alone. I forget where they said that Faith had got to. We sat around the dining table drinking coffee and eating digestive biscuits. Richard tried to draw them out, asking general questions about university life, the progress of their studies and the changing relationships between members of their social group.

John came across as a pleasant, easy-going young man – quite unlike his girlfriend who was forthright in her criticism of Timothy and dismissive of Niamh.

'He was a selfish bastard,' she declared. 'He cared for nobody but himself, and he expected everyone else to dance attention on him and worship the ground he trod on – especially if they happened to be female! And the worst part of it was that loads of them did! I don't know how Faith put up with him for so long. And then Niamh! I can't understand how she got taken in by him. Surely Faith must have told her … but I suppose she thought he'd changed.'

'Told her what, exactly?' asked Richard.

'Just the way he treated her. Standing her up. Taking her for granted. Talking about her behind her back – bragging about what they'd been doing together. You know the sort of thing.'

I thought of some of the banter that went on in the locker room at the police station. I could well imagine Sergeant Adams, for example, entertaining the lads with graphic accounts of his encounters with members of the opposite sex. "Of course, they can never resist a man in a uniform," he would say with that greasy smile of his, before describing some sordid encounter in the back of a police van while he was "checking her credentials".

Richard gradually brought the conversation round to the subject of Wendy and her relationship with Niamh. At first, Diane was more interested in giving us more evidence of Timothy's bad character. According to her, while he was supposedly going out with Faith, he attempted to get off with Wendy. Wendy wasn't having any of it, which was why he turned his attention to Niamh, who was far too trusting and naïve to suspect him of duplicity. Wendy had tried to warn her, but she was taken in by his flattery and believed him when he told her that everything had been over between him and Faith for some time.

But Wendy and Niamh remained good friends?

Oh yes! In fact, Wendy had become all the more protective of Niamh after she hitched up with Timothy.

John's take on that was slightly different. He saw Wendy's protectiveness as somewhat overbearing. In his opinion, Wendy liked being in charge and she wasn't keen on losing her influence over Niamh in favour of Timothy, who was, after all, "a mere man" as John put it.

Richard suggested that the friends might all have been drawn together by a common interest in nuclear disarmament. Diane laughed at this idea. She confirmed that Niamh had only rallied to the cause at Wendy's urging. As for Timothy! He cared for nothing and nobody except himself, but he knew a bandwagon when he saw one and had obviously calculated that jumping on it might ingratiate him with certain female company.

* * *

A loud beeping sound made Jonah break off his narration and look towards the array of rectangles on his computer screen, trying to work out where the noise was coming from.

'I'm sorry. I'll just have to get that.' Dot's face appeared to tilt alarmingly as Carys reached for her mobile phone and in doing so joggled the iPad. Everyone waited as she conducted a muffled and one-sided conversation. 'I'm sorry,' she repeated at last, 'one of the other residents has had a fall and they need me to go and help. I'm afraid that will have to be the end of your video call. I'll just turn the screen round now so that you can all say *goodbye*.'

Dot's face appeared on the screen again and she moved her head weakly, trying to focus on their faces on her screen. She smiled and seemed to be trying to speak, but no sound came. Everyone else called out cheerful goodbyes and waved their hands. Then Carys took over again, giving them an assurance that she would help Dot to join them for another videoconference the next day, before switching off the iPad. For a moment or two, everybody watched in silence as the rectangle representing Dot went black and then disappeared.

'What do we do now?' asked Dominic at last. 'I mean: does Jonah go on and finish his story or do we wait until tomorrow so that Aunty Dot can hear it too?'

'I vote we wait,' said Lucy at once. 'It's not fair us hearing it when Aunty Dot can't, and she enjoys it so much.'

* * *

'Do you think you could record the rest of your book?' Bernie asked Jonah as she and Peter prepared him for bed that evening. 'I've got a bad feeling about how things are going to turn out with Aunty Dot and I can't help thinking that she may not be able to join us on tomorrow's video call. If you made an audio recording, they could play it to her even if she's in hospital.'

Jonah opened his mouth to make a joking remark about wild horses not being able to drag the obstinate old lady into hospital. Then, seeing Bernie's sombre expression, he changed his mind. 'Yes, of course. That's a good idea. I'll do it first thing tomorrow, if you can set me up with the mike and everything.'

'Thanks.' Bernie pulled the duvet up over Jonah's slight form – very different from the muscular police officer whom she had first met at Richard's funeral all those years ago – and checked the settings on his special bed to ensure that it would tilt from side to side at intervals during the night to prevent pressure sores developing. 'I have a horrid feeling that she hasn't got long to go, and I'd hate her not to get to find out who done it!'

'Don't write her off quite yet,' Peter commented as he gathered up Jonah's discarded clothes and bundled them into the linen basket that stood in a corner of the room. 'You never know, she may surprise us all.'

'She's a tough old bird,' Jonah agreed. Then catching Bernie's eye, he added, 'but I know, she's a hundred and one and she's got a virus that kills older people disproportionately and the hospitals don't have enough beds for everyone ...'

'And she'd rather it was her than someone with their whole life ahead of them,' Bernie added in a low voice. 'She's ... she wouldn't want us to be clinging on to her, instead of ... It's just going to be so strange without her – even though we hardly ever see her anyway! Oh well! No point getting in a state about something that hasn't happened yet.'

She leaned across and kissed Jonah on the cheek. 'Good night. I'll sort out the mike for you first thing in the morning.'

13. THE END

The case conference that we held that Monday morning wasn't a particularly cheerful affair. Ten days after Timothy Sudbury's death, our attempts to establish who killed him seemed to be running into a brick wall. I was convinced that we now knew where the ketamine had come from, and Richard agreed that the Brotherton racing stables were the most likely source; but was it Wendy or Niamh who had taken some and brought it to Oxford? And, whoever brought it, why had they done so? If it was with the intention of killing Timothy then the murder must have been planned several weeks before it was executed. That was rather strange behaviour if it was a crime of passion.

Or were we wrong in thinking that there had been any evil intent? Had Timothy asked one of them – most likely Niamh – to get it for him, because he wanted to experiment with it? Despite the protestations from everyone who knew him that Timothy would never have considered taking drugs, Mac thought that was the most likely explanation.

'I know he's supposed to have been this clean-living, health fanatic,' he argued, 'but the other thing that everyone seems to agree about is that he was an arrogant bastard. In my opinion, he would have thought that he could take drugs without any ill-effects and without getting addicted. He sounds the sort who say they can stop any time – only they never do! I'd lay money he asked Niamh to get some for him and she was so besotted with him that she went ahead and did it.'

'But why on earth would he take it during the march?' I still wanted it to be murder, rather than an accidental overdose. 'Surely he'd have chosen a more suitable time and place – such as back home in his room? And why did he wipe the syringe clean afterwards?'

'Maybe Niamh got it for him and someone else got hold of it?' Mac suggested, obviously reluctant to give up on his theory. 'Any of them could've known he'd got it. I wouldn't put it past him to go round boasting about it.'

'The thing is though, Mac,' Peter remonstrated gently, 'if Niamh got the stuff for Timothy and then someone else used it against him, I'd expect her to have admitted to what she did by now. In fact, even if she thought he'd taken it himself after she gave it to him, I think she'd be having a crisis of conscience and coming to us to confess.'

'What about Wendy then?' I asked. 'She had the best chance of getting hold of the ketamine and we now have a good idea where the syringe came from too.'

'Oh?' Mac looked across at me enquiringly. 'Where's that then?'

'Wendy had a riding accident while Niamh was staying there during the summer and she was prescribed painkilling injections.'

'Which Niamh used to help her with,' added Richard. 'If we accuse her of killing Timothy, she may say that Niamh took the syringe away with her when she went home. In any case, it's a common enough type; anyone could have got hold of one. Without any fingerprints, we've no way of proving who used it.'

'And where's your motive?' demanded Mac. 'Why would Wendy care enough about Timothy to want to kill him? OK, she despised the man, but he was leaving Oxford anyway in a few weeks and she'd never have to meet him again!'

'Except at Niamh's wedding and every time she visited her friend,' I pointed out with sudden inspiration. 'What if she was so obsessed with the idea that Timothy was the world's worst creep that she just couldn't bear the idea of Niamh marrying him? Everyone agrees that she gets passionate about things; what if one of those things was the idea that marrying Timothy would be disastrous for her friend – her best friend – the only real friend she's ever had, according to her Mum?'

'I still think-,' Mac began, but he was interrupted by the ringing of the telephone on Richard's desk. He silenced us all with a look as he took the call. We listened intently to the one-sided conversation, trying to work out what was going on.

'When? ... And she's still there now? ... So, when can we ...? I see. ... Niamh O'Halloran? ... And her parents too? ... Right! Thanks. I'll come over right away.'

He turned to look at us. We gazed back expectantly. It was clear that something interesting had occurred involving Niamh.

'It's Wendy Brotherton,' he told us. 'She's taken an overdose.'

'Ketamine?' I blurted out.

'No. Paracetamol – and sleeping tablets. It looks like a suicide attempt. She's in the Radcliffe. Niamh found her and rang for an ambulance, which took her to Casualty. She's there now, and so are Mr and Mrs Brotherton. Peter! I want you to go round to the flat and see what you can find there. There's a uniformed officer at the scene who'll let you in. MacBride! Get over to New Hinksey and tell her friends what's happened, and see if they know anything about why she could've done it.'

I waited impatiently, wondering what job I would be assigned. I could hardly believe my luck when-

* * *

Jonah broke off in mid-sentence, distracted by the ringing of the telephone in the hall. He heard Bernie's feet descending the stairs to answer it. Straining his ears, he heard her opening words, 'Hello? Oh, hi Joey! Any news?'

The door from Jonah's private lair opened silently at a wireless command transmitted from the keypad on the arm of his wheelchair. Gliding into the doorway, intent on listening in on the conversation, he saw Peter on the opposite side of the hall watching from the door of the lounge.

'Thanks for letting us know. Have you told Dom and Lucy? ... OK ... Yes ... Yes of course ... Bye for now.'

Bernie replaced the receiver and looked round at them both. 'Aunty Dot's taken a turn for the worse,' she told them. 'The Home's rung for an ambulance to take her to hospital, but they said it could be an hour or more before there's one free.'

For what seemed like an age nobody moved and nobody spoke. There seemed to be nothing to do and nothing to say. Then Bernie took a deep breath and let it out in a slow sigh.

'I don't know about you lot,' she said, 'but I could do with a cup of tea.'

Then, without waiting for any response, she headed off for the kitchen. Peter followed her.

By the time Jonah had manoeuvred his chair round the tight corners into the room, Bernie was busy getting out china mugs from one of the wall cupboards and spooning loose tea into a large brown teapot. Peter emerged from the walk-in larder carrying a square cake tin.

'I made these while you were changing the beds,' he told Bernie. 'I thought we might need them.'

He set the tin down on the table and took off the lid. Bernie looked in and saw about a dozen butterfly cakes piled carefully to avoid smearing the cake papers holding the top layer with the generous portions of butter cream adorning those below.

'Thank you, Peter. I'll get us some plates.'

The kettle boiled and clicked off. Bernie filled the teapot and brought it over to the table. Then she turned back to fetch a brightly-coloured knitted tea cosy, which hung on a hook on the larder door. As she pulled it down over the pot she murmured, 'Aunty Dot knitted this ages ago. She made it for me when I came up to Oxford forty-odd years back. Whoever would have thought it would've lasted all this time!'

She put the pot down on the table and busied herself pouring milk into two mugs and Jonah's special plastic cup with the lid and straw to enable him to drink independently.

'How're you getting on with your recording?' she asked, making conversation to cover the awkward silence.

'I've done about half of that final chapter. It's taking longer than I expected. Somehow, whenever I'm speaking into the microphone, I start stumbling over the words the way I never do when I'm reading out loud normally. And once I get stuck on a phrase it can take ten or a dozen tries to get it right. Sometimes I've even had to go back to the top of the page and take a run at it, hoping I don't remember how tricky it is when I get to it. And then there's all the cleaning up and editing to do. It's a bit of a slog, I'm afraid.'

'I could do that for you,' Bernie offered, pouring the tea. 'Just send the raw audio files over to my computer and I'll process them for you. It'll give me something to keep my mind occupied while I wait for Joey to ring again.'

* * *

I waited impatiently, wondering what job I would be assigned. I could hardly believe my luck when Richard turned to me and told me to get my coat because we were going over to the hospital to talk to Niamh and, hopefully, also to Wendy herself.

To my delight, when we got there we found Margaret in conversation with Niamh. Mr and Mrs Brotherton were there too, looking very anxious and upset.

'With paracetamol poisoning, it's important that we know how long ago the tablets were taken and how many,' Margaret was saying to Niamh. 'What can you tell us about that?'

'We-ell,' Niamh seemed to be thinking hard. 'As far as how many tablets it was, it must have been nearly 200. It was the bottle that we kept in the bathroom for either of us to use, but I don't think we'd needed any. As far as I remember, it was still full – or almost full, anyway.'

'Good. That's useful for us to know. And the time?'

'I don't know. I'm sorry.'

'That's OK. Don't worry if you can't remember, but could you just think back. When did you see her last – before you found her unconscious?'

'This morning, at breakfast. We had breakfast together as usual, and then I went out to check some references in the Bod. Wendy said she was going to work on her thesis in her room for a bit. She asked me to pick up some bread for lunch on the way back.'

'And what time was it you found her?' Margaret pressed her gently.

It was at that point that Niamh spotted us approaching. Seeing her staring towards us, Margaret also looked our way. I could tell that the Brothertons, too, had noticed us. George Brotherton moved as if to get up, but his wife pushed him back into his seat. They both watched intently as Richard strode calmly across the room and addressed Margaret. He knew her from previous encounters in the emergency department, most recently of course though her having been the doctor who had confirmed Timothy Sudbury's death. He also knew her personally and had been instrumental, in a round-about way, in our having become engaged two years previously[19], but this was strictly professional.

'Dr Hulme! May we have a word?'

She looked round and smiled towards us. She liked Richard. 'Of course, Chief Inspector. What can I do for you?'

'You're treating Miss Brotherton? How is she?'

'Well, Dr Milner's in charge; but I saw her when she came in. We don't know yet how she is, because it all depends on how much of the paracetamol got into her system before we intervened. We've pumped out her stomach, but ... well, with paracetamol, there's not an awful lot you can do once it's in the bloodstream. So, we've got to hope that she was found before too much of it was absorbed. That's what I'm just trying to ascertain from Miss O'Halloran here. She was the one who found her.'

She turned back to address Niamh.

'Now, you were about to tell me what time it was that you found her.'

'Yes.' Niamh glanced round nervously. I suppose she was assimilating the fact that two police officers were taking an interest in her friend's condition. 'Let me see ... I suppose we finished breakfast around half past eight, and then I cycled into town. When I got to the Bod, I found myself a place to sit and work. I got my things out of my bag and put them on the desk, ready to make notes. And then I discovered I hadn't brought the list of references that I'd made last night. I suppose I spent a few minutes hunting through my bag for them before I convinced myself that they must still be in the flat. Then

---

[19] You can read about this in chapter 2 of *Changing Scenes of Life* © 2015, ISBN: 978-1-911083-09-2

there was nothing for it but to go back to get them; so, I packed up my bag again and came back. And that was when ....' She gulped and put her hand over her mouth.

'That was when you found Wendy?' Margaret asked gently, putting her hand out and resting it gently on Niamh's arm. 'Less than an hour after you left her?'

'It must've been about that,' Niamh nodded. 'I just popped my head round the door of her room, to let her know why I'd come back and that I was going out again right away, and ... and ... and there she was!'

'And she was already unconscious?' Margaret probed.

'Yes. She was lying on her back on the bed. She had all her clothes on – even her shoes – but her eyes were closed and she looked as if she was asleep. It seemed so strange when she'd told me she had lots of work to do on her thesis. I thought she must've felt ill and decided to lie down for a bit, but then – then I saw the pill bottles.'

Margaret looked down at her watch. 'That can't have been earlier than nine fifteen – probably later – and now it's still only the right side of ten thirty. And you're sure she was OK when you went out at eight thirty?'

Niamh nodded.

'That's great! You've done splendidly, calling the ambulance so quickly. I'll have to go now: Dr Milner needs to know about this right away. Now, I can't make any promises,' Margaret added, looking round at Mr and Mrs Brotherton, 'but I think she's going to be OK. Most of the paracetamol must've still been in her stomach when we got her here, and any that did get into the blood stream won't have reached her liver yet. Now, I'm sorry – I must go.'

'Miss O'Halloran?' Richard went over and sat down next to Niamh. 'I know it's difficult for you and you've probably already told everything to the doctors, but do you think *I* could ask you a few questions now?'

Niamh nodded and dabbed her eyes with a tissue. I sat down on another of the plastic-covered seats that were dotted about the waiting area and took out my notebook.

'You said just now that, when you came back from the library, you found Miss Brotherton lying on her bed, fully clothed. Have you ever known her to do that before?'

'No.' Niamh shook her head.

'And you mentioned some bottles of pills. That was a bottle of 200 paracetamol tablets and what else?'

'Her sleeping tablets. She broke her collarbone a couple of months ago and she had trouble sleeping because of the pain. I didn't know she still had them. I thought she'd finished with them ages ago.'

'And the bottle was empty? Do you have any idea how many tablets were in it?'

'No. I just assumed she'd finished them before coming back to Oxford this term.'

'OK. That's great. You're doing very well. Now, can you tell me how she seemed this morning – in herself?'

'What do you mean?'

'Did she seem happy? Sad? Was she worried about anything, do you think?'

'I don't know. She just seemed normal, I suppose. I didn't really think about it.'

'Did she leave a note at all?'

'Not that I noticed. There wasn't anything on the bedside cabinet. I think I'd have seen it if there had been, because that's where the pill bottles were and I looked at them to see what they were.'

'That's fine. Don't worry about it. Our officers will look for it. I'm afraid they'll have to search her room.' Richard looked round apologetically at Wendy's parents, who nodded their acquiescence. 'And what about you? Had you noticed any changes in her demeanour recently? Did she seem anxious at all or upset about anything?'

'No.' Both parents shook their heads.

'But then, we haven't seen her for three weeks,' Norma added. 'She came home for the weekend. It was three weeks ago, wasn't it George?'

'You mean the eleventh and twelfth?' I asked eagerly, after doing some quick calculations in my head. That was the weekend immediately before the demonstration and Timothy Sudbury's untimely demise.

'Yes. That's right.' George Brotherton confirmed. 'It was the day after Hebridean Sunset and Fanny Crosby came in first and second at Doncaster.'

I looked triumphantly across at Richard, but he stared back impassively, evidently determined not to give any hint that the date of Wendy's visit to the stables could be significant.

'And does she have any history of depression?' he asked looking towards Mrs Brotherton. 'Perhaps when she was a teenager? It's often a difficult time – boyfriends and that sort of thing.'

'No. I wouldn't say she was ever a particularly happy child,' Norma admitted. 'Not carefree the way Keith always was. She took everything too seriously for that. She always had some cause she was involved in. She was only about twelve when she went on her first demonstration: trying to stop the M4 motorway being extended beyond Reading. But she was never depressed! She always had far too much that she wanted to do to consider ... well, I just can't believe she'd commit suicide!'

'Obviously, we're hoping it won't be long before she'll be able to tell us all about it, but ....' Richard paused. I took it that he was struggling to find suitable words. 'But we can't rule out the possibility that her attempt on her own life is in some way connected with Timothy Sudbury's death.'

'You mean, you think she killed him?' George Brotherton demanded aggressively.

'Oh! I can't believe she'd do anything like that! Niamh gasped, wide-eyed.

'I was thinking more that she might have felt responsible,' Richard answered patiently. 'Timothy's death was caused by his having had an injection of ketamine following the imbibing of a quantity of alcohol. We don't know who was responsible for the ketamine injection: he may well have taken it himself. People do sometimes. It has hallucinogenic properties that some people enjoy. What we do know is that your daughter opened a bottle of wine when Timothy and her other friends were at lunch the day he died. She could have believed that he would still be alive if she hadn't pressed this on him.'

'And I suppose you think that the ketamine came from our stables?' George growled, clearly unconvinced by Richard's explanation.

'We haven't been able to rule out that possibility,' Richard replied smoothly. He turned to address Niamh. 'I'm sorry, Miss O'Halloran, but I do have to ask: did Timothy ask you to get ketamine for him?'

'No.' Niamh shook her head vigorously. 'He didn't ask and I wouldn't have done it if he had. And I don't believe Wendy would have either!'

'Alright.' Richard stood up and shook hands all round. 'I need to go and speak to the doctors now. Thank you for answering my questions, and I hope Wendy makes a full recovery. She's in the best place she could be for that.'

As we walked down the corridor in search of Margaret, I quizzed Richard on what he thought of Wendy's suicide attempt.

'Do you think it was remorse for killing Timothy Sudbury?'

'Possibly.'

'It must mean that she did it, mustn't it?' I persisted.

'It's not proof admissible in court,' Richard replied drily, 'unless she left a note containing a confession. And even then, she could easily retract it.'

'And she could've got the ketamine while she was at home the weekend before,' I went on. 'That makes a whole lot more sense than the idea that Niamh might have taken it, back in July.'

Dr Milner told us that he had given Wendy a sedative and we would not be allowed to speak to her for several hours. The good news was that she was expected to make a full recovery. Niamh's quick action had most likely saved her life. He went on to say that Margaret was waiting for us in the doctors' mess. She had spoken to Wendy in A and E, before she was rushed off to have her stomach pumped, and wanted to tell us about it.

At Richard's bidding, I knocked nervously on the door of the mess. I was relieved when it opened and Margaret's face appeared round it. She smiled when she saw us, and held it wide so that we could enter. We tiptoed in and followed her silently across the room to a corner where three chairs were grouped around a low table. Two young doctors in surgical scrubs stopped their conversation and stared at us as we walked gingerly, trying to look unobtrusive. We sat down and I got out my notebook.

'Thank you for coming,' Margaret said to Richard. 'I don't know if this is important, but I thought you ought to know.'

'Ye-es?' Richard prompted encouragingly.

'We managed to get her to wake up,' Margaret continued, 'but she was very drowsy from the sleeping tablets and we were concentrating on trying to get her to tell us how much paracetamol she'd taken and when, but ... Well, she said something about Niamh going to the police station, and something about a pair of gloves. I don't know if that makes any sense to you?'

'Yes,' I assured her, 'it does. Niamh did come to the station to tell us that Wendy hadn't given us a straight story about throwing something away in a litterbin while they are at the demo. I always *thought* it might be something to do with Timothy's death, and now I'm sure of it!'

'The gloves that she wore to handle the syringe?' Margaret suggested. 'Didn't you say that it didn't have any fingerprints on it?'

'Yes. That's right!' I was feeling very excited now. 'It all fits! Wendy goes home to her parents' stables and pinches some ketamine from their medicine cupboard. She's already got a hypodermic syringe from when she needed painkillers for her collarbone. She fills it with the drug and wipes it clean. Then, while nobody's looking, she puts on the gloves and injects Timothy with it. She pops it into his pocket to make it look as if he did it himself and throws the gloves away in the litterbin on the corner of Pembroke Square. Then she drags Niamh away before he collapses so that nobody will suspect that either of them had anything to do with it.'

'But why?' asked Richard. 'Of all the people we've considered, she seemed to have the least possible motive.'

'This may have nothing at all to do with it,' Margaret said cautiously, 'but there was something else that she said. Or at least I think that was what she was saying. As I said, she was rather rambling and incoherent. She said something about how she'd done everything for Niamh. I don't know what that meant, but she sounded a bit aggrieved – or maybe more disappointed. It was as if … as if Niamh had somehow failed her expectations, but it wasn't clear what those were.'

'Could she have killed Timothy to get back at Niamh?' I suggested.

'That sounds a bit drastic,' Margaret commented. 'I hope your friends wouldn't try to take it out on me if you offended them!'

'OK then,' I conceded, 'maybe it was Niamh's engagement to Timothy that upset Wendy. Do you remember, Sir, the way she kept telling Niamh that he wasn't good enough for her? It was almost as if she thought him dying was a lucky escape for Niamh. Perhaps she killed him to rescue her friend from what *she* thought was a fate worse than death!'

'And now Niamh isn't being suitably grateful?' Margaret murmured thoughtfully. 'Mmmm yes, I suppose that might fit.'

'It's a pity we were too late to find the gloves in the litterbin,' Richard commented. 'That would have been some hard evidence, which is what we're short of in this case. Everything's just circumstantial.'

'Yes,' I agreed. Then a thought suddenly struck me. 'But didn't someone search the bins earlier – looking for that vodka bottle that Timothy Sudbury was supposed to carry round with him? And that's another thing! Wasn't it Wendy who told us about it – after we started asking about how he could have drunk so much? *And* she was the one who produced the wine at lunchtime. It all fits! I bet she laced his wine with vodka and then made up the story about him having his own bottle to stop us following up on how he came to have consumed so much alcohol. She *knew* about the effect of combining ketamine with alcohol – or else she just wanted to get him mildly drunk so that he'd be less likely to notice her jabbing him with a hypodermic. It's all plain as a pikestaff!'

'Not as far as a jury's concerned,' Richard remarked. 'None of that is proof and a good defence barrister will be able to come up with half a dozen equally plausible scenarios to explain the facts.'

'But what if we could find the gloves? That's what I was going to say, Sir. After Wendy mentioned the vodka bottle, Peter said that we ought to go through the bins along St Aldates. Did anyone do that? And did they include the one on the corner of Pembroke Square?'

* * *

Peter put his head round the door of Bernie's study. 'Lunchtime!'

His wife removed the headphones through which she was listening to Jonah's audio-recording and looked towards him. 'Just give me five minutes. I'm almost through with this.'

Peter nodded and then backed out of the room again, closing the door silently as he did so. Bernie put back the headphones and clicked the computer mouse to resume editing. Jonah really did read remarkably well – just as he did practically everything else! Sometimes she wished that there were more things that he was *not* good at. It could sometimes be quite provoking having someone around who excelled at everything that he turned his mind to.

People of a certain religious disposition might say that this was why God had arranged for him to suffer a paralysing injury: to bring him up short and show him that, however talented and accomplished you might be, you were never self-sufficient. Bernie smiled to herself at this thought. More fool God, if that were the case! Any satisfaction He may have had at Jonah's come-uppance must have been short-lived. There might have been a few months – nearly a year, perhaps – when his self-confidence was shaken and he was teetering on the brink of serious depression, but it wasn't long before he had accepted his new situation and was determinedly making the best of things.

She saved the edited file to the computer hard drive and emailed it to Jonah for his approval. Then she headed downstairs to join the others in the kitchen.

'I think I'll give Joey a ring,' she announced, fishing her phone out of her pocket. 'In case there's any news.'

Before she could finish dialling, she was interrupted by an incoming call. It was Lucy, wanting to know if her mother had received any updates on Aunty Dot's condition.

'No,' Bernie told her. 'Joey's down as her next-of-kin, so that's who the Home will ring. I was just about to check with him again, but I'm sure he would have rung us if anything had happened.'

'It was hours ago that they called for an ambulance,' Lucy argued. 'Surely it must have come by now! Maybe they've been too busy to ring.'

'Well the Home can certainly do without lots of us pestering them for news. We'd better leave that to Joey. If you get off the line, I'll give him a bell and see if he's heard anything.'

Cousin Joey had no news to report. In fact, he'd been on the verge of ringing Bernie in case she had managed to get through to Dot by email or Skype or Zoom or whatever it was that she used to speak to her on her iPad.

'Ruth's going frantic with worry,' he confided to Bernie, 'and I have to confess I'm not much better now. How can they decide she needs to go to hospital and then not manage to get her picked up for more than four hours?'

'I suppose that's better than being stuck for four hours in A and E waiting to be seen,' Bernie suggested, trying to find some spark of light in this dark situation. 'Have you spoken to anyone at the Home? How *is* Dot?'

'I rang them again an hour or so ago. They said her temperature's up again, which is making her a bit dopey and confused, but their main worry is her breathing. They think she could do with oxygen, which is why they wanted her admitted to hospital. They told me that they're looking into getting it prescribed for her to take at home, but apparently there are all sorts of forms to fill in and it all needs to be signed off by her doctor, who won't be able to come until later this afternoon.'

'Well, it sounds as if they're doing the best they can.' Bernie tried to hit an optimistic note, but deep down she felt far from hopeful. 'What's Aunty saying about the hospital idea? She was adamant that she didn't want to go into ICU because she'd rather leave the space for someone younger.'

'I don't know. I haven't been able to speak to her. I'm only going on what the manager tells me. She seemed to think that she doesn't need intensive care – or not yet, anyway.'

'Good. Well, I'd better go now. Give my love to Ruth, and let me know if you hear anything more about Aunty Dot.'

Bernie looked round at the others. 'I assume you got all that. I'll just ring Lucy to let her know there's still no news, and then we can eat.'

* * *

It turned out that Peter had organised a team of PCs to go through the bins all along the route of the procession from Folly Bridge to Carfax. Moreover, they had made an inventory of all items of potential interest that they found there. This did not feature an empty vodka bottle – or a bottle of any other kind of spirits – which was why it hadn't been brought to Richard's attention previously. However, there was one very interesting entry in the list: *disposable latex gloves (1 pair)*.

These days, those gloves would have been off to the lab before you could say "forensic evidence" to be swabbed for possible traces of DNA; but back then the science was much less advanced and there was no chance of being able to identify the wearer from the few skin cells or drops of sweat that might still be adhering to the insides. Nevertheless, this did look remarkably like some sort of breakthrough in the investigation. Wendy had muttered something about gloves, and now here were some gloves of just the sort that the murderer might have chosen to avoid leaving fingermarks on the syringe.

Things started looking even better when we inspected the plan of the bins, which the sergeant who had overseen the operation had made. The gloves had been found in bin 5, which turned out to be the one on the corner of Pembroke Square – the self-same bin where Caroline Moreton had told us she had seen Wendy throwing something away only minutes before Timothy Sudbury collapsed!

'It must've been her!' I declared confidently. 'She must have done it.'

'It won't be so easy to convince a jury,' Richard said drily. 'It's all still very circumstantial, but I think we can justify searching her room – no, better go for the whole flat; she and Niamh could be in it together.'

* * *

Sensing movement behind him, Jonah paused in his recording and clicked a button to save the file. He looked round to see Bernie waiting for an opportunity to speak without interrupting.

'I finally got through to the Home,' she told him. 'They've given up on trying to get Aunty Dot into hospital. Her doctor's been out to see her and he's agreed she ought to have oxygen; so now they're running round trying to source the equipment. Luckily, they've had residents with chronic lung disease before, so a couple of staff are already trained to use it – if they can get hold of any.'

'I suppose it's all been taken to the hospitals,' Jonah sighed, 'which is understandable enough, but ...'

'Anyway, they said she's still conscious – just rather light-headed because of the fever – and they've promised to play her your recording if we can send it through to them as an MP3 file. I've finished what you gave me so far. How're you getting on with the rest?'

'I've got another chunk ready for you to process, but I could do with another drink before I do any more. My voice is starting to develop an unpleasant sandpapery quality to it.'

* * *

Mac and I searched the flat in Temple Street, while Peter visited the shared house in New Hinksey and Richard interviewed Niamh again at her family home in Headington, where she had retreated once the decision had been made to keep Wendy in hospital overnight.

We started with Wendy's room, which was very dark and felt rather cold and damp. The only natural light came from a small, rather dirty, skylight, and the only source of heat was a one-bar electric fire attached to the wall. Mac switched on the light and a forty-watt bulb came on in the centre of the ceiling, making not the slightest difference to the general gloom.

I walked over to the desk and switched on the table lamp that stood perched on a small pile of books there. That did emit sufficient light to enable me to examine the contents of the desk drawers and the books and papers that lay on its surface. While I sifted through stacks of incomprehensible notes, many of them in foreign languages and strange alphabets, Mac prowled round the room, opening cupboards and peering under the bed.

'Hey! Come and have a look at this!' he called out, picking up a sheet of paper from the floor, between the bed and the wall. 'It looks like a suicide note. I suppose it must've slipped down there when Niamh moved Wendy to try to revive her.'

I came over at once and we both stared down at the words: Dear Niamh, I'm sorry, but everything seems pointless after yesterday. I thought you understood, but now I know you don't. I hope you find someone better than Tim to spend your life with. Goodbye.

'Well, that seems clear enough,' Mac said, folding the paper and putting it in his pocket. 'I reckon she killed Tim, thinking she was saving her friend from a fate worse than death, and then yesterday she realised that Niamh wasn't grateful to her for doing it.'

'Are you suggesting that she told Niamh what she'd done?' I asked in surprise. 'Surely Niamh wouldn't have just kept quiet about it, if she had?'

'Maybe she told Wendy she was going to the Police; and maybe Wendy killed herself rather than face the consequences.'

'Maybe.' I was still not satisfied that this was a full explanation. 'But what does she mean about everything being pointless? And ... Well, look at this second sentence: *I thought you understood.* If she told Niamh yesterday that she'd killed Timothy, wouldn't she have said: *I thought you **would** have understood,* meaning *I expected you to understand why I did it (when I told you about it).* This sounds more like something that Niamh already knew about, which Wendy thought she understood, but it turns out she didn't.'

'That's too complicated for me!' Mac shook his head. 'What difference does it make whether she said *I thought you understood* or *I thought you would have understood*? It's all the same thing as far as I'm concerned.'

'It's a matter of tenses,' I began. 'You see, *you understood* is describing Niamh's reaction to something that has already happened, whereas *you would have understood* is conditional. It means that ...,' but then I decided to give up. Mac clearly didn't appreciate some of the finer points of English grammar; but then, I don't suppose there was much call for it in the back streets of the Gorbals (or wherever it was that he grew up). I returned to my task of searching through the contents of Wendy's desk.

The top drawer contained writing implements (pens, pencils, a pencil sharpener and a bottle of ink). The next one down had documents: a cheque book (with three stubs all for sums of twenty pounds drawn to "self"), a building society passbook, which revealed that she had a balance of £754.87 in her savings account, a pile of bank statements, and her passport, containing visas for trips to Turkey, Egypt and Jordan. I supposed that these probably related to her research work into ancient languages.

Digging down under a pile of letters from various anti-nuclear organisations and activists in the bottom drawer, I found a small black book, which turned out to be Wendy's diary. I sat down in the rather uncomfortable wooden chair next to her desk and began to thumb through the pages.

Things started to become interesting round about the middle of July with her account of the riding accident and the nursing care that Niamh had given her afterwards. I couldn't quite put my finger on it, but there was something rather strange – a bit unnerving – about the intensity with which she wrote about their friendship and how much she appreciated Niamh's attentions. For the three weeks of Niamh's visit to the family home, the daily entries hardly mentioned anything apart from what they had done together, what Niamh had said, how pretty Niamh was and how kind, and how much Wendy would miss her when she went to Ireland to visit her brother and his family.

Then they were back in Oxford together and Timothy started to feature fairly regularly – and never portrayed in a good light. Wendy seemed to view his presence as a distraction, something that kept Niamh away from her proper place, which was by Wendy's side. It would appear that Wendy resented every moment that Niamh and Timothy spent together – or perhaps it was that she resented every moment that Niamh spent apart from her.

Then came Niamh's false alarm, which prompted a torrent of abuse towards Timothy. There was also some disappointment that she had chosen to confide in her mother rather than in Wendy, but then satisfaction that Niamh's parents had entrusted their daughter to her safe-keeping once the scare was over.

At the beginning of September, Niamh went off to Coleraine to stay with her brother Patrick. It was during that time that Timothy made his play for Diane – or perhaps that was one occasion out of a number of them. Anyway, whatever happened between them seemed to have hardened Wendy's feelings towards him all the more.

There was a veiled hint in the diary that the incident between Timothy and Diane prompted Wendy's weekend trip home, just before Niamh was due to return to Oxford on the Monday. There were no entries for that Saturday and Sunday: presumably she had left the diary in the Temple Street flat while she paid her flying visit to Lambourn.

'Pity that,' Mac commented when I showed him the pages that led up to that fateful Thursday when Timothy Sudbury had met his doom. 'A nice detailed account of how she stole the ketamine and what she planned to do with it would have suited us just fine.'

Nevertheless, the diary provided us with a good deal more evidence that Wendy not only harboured a hearty dislike of Timothy, but also resented his attachment to Niamh, to whom she seemed to be obsessively devoted. Here at last was someone with a strong motive – albeit a rather weird one in our young and inexperienced minds – for wanting Timothy Sudbury out of the way.

Richard agreed with this assessment of the situation, when I showed him the diary after we all re-convened back at the police station on St Aldates. His interview with Niamh hadn't revealed much new information. Niamh had confirmed that Wendy had physically pulled her away from Timothy during the demonstration, but she insisted that it was just because she wanted to save her from the crush. She still maintained that she didn't know what it was that her friend had thrown away in the bin on the corner of Pembroke Square and to deny having any idea what Wendy had meant when she spoke to Margaret about gloves.

In a separate conversation, Siobhan O'Halloran had admitted that Wendy did occasionally appear to be a bit overbearing towards Niamh, but she was adamant that it was only because she, as the stronger character, was worried for her and wanted to protect her.

Peter had found John Goodey alone when he called at the house in New Hinksey. Faith and Diane were meeting with their supervisor in the university archaeology department. This was probably fortunate, because John opened up in the absence of those dominant females and spoke more freely than previously about the relationships between the six friends. He admitted that Timothy, "liked to have a good time" but insisted that he wasn't the Casanova that Diane would have us believe.

He was shocked to hear about Wendy's attempted suicide, repeating over and over that she was the last person that he would have expected to take her own life. When Peter asked him why, he talked about how she always seemed so sure of herself: so dedicated to changing the world. Why would she end it all when there was still so much left for her to do?

What exactly did she want to change?

Well, she wanted to get rid of the nuclear threat for a start.

Anything closer to home – more personal?

John didn't understand what Peter was getting at.

Might she have felt a need to intervene in any of the things going on around her in their little group? Could she, for example, have been worried about Timothy's relationship with Niamh?

If Peter was suggesting that she killed him, then absolutely not!

But …?

Well, he supposed that Wendy did seem quite keen to dissuade Niamh from looking for jobs in Leicester.

She would prefer her to stay in Oxford, perhaps?

Yes … or … well, John wasn't sure that he was supposed to know about this, but he'd overheard Wendy talking about a plan for them to open a riding school together at her parents' place in Berkshire.

* * *

'Thank you for emailing that audio file across.' The voice of the Care Home manager sounded strained and tired. 'Your aunt's sleeping at the moment, but we've got it all set up to play it to her when she wakes.'

'How is she?' Bernie asked anxiously.

'I'll be honest with you: we don't think it'll be long now. The oxygen has helped her a bit, but her blood pressure's way down now. It looks like her heart can't cope any longer.'

'But how is she?' persisted Bernie. 'I mean: is she in any pain? Can she breathe OK?'

'No, she isn't in pain. We're doing our best to manage her breathing, but it isn't easy. This virus … I'm afraid it isn't a nice way to go. I'm sorry.'

* * *

We decided that we finally had enough evidence to justify bringing Wendy in for questioning under caution. Richard and Peter waited at the hospital for her to be discharged and intercepted her before her parents could whisk her away to Lambourn. I was delegated to sit with them in the police station reception area while Richard and Peter questioned her about her diary entries, the gloves in the litterbin and a last-minute recollection from John that Tim had cried out in pain and clasped at his thigh just before Wendy and Niamh disappeared into Pembroke Square.

The Brothertons looked terribly shocked. I suppose no parent likes to think that their offspring could be a murderer. George Brotherton sat in silence, apparently deep in thought, while his wife plied me with questions about what would happen next. I tried to answer, but to be honest, I wasn't sure about that myself. So much depended on whether Wendy could be persuaded to confess to killing Timothy. If she did, there was a good chance she'd be allowed out on bail, since I couldn't see that she was likely to be considered a risk to anyone else. If not ...? Would we apply for more time to question her? Or let her go while we tried to find more evidence against her? I was convinced in my own mind that she was guilty, but if we went ahead with a prosecution and the jury found her innocent then we would have no second chance to convict.

Eventually, the family lawyer emerged and informed Mr and Mrs Brotherton that Wendy was being kept in police custody overnight with a view to questioning her further in the morning. The police had applied for a search warrant for the stables, and wanted to see all the records of drug supplies there dating back to June. He advised that the family co-operate fully with the police investigation, since any failure to do so might imply that they believed their daughter to be guilty, or even that they had conspired with her to kill Timothy Sudbury.

I won't bore you with the details, but the upshot of those enquiries was that a discrepancy was discovered between the quantities of ketamine recorded as being present in the drug cupboard before and after Wendy's hastily-arranged visit the weekend prior to Timothy's death. At last we had sufficient evidence to charge her with his murder.

* * *

'And that's the end of the recording,' Carys said, putting down Dot's iPad and leaning forward to wipe a dribble of saliva from beneath her open mouth. 'It was kind of him to make it for you, wasn't it? Maybe he'll release it as an audiobook one day.'

Dot had given up even trying to speak; it took too much effort. But she looked up at Carys and managed a weak smile.

'I'm afraid I'll have to go now,' Carys continued, 'but I'll look in again in a few minutes, and you've got your buzzer there in your hand in case you need anything.'

Dot nodded almost imperceptibly and smiled again. She watched Carys out of the door and then tried to focus her eyes on the crucifix that hung on the wall opposite the bed. She had missed her usual morning devotions that day – or she thought she had – or was that yesterday? What day was it anyway? She ought at least to say the Our Father. She began silently reciting the familiar words, her lips moving as she tried to concentrate. Thy Kingdom come; thy will be done, on Earth as it is in Heaven … What came next? Thy Kingdom come … Thy Kingdom … It was no good. She would have to wait until she was less tired. But it was so frustrating not to be able to remember … Thy … thy … She closed her eyes and drifted off into a doze.

* * *

The telephone in the hall rang. Bernie immediately put down the spoon that she had raised to Jonah's mouth to feed him his next mouthful of Peter's rhubarb pie and raced out to answer it.

'Joey?'

'No. Sorry to disappoint you. It's Father Damien. Just ringing round my flock, checking you're all OK. I gather you were expecting a call from someone else?'

'My cousin Joey in Liverpool,' Bernie explained. 'I'm sorry if I didn't sound pleased to hear you. It's just that our aunt has COVID-19 and we're expecting to hear from the Care Home any time.'

'That'd be your Aunty Dot?' Damien enquired gently. 'Peter told me she was ill. You're not expecting good news then, I take it?'

'No. They've said it's only a matter of time before her heart gives out under the strain. She's a hundred and one, so she's had a good innings. We've known for years that a bout of flu or even a bad cold could carry her off. It's just ...'

'However long you have to prepare, it's always a shock when the time actually comes,' Damien finished for her. 'Well, I won't keep you on the phone in case your cousin's trying to get through, but if there's anything I can do – even if it's just someone outside the family to have a chat with – you know where to find me. I'll remember your aunt when I say my prayers before the blessed sacrament this evening.'

'Thanks. And ... maybe you could light a candle for her. I think she'd like that. She always used to light one in church for my mam every week when I was little.'

'Yes, of course. I'll do that. Now I'll let you go. Keep safe, all of you, and be sure and tell me how things turn out with your aunt.'

Bernie had hardly got back to the table and finished explaining to the others who the caller had been when the telephone rang again. Bernie leapt to her feet, then stood frozen to the spot as Peter and Jonah stared up at her. She somehow knew that this time it would be Joey.

'Shall I get it?' Peter asked at last.

'No. I'll go.' Bernie pushed back her chair and hurried out into the hall.

'Hello?'

'Bernie? It's Joey.'

'Yes. Thanks for ringing.'

'Mrs Radcliffe rang – you know! From the Home. Aunty Dot passed away this afternoon.'

'She told us, when we emailed over Jonah's audio recording, that she didn't think she'd last much longer.'

'Yes. She told us that too when we rang this morning.'

There was a long silence as they both struggled to think of anything else to say.

'Oh,' Joey said at last, 'speaking of Jonah's recording: she said that Carys played it all to her and she seemed to enjoy listening to it.'

'That's good. I'll let Jonah know. He was afraid he wouldn't get it done in time and she'd never know how things turned out. I bet she was disappointed that she was wrong about who done it!'

'I'll let you know when we've got the funeral sorted out,' Joey went on. 'There's all sort of restrictions on who can go and stuff; so it'll be a bit strange. Mrs Radcliffe said the undertaker'll have to dress up in full protective gear just to come and take her to the chapel of rest; and the churches are all closed, so she can't have a proper requiem mass like she'd wanted. Ruth's quite cut-up about that.'

'Tell her Aunty wouldn't have minded. She'd have said, "I was a nurse for over forty years and I know all about preventing disease transmission!"'

'Yes, she probably would.'

'Anyway, I'd better let you go. I suppose you've probably got lots of other calls to make.'

'Yes … well … like I said, I'll be in touch when I know about the funeral.'

14. EPILOGUE

The funeral seemed very strange. Only six mourners were allowed inside the crematorium chapel, which created unexpected debate as to who those select few should be. Bernie, far away in Oxford, was immediately ruled out of the picture through the COVID-19 travel restrictions. The same went for Joey's brother, George, who had married into a farming family in Devon. Ruth desperately wanted to be present, but agreed with Joey that they ought to stay at home in order to shield his mother, who lived with them and was classed as extremely vulnerable due to her age and a range of underlying health conditions. That left the younger generation: Joey's three offspring and Lucy.

Dominic made known his intention of bringing Mariam with him, at which his sister Chloë declared that she must have the support of her long-standing boyfriend, Chris. Ruth wasn't sure that she wanted Chloë to draw attention to the fact that she had been living with Chris for three years without having made any plans for a marriage ceremony, to which her daughter retorted that nobody would know and even fewer would care.

James, the oldest of the Fazakerley brood, agreed with Chloë's stand, but pointed out that he, too, had a partner and, since it was clearly impossible for all three of them to bring their other halves without excluding Lucy, it might be better to restrict invitations to Dot's blood relatives: Dominic, Chloë, Lucy and himself. That was

Lucy's cue to remind them that, since Ibrahim was going to drive them to the crematorium, it seemed only fair that he should be allowed in. Her plan was for the guests to be: James, Chloë, Dominic, Mariam, Ibrahim and herself.

Chloë immediately objected to this suggestion, saying that, since she and Chris had been together for far longer than Dominic and Mariam, Chris clearly ought to have priority. Dominic, backed by his mother, retorted that he and Mariam were officially engaged, whereas Chloë had repeatedly refused to be drawn into talking about regularising her relationship with Chris.

Ibrahim insisted that he was fine about waiting in the car or in the grounds of the crematorium, if that was allowed. Mariam said that she would be happy to give way to Chris. After all, the rules said that the ceremony had to be as short as possible and she could easily wait in the car with her brother. The funeral director had promised to record the service; so they could all watch it together later that day.

In the end, it was Ruth who came up with the solution: James, Chloë, Dominic and Lucy would attend the service, leaving two spaces free for Carys and Jonathan, the two Care Home staff who had looked after Dot during her final hours.

'They were so good with her,' she said, 'making sure she was never alone and helping us to see her even though we couldn't visit. I'm sure Dot would have wanted them to come, if they'd like to.'

Fortunately, April was unusually dry and sunny that year, so Mariam and Ibrahim were able to wander round the Garden of Contemplation at Springwood Crematorium, exchanging occasional socially distanced greetings with Chloë's Chris and James's Kim, while Lucy and Dominic paid their last respects to the last of the thirteen Fazakerley siblings who had grown up in Liverpool between the wars.

'I'm surprised they went for cremation,' Ibrahim murmured, as they watched the coffin being taken out of the back of the hearse. 'I thought Catholics favoured burial – like Muslims.'

'Dom told me Dot asked for cremation in her will,' Mariam told him. 'She didn't want anyone feeling obliged to look after her grave.'

'That sounds like Dot,' Ibrahim nodded. 'She never liked to impose on people – and she was so practical! I think she must've been a good nurse.'

'Dom said she was very strict when he was little. He used to be afraid of her, even though she must have been quite old even back then.'

'Lucy says that her mum told her that Dot was like a sort of second mum to her. Bernie's mum had … motor neurone disease, I think it was. Anyway, she got so she couldn't look after Bernie, and Dot stepped in to help.'

'Mmm. Lucy told me that too. It's a pity Bernie can't be here. It must've been awful for her, stuck down there in Oxford while her aunt was so ill.'

The hearse moved off, giving them a clear view of the coffin disappearing inside the chapel.

'Lucy said she'd never even met her Aunty Dot until about four years ago,' Ibrahim continued. 'And then, all of a sudden, her mum decided she ought to know more about her roots.'

'I suppose she must've been busy,' Mariam suggested, 'with Lucy's dad dying and having to bring her up on her own as well as holding down a full-time job at the university. It's not surprising if she didn't have time to make trips up here.'

'Mmm. It still seems strange, though. Bernie's so proud of being a Scouser and so keen to say that there's nowhere as good as Liverpool, and yet she never came back here for more than sixteen years – at least, that's how old Lucy was the first time she visited.'

'Only like our Grandad,' Mariam pointed out. 'He's always talking about how great it was in Pakistan, but he never goes back there.'

'It's not quite the same,' Ibrahim argued. 'There're trains to Oxford. And I know everyone complains about the fares, but it's still not like flying out to Pakistan.'

'I think he knows it'd be a disappointment if he did go back. Tahira went there with her family a few years back, and she told me there was dreadful inequality and anyone who looked as if they came from the West was considered fair game for begging, or even mugging.'

'Knowing Tahira, she probably didn't make any effort to fit in with the local culture,' Ibrahim laughed. 'She probably started out by lecturing them on how their style of Islam was hardly more than folk religion and not at all true to the Prophet (peace be upon him)!'

'Yes,' his sister smiled. Her friend had been a founder member of their little club, the Feminist Sisterhood of Islam, and fancied herself as an Islamic scholar equal to, if not superior to, most Muslim men. 'Tahira never knows when to pull her punches. She's got this ... I was going to say "*crusading* spirit", which must say something about how I've been brainwashed into adopting the language of our oppressors. I guess I'd have to watch my step too if I went to Pakistan! Dom would be horrified: he's always talking about how Christians use the word *crusade* without realising how offensive it is to Muslims.'

'Probably because most of them don't know what the crusades were. Anyway, we'd better be getting back to the car. They'll be out any minute.'

They walked across the grass and through a line of trees to where they could see both the chapel and the car park. Lucy and Dominic were standing close together under the canopy outside the door of the chapel, keeping the statutory two metres away from Chloë on the other side of the parking space reserved for funeral cars. As they watched, James emerged, followed after appropriate intervals by Carys and Jonathan.

Lucy looked across at Ibrahim and Mariam and waved. Then, pulling her cousin by the arm, she hastened across to join them in the car park.

'The funeral director's going to email us the video,' she told them, 'and Father Nat's going to video his requiem mass too. He was ever so good in what he said in the service just now. He remembered all sorts of things about Aunty Dot, even though she hadn't been to his church since she moved into the Home.'

'Everyone's doing their best,' Dominic agreed. 'It's just so … well so weird, I suppose.'

* * *

'Everyone did their best.' Bernie echoed her cousin's words as the video of Father Nathaniel's solitary mass ended and the faces of Lucy, Dominic and their friends came back into view on the computer screen.

'I'm glad Aunty Ruth had the idea of inviting Carys and Jonathan to the crematorium,' Lucy chipped in. 'They seemed ever so pleased to be there and I know Aunty Dot would have wanted them. She was very fond of Jonathan especially.'

'And they were very good with Aunty Dot while she was ill,' Dominic added. 'It must've been really difficult for them these last few weeks.'

'Yes,' agreed Lucy. 'And it's not over yet. There were two more COVID-19 deaths in the Home this week. One of them was Eric: the talkative old man in the wheelchair who gave us each a lace hankie.'[20]

---

[20] You can read about this in *In my Liverpool Home*, the 8th Bernie Fazakerley Mystery, © 2017, ISBN: 978-1-911083-35-1

'I suppose that must have been on the cards, once the virus got in the Home,' Jonah observed. 'After all, he had diabetes.'

'I suppose they still don't know how it got in?' Peter asked.

'No,' Dominic confirmed. 'The best bet is that it may have been one of the agency staff who was working across several different homes, but it could've been a visitor before they locked down or ... well, anyone really who had contact with the outside world.'

'Oh! I nearly forgot,' Lucy said suddenly. 'Jonah! Jonathan said to thank you for recording the last chapters of your book. He says Dot loved hearing the story and everyone in the Home wants a copy when it comes out in print!'

'So you're going to have to get it published now,' chipped in Dominic. 'Will we get our names on it as editors?'

'Are you going to leave it there, finishing with Wendy's arrest?' Ibrahim asked. 'Or are you going to tell the readers what happened afterwards?'

'The trial, do you mean?'

'No, not so much that as where everyone is now. Did John and Diane get married? What happened to Niamh after she found out her best friend had murdered her fiancé? Which out of Faith and Diane got the postdoc job? That sort of thing.'

'But I don't know the answers to those questions,' Jonah objected. 'Once the police investigation was over, it was none of my business what happened to them.'

'Mam knows!' put in Lucy eagerly. 'Don't you, Mam? You hinted that you'd read about Niamh in that Shrewsbury Alumni magazine you waffled on about. Go on! Tell us what happened to her.'

'OK,' Bernie smiled, 'I'll spill the beans – as far as I know them, which is only what was in her obituary in *the Shrew*.'

'Her obituary?' Dominic exclaimed. 'Don't tell me – she couldn't face going on without Timothy and she took her own life?'

'Don't be stupid!' Lucy was scornful at this suggestion. 'If she was going to do that, it'd have been straight after Wendy was arrested or at most after her trial, and Jonah would've known about it. And if Mam read her obituary, that must've been years later, when she'd done enough for it to be worth writing about her. Go on, Mam! Tell us what happened to her.'

'She finished her doctorate and was awarded her degree in July 1984; and then she joined a religious order in County Wicklow.'

'You couldn't make is up!' crowed Dominic. 'The lovelorn maiden loses the love of her life and retreats to a nunnery!'

'No, Dom, it wasn't like that,' Bernie protested. 'Her old theology tutor at Shrewsbury wrote the obituary. She said that Niamh had always felt called to do something to spread the faith. That's why she studied theology. She felt strongly that women were undervalued in the Church and that it was partly because they were excluded from the seminaries, so that male priests had a monopoly on the detailed theological knowledge that you needed in order to promote change.'

'It sounds as if she and Tahira would have got on like a house on fire,' Mariam observed, with a quick glance towards Ibrahim.

'That doesn't sound the least bit like the Niamh that Jonah portrayed,' objected Lucy. 'She sounded like a little mouse who wouldn't have dared to stand up to anyone, least of all the Church establishment.'

'That's because he never really got to know her,' Bernie replied. 'If you think about it, he only met her a few times – half a dozen at the most – and only at a time when she'd just been knocked sideways by the sudden death of her boyfriend.'

'But even her parents said she was vulnerable,' Lucy persisted. 'They even asked Wendy to keep an eye on her, they were so worried about her.'

'She was the baby of the family and the only girl,' Bernie argued. 'I reckon even they underestimated her. It's a big mistake to confuse meekness with weakness. Don't forget, I actually knew her. She may have been tiny and looked like a china doll, but she could be tough too. She had a very fine logical mind and she knew her stuff. You should have heard the way she pulled apart St Paul's letters in the CU Bible study group!'

'So what happened after that?' asked Ibrahim. 'Did she stay in the nunnery for the rest of her life?'

'In a way. Incidentally, she'd have taken you to task for calling it a nunnery. She joined an order of nuns that ran schools and colleges. That sort of nuns is like the equivalent of friars: they live together but they go out into the world to do stuff. They live in a convent. The other sort – the ones who hide themselves away from the world like monks – live in a monastery. Anyway, Niamh became deputy head of a college that trained teachers, and she wrote books – some of them very well-thought-of in theological circles. She died of cancer a couple of years ago, which was when the obituary was published.'

'Do you know anything about any of the others?' demanded Dominic. 'Did your alumni magazine have anything about them in it?'

'I did have a look back through some of the past editions,' Bernie admitted with a smile. 'I found an entry in the Births, Marriages and Deaths section of the Green Book, which reported that John Goodey had married Octavia Pritchard at a ceremony somewhere in London.'

'So he didn't stay with Diane then,' commented Jonah. 'I always thought they weren't very well suited. He was too easy-going; she'd have dominated him.'

'And there was a very interesting entry in the *Shrew* about Dr Faith Loftus, née Nelson, and her seminal work (published jointly with her husband) on Phoenician influences on pre-Roman communities in Southern Britain.'

'So she not only seduced her supervisor but persuaded him to marry her?' exclaimed Peter.

'What about the wife and family down in Dorset?' demanded Ibrahim.

'Divorced, presumably,' Bernie shrugged. 'Look, I don't know the full history or even what order things happened in. All I know is that, by 1997, Faith had changed her name to Loftus and was writing books and research papers with Professor Arthur Loftus of Henderson College.'

'So much for all those histrionics when she told me and Mac about her liaison with her supervisor,' Jonah snorted. 'To think I felt sorry for the girl!'

'Poor Colin,' commented Lucy. 'I don't know who he was, but it sounds as if she was keeping him on a string, using him as her toy boy, while all the time she was having it off with that Dr Loftus.'

'We don't know that,' Bernie pointed out. 'She could've been speaking the truth. Maybe she *was* ashamed of using her body to try to persuade Dr Loftus to give her the postdoc. And maybe she *did* only do it in order to be in Oxford with Colin. Her relationship with Loftus may have blossomed much later – after she and Colin had already split up.'

'Tell that to the marines, as my Dad used to say,' scoffed Jonah. 'The more I think about it, the more I think the only thing she was really upset about was that Timothy had found out about it and might spill the beans to Colin or Diane.'

'I will never cease to be amazed at the shenanigans that these Oxford academics get up to,' sighed Peter, shaking his head. 'I thought all these posts were supposed to be awarded on merit.'

'So they are,' agreed Bernie, 'and I'm sure these days there would be a lot more checks in place to make it more difficult for the likes of Loftus to go choosing his fancy woman to be his research assistant, but don't you try to deny that this sort of thing goes on in the police service too!'

'Yes, I suppose it probably does,' Peter admitted grumpily. 'But it's not so easy. We have exams to pass to get promotion.'

'And so had Faith passed exams. She was qualified for the job. It's just that so was Diane and probably several other people. Anyway, what I *do* know is that Colin doesn't bear her any grudge and he's happily married to an American mathematician that he met while he was over there on his Fulbright scholarship. When this COVID-19 business is all over, I'll invite him round and you can all meet them both.'

'What about the others?' persisted Dominic. 'We know what happened to Wendy, Niamh, John and Faith. That still leaves Diane and Dawn.'

'I'd forgotten about Dawn,' admitted Lucy. 'She didn't really come into it at all in the end. Why did you make such a big thing of her, Mam? Were you just trying to put us off the scent?'

'Well, sort of,' Bernie smiled. 'But mostly it was just that she was the main person that I remembered from the whole thing, and I was curious to know what the police made of her. I was expecting her to go on to become something big in politics. I'm surprised she didn't.'

'She did in a way,' Ibrahim informed them. 'I tried to look them all up on Google. 'I suppose I must've missed Faith because of her name change, and John and Niamh haven't done anything important enough to get on there, but I did find Dawn Farmer listed as a Green Party candidate in last year's general election.'

'So that only leaves Diane,' commented Dominic. 'Did you find anything about her?'

'According to Colin Anderson, she's an associate professor in the archaeology department at the University of New South Wales,' Bernie told them.

'Getting as far away from Oxford as she can,' Lucy commented.

'And Wendy's out of jail,' Ibrahim went on. 'She was released in 2003 after serving twenty years of her life sentence. I read about it on the Oxford Mail website.'

'I still don't get why she did it,' Lucy said, screwing up her face in a puzzled frown. 'Was she a lesbian? Did she fancy Niamh? She surely can't have thought there was any possibility of Niamh reciprocating?'

'We didn't think about things the same way in those days,' her mother told her. 'I suppose I had heard of lesbians, but it would never have occurred to me that I might actually come across one. Looking back, I can think of a few "best friends" at college who went around together a lot, but it would never have crossed my mind that they were anything other than best buddies.'

'She probably didn't even think about it that way herself,' Jonah added. 'I think she just wanted Niamh to be her exclusive friend and she was afraid that Timothy was stealing her away from her. Don't you remember? Her mother said she'd never really had any friends before. She was probably frightened that she was losing the only friend she'd ever have.'

'I wonder what Richard thought about them,' Bernie mused. 'I mean, did he see the parallels with what his mother did? Did he even know?'

'Know what?' asked Dominic.

'When he was eight years old, his mother – Lucy's grandmother – ran off with a woman friend. They set up home together. She was a journalist and Eleanor became her photographer. They travelled the world together. She only came back to Oxford after both her "lady friend" and her husband were dead. I was wondering whether Richard knew about any of that. Eleanor never said anything to me about it, but she might have told him.'

'How do you know all about it, if neither of them said anything?' asked Ibrahim.

'Mam found out for herself, didn't you Mam? Jonah's not the only one in the family who can do detective work!'

'That's right,' Bernie smiled. 'Has Lucy shown you her book? It's a collection of stuff about Richard. I started making it before she was born, so that she'd know something about her dad. Lots of the people who knew him wrote stories about him: Peter did – and Jonah! I started looking into his family[21] and almost the first thing I found was this big mystery of where his mother disappeared to for all those years. I got to the bottom of it in the end – with a little help from my friends!' she added looking towards Peter and Jonah.

'I think I get what you're driving at,' Mariam murmured thoughtfully. 'This Eleanor – Lucy's gran – got married and lived with her husband for years before admitting that she was gay. Are you saying that Niamh could've been like that – in denial?'

'You mean, Wendy could've been right?' demanded Dominic excitedly. 'Marrying Timothy would have been a disaster – for Niamh as well as for her?'

'That would certainly make sense of her becoming a nun afterwards, wouldn't it?' Mariam nodded

'No, I'm not sure I was thinking that exactly,' Bernie answered. 'I'm not sure what to think about them. Like I said, we all thought differently back then – and it must've been even more different in Eleanor's time when homosexuality was illegal. I'd be very surprised if Niamh

---

[21] You can read about Bernie's quest for the truth about Richard's mother in *Despise Not Thy Mother* © 2015, ISBN 978-1-911083-14-6

had any idea – even if she was. And Wendy … she may not have thought of it that way either – or maybe she did. But I *am* sure that becoming a nun won't have been just a way for Niamh to escape. I'm sure she will have been convinced that it was her vocation.'

'I think Bernie's right,' Peter agreed. 'I don't suppose either of them had a clear idea of their sexuality. In those days, people thought nothing of little girls holding hands or a pair of women sharing a flat. Wendy may have been attracted to Niamh, but the chances are she didn't think beyond them being mates and running a riding school together.'

'She'll have had plenty of opportunity to sort herself out in that respect, shut up in a women's prison for twenty years,' Jonah observed.

'And now she's been out again for nearly as long,' Lucy mused. 'I wonder what she's been doing. It must be weird going into prison in your twenties and coming out in your forties. She's missed out on the bit of her life where most things happen. I mean getting married, having children and all that sort of thing.'

'Forty isn't too late for those things,' Bernie pointed out. 'I was forty-one when you were born, remember.'

'At least Wendy had a chance to make a new start,' Mariam pointed out. 'Timothy didn't just miss out on twenty years of his life; he had it cut short before it had really started. And what about his family? Does anyone know what happened to them?'

'I saw his mother at Wendy's trial,' Jonah answered. 'She seemed to be bearing up OK. There was a younger woman with her – Timothy's sister, I think. I assume his father was there too, but I didn't notice him. Of course it must have had a profound effect on all of them, but …'

'Did Wendy plead guilty in the end?' Bernie asked. 'That would've made the trial a bit less traumatic for the family, I should think.'

Jonah shook his head. 'Only to manslaughter. She claimed that she never intended to kill him, only to give him a fright. The prosecution maintained that the way she plied him with alcohol at lunchtime proved that she was deliberately trying to increase the risk of death, and the jury accepted that argument.'

'Well, I think Jonah made a very good story of it all, anyway,' Dominic declared.

'Yes!' Ibrahim agreed. 'When's the movie coming out?'

THANK YOU

Thank you for taking the time to read Crowd of Witnesses. If you enjoyed it, please consider telling your friends or posting a short review. Word of mouth is an author's best friend and much appreciated. Thank you,

Judy

ACKNOWLEDGEMENTS

I would like to thank all the Facebook friends who contributed suggestions during the planning stages of this book.

As with previous books, I am grateful to Gillian Gilbert for reading the manuscript, giving helpful comments and pointing out typographical errors.

I am indebted to the authors of a wide range of internet resources, which have been invaluable for researching the background to this book, including:

- Wikipedia (https://en.wikipedia.org/)

- Google Maps (www.google.co.uk/maps)

- The Crown Prosecution Service (www.cps.gov.uk)

- Policing Insight (https://policinginsight.com)

- The National Institute of Health and Care Excellence (www.nice.org.uk/)

Every effort has been made to trace copyright holders. The publishers will be glad to rectify in future editions any errors or omissions brought to their attention.

DISCLAIMER

This book is a work of fiction. Any references to real people, events, establishments, organisations or locales are intended only to provide a sense of authenticity and are used fictitiously. All of the characters and events are entirely invented by the author. Any resemblances to persons living or dead are purely coincidental.

Many of the locations and institutions that feature in this book are real. Their inhabitants and employees, however, are purely fictional. In particular:

- Henderson, St Luke's, Holy Cross and Lichfield colleges do not exist and are not based on any specific college in Oxford or elsewhere;

- Shrewsbury College, which I have taken the liberty of making into Bernie's Alma Mater, exists only as a fictional women's college in Dorothy L Sayers famous novel, *Gaudy Night*;

MORE ABOUT BERNIE AND HER FRIENDS

There are fourteen **Bernie Fazakerley Mysteries**:

1. **Two Little Dickie Birds**: a murder mystery for DI Peter Johns and his Sergeant, Paul Godwin.

2. **Murder of a Martian**: Peter and Jonah solve a double murder and Peter meets Martin Reiss for the first time.

3. **Grave Offence**: Peter investigates an assault and a suspicious death, while Jonah is in rehab in the spinal injuries centre.

4. **Awayday**: a traditional detective story set among the dons of Lichfield College.

5. **Death on the Algarve:** a mystery for Bernie and her friends to tackle while on holiday in Portugal.

6. **Mystery over the Mersey**: a murder mystery set in Liverpool.

7. **Sorrowful Mystery**: Jonah investigates a child abduction and Peter embarks on a new journey of faith.

8. **In my Liverpool Home**: Bernie and her friends return to Liverpool to investigate a suspicious death in Aunty Dot's Care Home.

9. **Organ Failure**: a body is discovered under the organ in St Cyprian's Church and Jonah is called in to investigate.

10. **Rainbow Warrior**: One of their friends is injured in a hit-and-run incident and Jonah is convinced that this is attempted murder.

11. **Admission of Innocence**: Father Damien calls Peter and Jonah out of retirement to solve a murder case and prevent a miscarriage of justice.

12. **Lethal Mix**: Three of Lucy's student friends are injured in an anti-Muslim hate crime in Liverpool. Jonah, Peter and Bernie assist Merseyside Police to bring their attacker to justice.

13. **A Secret Gardener?** Bernie's friend Martin discovers a body in the Fellows' Garden of his Oxford College.

14. **Crowd of Witnesses**: Jonah decides to write his memoirs, beginning with a murder investigation from 1982.

Bernie also appears in three other novels:

- **Changing Scenes of Life**: Jonah Porter's life story, told through the medium of his favourite hymns.

- **Despise not your Mother**: the story of Bernie's quest to learn about her dead husband's past.

- **Weed Killers**: the first of a trilogy of novels about the death of PC Kenny Hughes.

There is also a book of short stories, in which Peter narrates his side of the story:
- **My Life of Crime**: the collected memoirs of DI Peter Johns. This includes some episodes that appear in other books, but told from a new perspective, as well as some completely new stories.

You can find them all on Judy Ford's Amazon Author page:

www.amazon.co.uk/-/e/B019315B1M

Visit the Bernie Fazakerley Publications Facebook page here:

www.facebook.com/Bernie.Fazakerley.Publications.

Follow Bernie on Twitter:

https://twitter.com/BernieFaz.

GLOSSARY OF OXFORD
UNIVERSITY JARGON

This glossary is by no means exhaustive. A fuller list of Oxford terminology may be found on the University website www.ox.ac.uk.

BA – Bachelor of Arts, the degree that is awarded to students completing an undergraduate degree programme. (Even those taking science degrees receive a BA).

Battels – The charges made to members of a college for accommodation, meals etc.

Blue – Sporting award for those who have competed in the annual varsity match for some sports. In less prestigious sports, competitors are awarded a "half blue".

Bod – "The bod" is a nickname for the Bodleian Library.

Bodleian Library – The Bodleian Library is the main university library.

Bursar – The member of staff responsible for the finances of a college.

Buttery – A college shop where members can purchase provisions.

Chancellor – The ceremonial head of the university

Collection – College examination usually set at the beginning of term to test students on work covered the previous term.

Coming up – Arriving at Oxford at the beginning of term

Commoner – A student who does not have a scholarship or an exhibition

Don – A member of the academic staff.

DPhil – Doctor of Philosophy, the postgraduate research degree that is known as a PhD at almost all other universities.

Fellow – A member of staff holding a Fellowship at one of the colleges. Fellowships may be Tutorial (i.e. teaching) or Research.

Finals – Also known as "Schools". Both terms are abbreviations of "Final Honours School". These are the examinations taken by undergraduate students at the end of their final year of study.

First – Abbreviation for "First class degree". This is the highest class of undergraduate degree.

Freshers – first year undergraduates, particularly during their first few weeks at Oxford.

Going down – Leaving Oxford at the end of term

Gown – Members of the university are entitled to wear gowns that indicate their level of scholarship. The term may also be used to refer to the university community as a whole, as in "Town and Gown" which expresses the, sometimes uneasy, relationship between the residents of Oxford and the members of the university,

Greats – The commonly-used term for *Literae Humaniores*, which is an undergraduate degree programme comprising classical languages (Latin and

Greek), philosophy and ancient history. It is a four-year course, one year more than most undergraduate courses.

Hall – the dining hall of a college. This term may also be used to denote the evening meal ('dinner') served there. 'Formal Hall' means that staff and students are required to dress formally in gowns when attending.

High Table – The table in a college dining hall, often on a dais, at which the Head of House and Fellows dine.

MA – Master of Arts. A "courtesy" degree awarded to graduates of the university when they have completed twenty-one terms from Matriculation.

Matriculation – The ceremony at which students are formally made members of the university.

Michaelmas Term – The first term of the university year, which starts in October.

Mods – Abbreviation for "Honour moderations". This is an examination taken, usually at the end of the first year of undergraduate study, which must be passed in order for a student to progress.

Pigeon Post – Nickname for the University Messenger Service, the internal mail system.

Prelims – An alternative examination to *Moderations*, taken by students in certain subjects during their first year. Unlike Moderations, Prelims are not classified.

Scholar – A student who has been awarded a scholarship. Scholars wear a different design of gown from commoners. Scholarships may be "open" (i.e. based purely on merit) or "closed" (restricted to a limited group of candidates, such as those from a particular school or with a particular religious affiliation).

Schools – Also known as "Finals". Both terms are abbreviations of "Final Honours School". These are the examinations taken by undergraduate students at the end of their final year of study.

Scout – A college servant responsible for cleaning. Each scout is usually assigned to a specific part of the college. A student may refer to "my scout" meaning the scout responsible for cleaning his or her room.

SCR – Senior Common Room. This may either refer to a room for the academic staff (Fellows) belonging to a college to meet or to the academic staff of a college collectively.

Second – Abbreviation for "Second class degree". Until the nineteen-eighties, Oxford University, unusually in the UK, did not divide the second class. Now, students are awarded degrees designated "first", "upper second", "lower second" or "third" class. These are abbreviated as 1, 2:1, 2:2 and 3, respectively.

Senior Member – Anyone who has achieved an Oxford MA automatically becomes a Senior Member of the University. The Senior Members of a college are its fellows.

Staircase – The older Oxford colleges are designed on a 'staircase' system, in which a group of rooms is accessed by a staircase that opens on to one of the quadrangles around which the college is built. Typically, rooms are identified by a combination of the name of the quad, the number of the staircase and the room number within the staircase group.

Subfusc – Formal attire worn by students and academics on formal occasions, including matriculation, examinations and graduation.

The Union – The University debating society, which also has a building housing a library, bar and various other facilities for its members.

Third – Abbreviation for "Third class degree". This is the lowest class of undergraduate degree normally awarded. There are, however, three lower classes for students who fail to reach the required standard: Pass, Honours Pass and Unclassified Honours

Tutor – A member of staff (or a postgraduate student) who gives tutorials to undergraduate students.

Tutorial – A session in which one or two (or occasionally more) students are taught by a Tutorial Fellow or some other person appointed by their college. Typically, this involves students preparing work in advance and talking about it during the tutorial.

Tutorial Fellow – A member of staff holding a Tutorial Fellowship at one of the colleges

Vice-Chancellor/VC – The senior academic officer of the university.

Viva – abbreviation of viva voce, an oral examination. All doctoral students take a viva at the end of their course. Undergraduates may be given a viva to establish the class of their degree if their examination marks are borderline.

GLOSSARY OF UK POLICE RANKS

Uniformed police

Chief Constable (CC) – Has overall charge of a regional police force, such as Thames Valley Police, which covers Oxford and a large surrounding area.

Deputy Chief Constable (DCC) – The senior discipline authority for each force. 2nd in command to the CC.

Assistant Chief Constable (ACC) – 4 in the Thames Valley Police Service, each responsible for a policy area.

Chief Superintendent ('Chief Super') – Head of a policing area or department.

Police Superintendent – Responsible for a local area within a police force.

Chief Inspector (CI) – Responsible for overseeing a team in a local area.

Police Inspector – Senior operational officer overseeing officers on duty 24/7.

Police Sergeant – Supervises a team of officers.

Police Constable (PC) – 'Bobby on the beat'. Likely to be the first to arrive in response to an emergency call.

Police Community Support Officer (PCSO) – A uniformed civilian member of the police service.

Crime Investigation Department (CID) – Plain clothes officers

Detective Superintendent (DS) – Responsible for crime investigation in a local area.

Detective Chief Inspector (DCI) – Responsible for overseeing a crime investigation team in a local area. May be the Senior Investigating Officer heading up a criminal investigation.

Detective Inspector (DI) – Oversees crime investigation 24/7. May be the Senior Investigating Officer heading up a criminal investigation.

Detective Sergeant (DS) – Supervises a team of CID officers.

Detective Constable (DC) – One of a team of officers investigating crimes.

These descriptions are based on information from the following sources:
[1] Mental Health Cop blog, by Inspector Michael Brown, Mental Health co-ordinator, College of Policing. https://mentalhealthcop.wordpress.com/, accessed 31st March 2017.
[2] Thames Valley Police website, https://www.thamesvalley.police.uk , accessed 31st March 2017.

BERNIE'S "FAMILY"

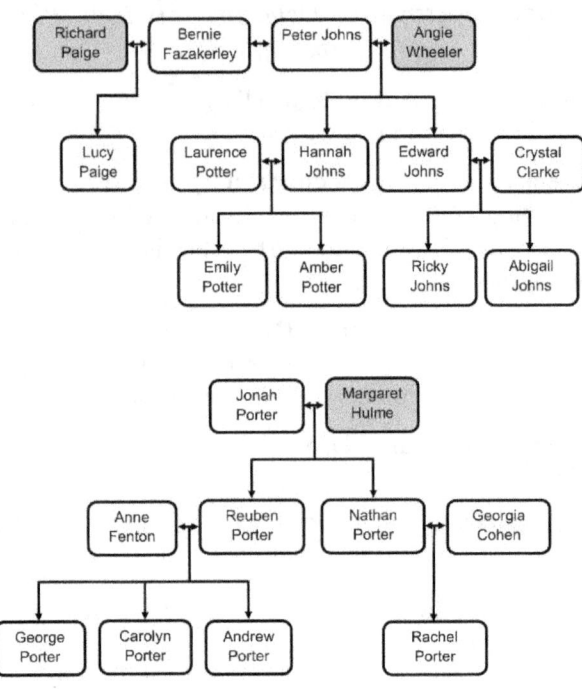

FAZAKERLEY FAMILY TREE

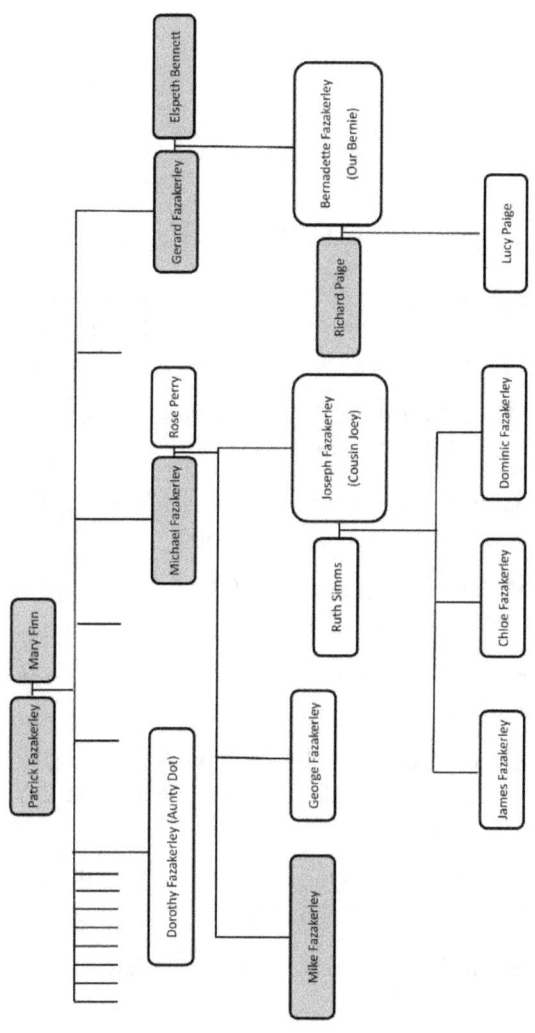

POLICE PERSONNEL

The following police officers recur in many of the Bernie Fazakerley Mysteries. This alphabetical list is provided to give some background to them and for reference.

- **Mark Adams:** (Thames Valley) Police Constable 1967, Police Sergeant 1981.

- **Rupert Andrews:** (Thames Valley) Detective Sergeant 2000, Detective Inspector 2012.

- **Malcolm Appleton:** (Thames Valley) Police Constable 2007, Sergeant 2018.

- **Penelope Black:** (Thames Valley) Forensic anthropologist

- **Eileen Brookes:** (Thames Valley) Secretary to the Chief Superintendent. Joined the force in 1958 as an office junior. Retired 2006.

- **Alison Brown:** (Thames Valley) Detective Inspector 1989, DCI 2004, Chief Superintendent 2015.

- **Amanda Burgess:** (West Mercia) Detective Constable 2016.

- **Tracy Burton:** (Thames Valley) Police Constable 1999, Sergeant 2005.

- **Michael Carson:** (Thames Valley) Forensic Pathologist

- **Anna Davenport:** (Thames Valley) Detective Sergeant 2007, Detective Inspector 2015. Married in 2001 to Philip Davenport. Separated in 2017. 3 children: Jessica (2001), Marcus (2002), Donna (2017). Archaeology and Anthropology graduate from Cambridge.

- **Brian Eddleston:** (Thames Valley) Police Constable 1958, Police Sergeant 1965, Inspector 1976, Chief Inspector 1981.

- **Karen Evans:** (West Mercia) Police Constable 2010, Detective Constable 2011 Detective Sergeant 2013. Married Paul Godwin in 2018.

- **Sarah Farrow:** (Merseyside) Police Constable 2003

- **Bryony Foster:** (Merseyside) Detective Constable 2016

- **Jordan Fox:** (Thames Valley) Police Constable 2001, Sergeant 2006, Inspector 2018

- **John Gamble:** (Thames Valley) Police Constable 2017

- **Paul Godwin:** (Thames Valley / West Mercia) Detective Constable 1993, Detective Sergeant 2002, Detective Inspector 2008, Detective Chief Inspector 2017. Moved from Thames Valley to West Mercia Police 2008. Married Karen Evans in 2018.

- **Luke Gray:** (Thames Valley) Senior SOCO.

- **Pamela Gregson:** (Thames Valley) Custody Sergeant.

- **Toby Hitchin:** (Thames Valley) PC 2014. Trained with Kenny Hughes.

- **Gavin Hughes:** (Thames Valley) Police Constable 1988. Specialises in community policing and building bridges with rough-sleepers.

- **Kenneth Hughes:** (Thames Valley) Police Constable 2014. Gavin's son. Killed while on duty in 2019.

- **Peter Johns:** (Thames Valley) Police Constable 1969, Detective Constable 1973, Detective Sergeant 1978, Detective Inspector 1993, retired 2011. Married to Angie in 1978 and to Bernie in 2006. Father of Hannah (1980) and Eddie (1982). Stepfather to Lucy (2000).

- **Lee Jones:** (Merseyside) Police Constable 2015

- **Arshad Khan:** (Thames Valley) Detective Sergeant 2002, Detective Inspector 2006, Detective Chief Inspector 2014. Specialises in cases involving ethnic minority victims.

- **Aaron King:** (Thames Valley) Police Constable 2001, Sergeant 2009.

- **Janet Kingman:** (Thames Valley) Forensic photographer

- **Sandra Latham:** (Merseyside) Detective Chief Inspector 2014.

- **Christopher Lucas:** (Greater Manchester / Merseyside) Detective Inspector 2009.

- **Andrew Lepage:** (Thames Valley) Detective Constable 2007, Detective Sergeant 2015. Graduate in criminology (1st class) from Leicester University

in 2005. Lives with his mother in Headington
Quarry.

- **Ruby Mann:** Senior SOCO. Specialises in Crime
Scene Management.

- **Callum McLaughlin:** (Thames Valley) PC 2018.

- **Jennifer Moorehouse:** (Thames Valley) Civilian
staff member

- **Janet Morecambe:** (Merseyside) Police Constable
2010

- **John O'Connor:** (Merseyside) Police Constable
2016

- **Monica Philipson:** (Thames Valley) Detective
Constable 2002, Detective Sergeant 2008. An
ambitious police officer, who studied at Keble
College, Oxford.

- **Richard Paige:** (Thames Valley) Detective
Constable 1960, Detective Sergeant 1967, Detective
Inspector 1973, Detective Chief Inspector 1981,
Detective Superintendent 1995, died 1999. Married
to Bernie in 1997. Father of Lucy (2000).

- **Joshua Pitchfork:** (Thames Valley) Detective
Constable 2015

- **Jonah Porter:** (Thames Valley) Police Constable
1977, Detective Constable 1979, Detective Sergeant
1983, Detective Inspector 1987, Detective Chief
Inspector 1996. Married to Margaret in 1982.
Widowed in 2014.

- **Louise Otterbourne:** (Thames Valley) Police
Constable 2017

- **Thomas Pullinger:** (Merseyside) Police Sergeant 2012

- **PD Q:** (Thames Valley) Police Dog 2014. General Purpose dog. German Shepherd Dog.

- **Oliver Ransom:** (Merseyside) Detective Constable 2015

- **Alice Ray:** (Thames Valley) Police Constable 2015, Detective Constable 2016

- **Charlotte Simpson:** (Merseyside) Detective Sergeant 2015

- **Melanie Stanton:** (Thames Valley) Police Constable 2009 and Dog Handler 2014

- **Ben Timpson:** (Thames Valley) Police constable 2018

- **PD Wesley:** (Thames Valley) Police Dog 2015. Drug and firearms search dog. Spaniel.

- **Melanie Wharton:** (Merseyside) Police Sergeant 2010.

- **Scott Wilding:** (West Mercia) Joined the police from the army in 2008. DI 2016.

ABOUT THE AUTHOR

Like her main character, Bernie Fazakerley, Judy Ford is an Oxford graduate and a mathematician. Unlike Bernie, Judy grew up in a middle-class family in the South London stockbroker belt. After moving to the North West and working in Liverpool, Judy fell in love with the Scouse people and created Bernie to reflect their unique qualities. She has worked in academia and in the NHS.

As a Methodist Local Preacher, Judy often tells her congregation, "I see my role as asking the questions and leaving you to think out your own answers." She carries this philosophy forward into her writing and she hopes that readers will find themselves challenged to think as well as being entertained.

www.ingramcontent.com/pod-product-compliance
Lightning Source LLC
Chambersburg PA
CBHW060543180626
46817CB00002B/704